PRINCE IN EXILE

PRINCE IN EXILE

BOOK 2 IN THE SWAYAMVARA ROMANCE SERIES

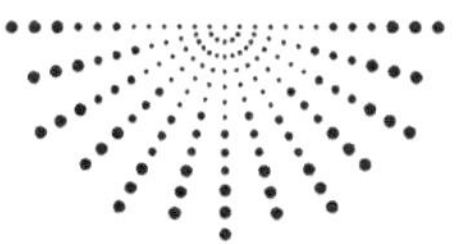

ANNA BUSHI

Library of Congress Control Number: 2025903511

ISBN 978-1-967291-01-4 (paperback) — ISBN 978-1-967291-02-1 (hardback)

Cover designed by GetCovers

First Printing, 2025

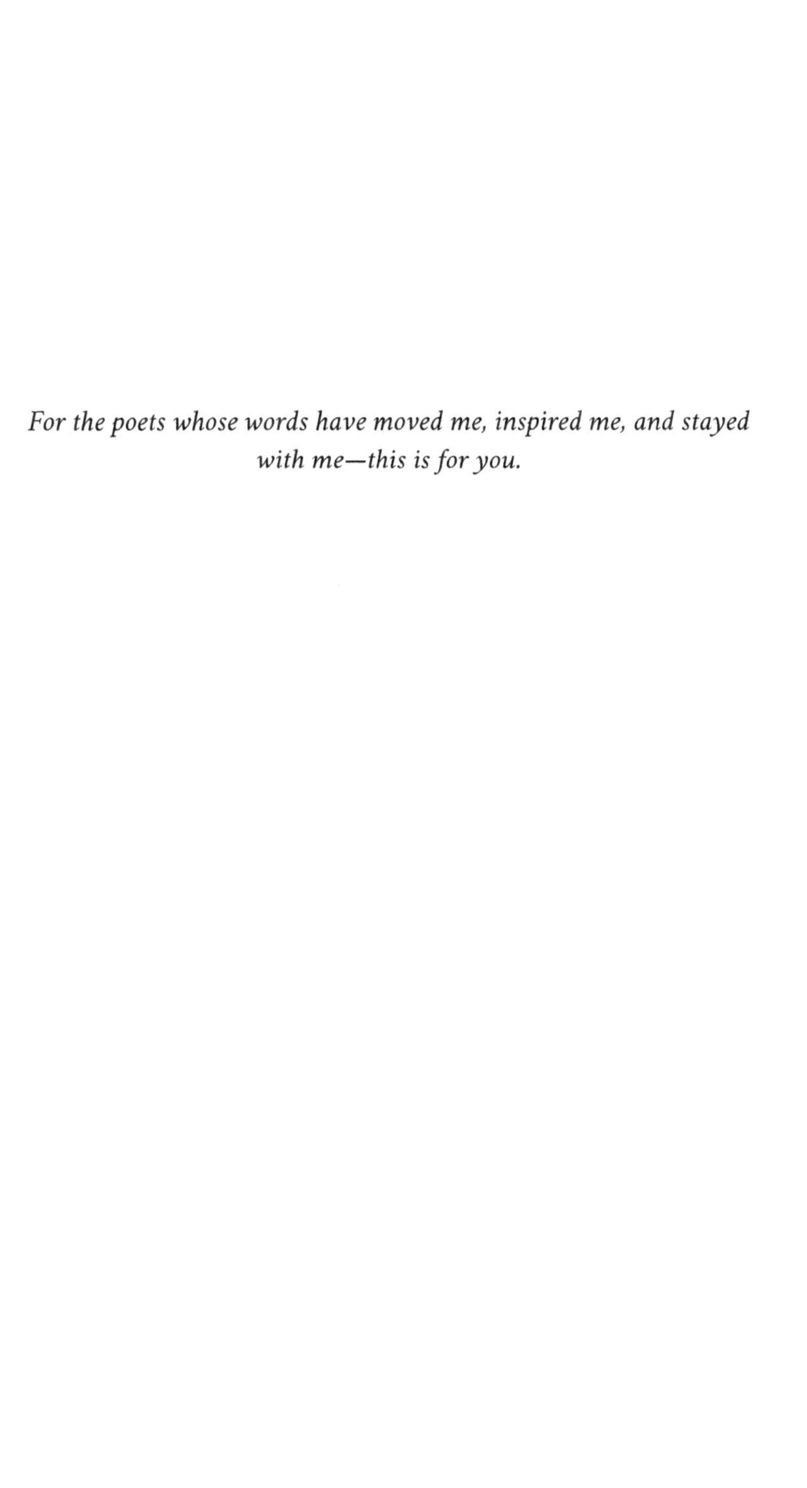

For the poets whose words have moved me, inspired me, and stayed with me—this is for you.

CHARACTERS

VIDARPUR KINGDOM

King Dushyant
    Queen Lalitha, wife of Dushyant
    Princess Kanika, sister of Dushyant
    Princess Ambika, sister of Dushyant
    King Lambhodara, father of Dushyant
    Queen Neelambari, mother of Dushyant

* * *

JAISALPUR KINGDOM

King Vibudha
    Queen Urmila, wife of Vibudha
    Prince Vikaran, brother of Vibudha
    Prince Mahabahu, son of Vibudha
    Princess Suryavati, daughter of Vibudha
    Prince Abhayan, son of Vibudha

* * *

King Bhadri
    Prince Giridhar, brother of Bhadri

1

SURYAVATI

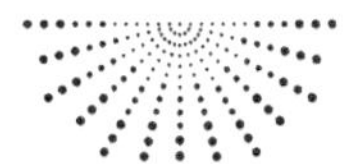

The air was hot and dry, but Suri took no notice, except to be thankful it was clear enough to see. Her gaze was not fixed on the actor on stage as he sang the lament. Instead, her eyes settled on the man standing beside the stage, silently mouthing the words along with the performer—the playwright who had somehow discovered her poem and woven it into his play.

She shone like a star in the sky
Sparkling like a diamond from up high
Now, her skin shriveled
Her beauty long withered
Death may have her quelled
But in my heart she still dwelled
Soon, she will be only dust
But continue to love her I must

The actor's voice broke as he crooned the final line, holding the hand of the dead girl lying on the floor. Since all the performers were male, the actor struggling to hold his breath was also a man. Though Suri knew this was just a play, the music emanating from the lone flute pressed all her anguish into her throat, and tears misted her eyes. The dark act unfolded in front of a colorful mural of a spring garden, flowers spilling everywhere. The contrast between the vibrant blooms and the fading lives was impossible to ignore. A sob escaped the actor's throat as he plunged a dagger into his chest and collapsed onto his lover's body.

The light from the flaming torch cast a golden glow on the playwright as he watched the scene unfold, while Suri watched him, her throat so tight she thought she might choke. She had dreaded coming here, worried about how the audience would react to the outpourings of her mind. The night was dreadfully silent, with no chatter from the crowd. She assumed that was a welcome sign.

"Is that your poem?" her cousin Kanika whispered, breaking her reverie.

She nodded slowly, still stunned to hear her own words. Her words. It felt like standing in a rain shower on a hot day.

"It is heartbreaking. When did you ever encounter such pain?" murmured Kanika.

Is being mute, unable to say a word, not pain enough? Suri thought.

The play ended, and the audience rose in hushed silence, seemingly enthralled by the tragic story they had just witnessed.

Suri stood with them, tugged her cousin's arm, and pointed in the direction of the playwright.

Kanika sighed, giving her a knowing look. "He is handsome, but you will never have a future with a playwright—not when you are the only daughter of King Vibudha."

Suri nearly laughed at how Kanika had misinterpreted her intentions. Shaking her head vehemently, she mimicked the act of writing. Marriage was not on her mind, nor did she believe any man would want to marry her for anything other than her wealth. What she truly desired was to collaborate with him. That was why they were in disguise, both dressed as ordinary men—rather, boys—instead of their royal attire.

Kanika's eyes narrowed as she studied her. "What mad scheme have you concocted now?"

Suri shrugged. The playwright had already given her a monumental gift by bringing her poem to life. She should be content with just that. But she wanted more—to write more and see him weave her poems into his tales. He was a natural storyteller who knew how to use even the silences to create dramatic pauses. Though she loved pouring her heart out into poems, she was not skilled at telling stories.

"If I have to sit through more of these, may I suggest you write merrier stuff? Otherwise, I'm returning to Vidarpur," said Kanika as they made their way through the dispersing crowd. A faint smell of flowers adorning the women's hair wafted through the air.

Suri did not respond to her cousin because she had arrived in front of the playwright. All thought fled her mind as she gazed into his eyes. The sorrow pooled in them shocked her. A play he had witnessed several times should not have caused such an effect on him.

The playwright glanced at them briefly before moving away to greet someone in the audience.

"If we were wearing our silk saris and gold jewelry, we would have received a different reception," mumbled Kanika, while Suri stared at the man's retreating back.

A sudden sneeze burst from her, drawing Kanika's attention. Her cousin's brows knitted with concern. "Are you falling ill? That's not the first sneeze I've heard from you today."

Suri shook her head, offering a reassuring smile to dismiss Kanika's worry. Her focus sharpened on the moment; she couldn't afford to lose this chance to speak with him. Suri strode forward and grasped his wrist. Her entire body hummed from that single contact, and she pulled her hand back as if it burned.

The playwright spun around. The moon hung low just above his head, tinting everything around him in silver. Suddenly, she couldn't bring herself to look at him and stared at her feet instead.

She must have trembled because he asked, "Are you okay, lad?" and placed a hand on her shoulder.

Heat rushed into her face from the warmth spreading from his skin. He would think it odd for a boy to blush from a mere touch, so she took a deep breath to calm herself. Mired in her own emotions, she missed his question until he repeated himself.

"What do you need?"

She moved away from him, pulled a palm leaf scroll out of her cloth pouch, and handed it to him.

"I know the poet," he read aloud. He repeated it as if saying an incantation, then stepped closer, placing both his hands on her shoulders and looking at her as though trying to read her mind. His gaze nearly melted her insides. "You know the man?"

Man? She stepped back from him, squashing the temptation to scowl at his assumption. Of course, he thought the poet was a man. Why wouldn't he? Women usually lacked the learning and leisure for such pursuits. Except she did. The leisure part would vanish once she became a wife, a prospect she wanted to delay for as long as possible.

Kanika cleared her throat, and Suri realized she had not answered his question. She nodded, while her cousin blurted, "Yes."

His eyes danced in eagerness as he grasped her hand. She would be crazy to assume her writing evoked such passion in him. "Can I meet him?" the playwright asked, squeezing her hand.

Tiny shockwaves traveled from her fingers to her heart. She

ignored the foreign sensations. She had never been touched by a man who was not her family. Her reactions to him did not mean anything.

Kanika answered sternly, "No, he is a recluse who avoids meeting anyone."

He dropped her hands as someone approached them. "Giri, are you joining us?" a man asked. She guessed he was a member of the drama troupe, based on the makeup and costume he wore.

"In a moment," Giri answered. Then he turned to her. "Will you give the poet a message from me?"

Suri nodded, while Kanika looked as if she might burst into laughter. She dared not silence her cousin with a stern glance, hoping the girl had the sense not to spoil this moment for her.

"Come back tomorrow and I will give you a letter," Giri said.

She grabbed his hand again, unable to contain herself. Then she started mouthing her words slowly while also tracing them on his hand.

Do you like...

He watched her fingers move with careful intent. While a part of her felt like a child waiting for her father's approval, another part noticed the young man's attention, causing heat to rise in her face.

Before she even finished, he said, "Do I like the man's poems?" She reluctantly let go of his hand as a slow smile spread across his face, dispelling the sadness that had engulfed him earlier. "His words speak to my heart. Don't forget to visit me tomorrow," Giri said and departed. He liked her work. A strange elation blew across her throat, fluttered down her chest, and settled in her stomach.

GIRIDHAR

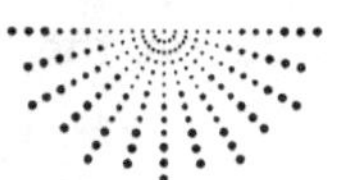

Giri stood alone in the courtyard, breathing in the crisp night air. In the moonlight, the raised platform that functioned as the stage glowed yellow. His brother would say he was wasting his life, but Giri disagreed. What was the use of fighting wars to acquire wealth if one did not enjoy poetry and plays during times of peace?

Mooka, a stray dog Giri had befriended, found him then, lumbering over to sniff his hands. Giri bent down to rub Mooka's neck absently.

He had stumbled upon two of Poet Ravi's poems and fallen in love with the shattered hearts depicted in them. Their sorrow mirrored his broken self, prompting him to write a play.

Giri would have preferred to simply write a story and share it with friends, watching them read his tale and discuss its merits. That alone would have filled his heart. But there was one problem: as the Crown Prince, his friends would one day be his subjects. They would not be honest with him about their thoughts—certainly not about the merits of a story. Worse, they would see too much of him in his characters and attribute their actions to him. He was not ready for that kind of scrutiny. Most others he encountered were too unlettered to truly appreciate his tale.

A staged play was his best alternative for sharing the stories crowding his mind. Watching the actors on stage brought him to life, satisfying his hunger to belong. His brother would say he was hiding from his responsibilities, and Giri couldn't deny it. He had spent weeks courting Princess Lalitha of Garthapuri, only to burn all the goodwill he had earned by attempting to kidnap her against her will. That he had been following his aunt's orders did not excuse his actions. Fortunately, Lalitha had more sense than he did and rejected him. Shame over betraying the lady's trust drove him into hiding, and for the past two months, he had sought refuge in Jaisalpur. Here, no one knew him as Prince Giridhar. Instead, he could simply be Giri, the playwright.

"There was something strange about the two boys who spoke to you," Sangu said, standing behind him. Giri mentally corrected his earlier thought: no one but Sangu knew him as Prince Giridhar. Sangu, his personal guard sworn to protect him with his life, had accompanied him to Jaisalpur.

"Those two beardless boys? One of them didn't say a word. He must be mute. Otherwise, I didn't notice anything unusual. They seemed harmless. The mute one indicated he knew Poet Ravi, though that could be a lie."

Sangu rubbed his chin thoughtfully. "Maybe. Still, I sensed something off."

Giri considered his words. Sangu wasn't accustomed to being his only guard, which might be causing him to see danger where there was none.

"I asked them to come tomorrow. I plan to send a message to the poet. We can follow them afterward—they might lead me to him."

"We are far from home. In a few days, the drama troupe will move on to a new city. Should we think about returning?"

Sangu asked, barely concealing his concern for Giri's well-being.

It must seem strange for Sangu to see his prince eating simple food, sleeping on the thinnest mats, and spending his days writing. Giri knew he couldn't hide from his brother forever. At nineteen, he needed a few more days of this freedom —to live his own life before surrendering to the whims of a brother who was also his king. After four years of marriage to two different women, his brother had only a daughter, making Giri the heir—a burden Giri did not relish.

Two men passed by, talking loudly about the play, pulling Giri back to the present.

"Are you tired of prancing around on stage?" Giri asked.

"It could be worse. I could be chasing enemies on a battlefield."

The moment those words left his mouth, Sangu knew he had made a mistake. "My apologies," he began.

Giri pressed his lips into a thin line but managed to wave him off. He wasn't a coward deserting his king in a time of need. When the occasion arose for him to lead the Nidhapur army, he would do so willingly. But not all men knew him as well as Sangu; they would think him a coward.

"When this play ends, we can return home." *To a life of serving his king.* "If I can meet the poet before then, I will urge him to come to Nidhapur." Maybe then, that place would not feel so desolate.

"If I may, I never doubted your bravery," Sangu whispered as they made their way back to the troupe.

Giri patted his shoulder in acknowledgment. They walked down the gravel lane, past the temple, and reached the open meadow. Actors and musicians squatted in front of a fire, motionless as statues, tired after a long day of singing and dancing.

Giri strode past the men without greeting them, not noticing the familiar smell of the burning wood. His mind was on the small changes he wanted to make during tomorrow's rehearsal.

The next day, a cat purred and swatted its tail against Giri's nose. Yawning, he gently pushed the animal aside and opened his eyes. Their camp bustled with morning activity: the cook blowing into his coal fire, a musician humming a tune, and leaves whispering in the breeze above.

After a meal of hot porridge, Giri gathered his actors. The first scene they practiced was between the girl and her father.

"Have I offended thee, Father? Thou grant thy blessings to the adulterer who cheats on his wife while denying them to your own daughter. What crimes have I committed to merit this? Have I not been devoted to you? Father, art thou here to rob a poor girl of her love?" cried the actor playing the girl.

"You dare ask me these questions? You defied—" began the actor portraying the father.

"Stop," Giri interrupted the actor. The older man paused, raising his eyebrows in question.

"Add *Ungrateful child* right after the first line," Giri said.

"Why? It's already very good," the veteran actor exclaimed dramatically, as though performing for an imaginary audience, visibly upset at yet another change.

Giri laughed self-deprecatingly. The lines were good, but not great. "Could you please add *Ungrateful child?*" he repeated, momentarily wishing he could command the actor instead of pleading with him. He had no one to blame but himself for hiding his royal title. As a mere playwright, he could no longer expect obedience as his birthright.

The veteran actor seemed to contemplate protesting further but ultimately inclined his head.

"You dare ask me these questions? *Ungrateful child!* You defied my orders. I have given all my love to raise you, and yet that boy is dearer to you than I am," the actor playing the father declared sternly.

Giri nodded, satisfied with the change.

Evening arrived, bringing with it a crowd eager to watch the play. There was no sign of the two boys, but Giri pushed them from his mind. The actors slipped seamlessly into their roles, allowing Giri to focus on the audience. He had worried that the people of Jaisalpur, accustomed to the familiar tales of the *Ramayana* and *Mahabharata*, might reject his creation. His fears, however, proved unfounded. Captivated by the story of the two young lovers, the audience watched each scene with rapt attention.

Toward the end of the musical drama, a light rain began to fall, mirroring the tears of the lead actor as he collapsed with a dagger protruding from his chest. The audience, still murmuring about the tragic ending, pulled coverings over their heads and began to disperse.

Giri remained, standing motionless as he watched the rain drip from the edges of the raised platform onto the ground. A deep contentment spread through his chest, keeping him warm despite the chill in the air. Frogs croaked their rhythmic calls, answering one another from the shallow creeks now flowing between the tree roots.

The rain began to hiss as it fell. Resigned to being soaked to the skin, Giri turned around and saw the boy from yesterday, standing under a tree. Black eyes met his gaze, and Giri stared back, surprised by what he had missed the day before. The boy was young, petite, and beautiful—an unusual kind of beauty that inspired poets to write verses. Then Giri noticed the boy gesturing and hurried toward him.

The boy waited warily, a furrow etched between his brows. "You have my thanks for coming," Giri said.

The boy took a step toward him, but then his knees buckled, and he sank to the ground.

3
SURYAVATI

Giri rushed to Suri and wrapped an arm around her shoulders as she knelt on the ground. A tremor shook her body, and she felt faint. Gently, he eased her back against a sturdy tree trunk and placed his fingers against her forehead to check her temperature, concern etched across his face.

"You're burning up," Giri whispered. "I'll take you to a physician."

She grabbed his upper garment and shook her head, her grip firm despite her weakness. A physician would undoubtedly discover she was no boy—and might even recognize her.

"No physician?"

She nodded, her head drooping slightly, and then shivered violently. The thin garments she wore offered little protection against the rain.

He scowled at her. "Fine, no physician. But you can't stay out in this rain. Let me take you to an inn—"

Her fingers dug into his arm, and she shook her head firmly. She couldn't risk being seen by her father's men.

At that moment, another man approached them. "Pitch a

tent for tonight. This boy will shelter with us," Giri said. The man glanced between her and Giri before walking off to carry out the order.

Giri slipped his hands under her shoulders and knees, lifting her with ease. Too drained to resist, she leaned against his broad chest and closed her eyes. He smelled of rain and earth.

It had been foolish of her to come tonight, but she couldn't resist the chance to see him again.

The previous evening, Queen Urmila had noticed her absence. When Suri tried to explain it away with a story about strolling in the garden with Kanika, her mother's skeptical gaze lingered. The queen wasn't easily convinced, especially with Suri's sneezing and sniffing raising her suspicions. Knowing her daughter too well, the queen kept a watchful eye on her after their evening meal. That forced Suri to enlist Kanika's help to distract her mother while she slipped out alone.

When she arrived in the city center to watch the play, the sky wept with her. After a few moments of exhilaration, cold wrapped around her like a cocoon, leaving her wet and miserable. If she fell ill, she would face a world of trouble with her mother.

Unaware of her turmoil, Giri placed her on a mat inside the tent, worry etched into his brow. The concern in his eyes caught her attention, and she couldn't pull her gaze away, her heart thudding loudly in her chest. The air was still crisp, but a warmth crept along her limbs. Maybe it was just her fever. A lone lantern flickered, casting shadows as he turned away.

"Here are some dry clothes. Let me help you remove your wet ones," Giri said, reaching to lift her tunic.

She let out a harsh cry and pulled away, clamping her hands under her arms in a defensive posture. He would wonder at her strange behavior, but she had acted instinctively.

Giri frowned, studying her intently, as though she were a puzzle he needed to solve. Fortunately, he asked no questions.

Instead, he rose reluctantly. "I'll leave the dry clothes by your side and wait outside."

She waited for his footsteps to recede before letting out her breath. Quickly, she changed out of her wet garments, her fingers trembling with haste, cursing her foolishness for coming that night.

Before her breathing could return to normal, Giri cleared his throat outside the tent. "I brought you some medicine," he said.

Suri hesitated, debating whether to cry out in response. Her inhuman voice often drove people away, and she didn't want to push him away. Instead, she clapped her hands, hoping he would understand the signal.

Giri entered, closing the tent flap behind him. He seemed to fill the small space as he approached, carrying a steaming pot. "A broth with ginger and other herbs. The cook promised it will help you sleep tonight."

She hadn't realized she was inching away from him until he stopped, the pot balanced in one hand. "You have nothing to fear from me, lad," he said gently.

She feared her own reaction to his presence. The tent felt far too small for the two of them. She held out her hand, keeping a careful distance between them.

He pressed the clay pot into her palm. "Drink," he whispered.

She inhaled the fragrant steam rising from the vessel and took small sips. The warm liquid soothed her throat and lent her strength. Once she had emptied the pot, she placed it on the ground and wiped her mouth with the back of her hand, acutely aware of his watchful gaze.

He remained still, his arms crossed over his chest, as though he didn't want to startle her. Her eyes drifted to the defined muscles of his arms, and she found herself wondering how a playwright had gained such strength.

"You'll be safe here tonight," he said, his voice reassuring.

"Get some sleep. The rain has stopped, so I'll be right outside this tent if you need anything."

She lowered herself onto the thin mat, her eyes never leaving him. He spread a blanket over her, his movements careful and deliberate. A shadow passed outside the tent, and she instinctively pulled the blanket up to her chin.

A moment later, a dog padded inside, heading straight for Giri. His face softened as he reached down to scratch behind the dog's ear. "I can leave Mooka for your company," he said with a faint smile.

The dog immediately flopped down beside her, pointing his nose toward the sky as if demanding attention. She couldn't help but smile as she reached out to scratch his ears, accommodating his silent request.

"I think he likes you," Giri remarked, as he picked up the empty pot and stepped out of the tent, leaving her alone with the dog.

Even as she nestled closer to the warm, furry companion, unease churned in her stomach. If her mother discovered her absence, there would be consequences in the palace. Suri prayed silently that any punishment would fall on her and not Giri.

She briefly considered sending a message to her cousin but quickly dismissed the idea. To do so, she would have to reveal her identity, and the thought of that left her uneasy.

Whether from her illness or the broth, Suri drifted into a restless sleep. In her dreams, voices murmured in despair.

Poor King. Look at her. She is cursed. She killed her brother. She will destroy the kingdom.

The camp stirred with the arrival of dawn. Crows cawed harshly, men chattered, and the clang of a metal pot hitting the ground jolted her awake. She rolled to one side, trembling as the remnants of the dream clung to her.

She exhaled sharply, trying to steady herself. Cursed, they

might call her, but she knew deep in her heart she had not caused her older brother's death.

"Where is he?" asked a voice she recognized instantly.

Kanika?

"My lady, he fell ill, so I offered him shelter," Giri replied. *My lady?* That title confirmed her fear—Kanika had come dressed as a royal princess.

Every muscle in her body tensed, urging her to flee.

4

GIRIDHAR

Giri stared at Princess Kanika of Vidarpur, standing before him in her royal splendor. Her resemblance to her brother, King Dushyant, was unmistakable. Dushyant—the man who had won the hand of Princess Lalitha, now Queen Lalitha of Vidarpur. For a brief moment, Giri's thoughts drifted to the spirited princess who had followed her heart. Lalitha was better off for choosing Dushyant. Though the whole incident had left a bitter taste in his mouth, he bore no grudge against Dushyant. No, all the fault lay solely at his own feet.

"Where is he?" Kanika demanded, tapping her foot impatiently.

"My lady, he fell ill, so I offered him shelter," Giri replied, puzzled by the princess's concern for the sick lad.

"He is a distant cousin of mine and had accompanied me from Vidarpur," Kanika explained, her words spilling out in a rush. "I knew he loved watching musical dramas, but I didn't realize he had snuck out from the castle last night. I will never forgive myself if any harm befalls him."

As they walked toward the tent, the grass beneath Giri's feet was still damp with morning dew. A warm, flowery fragrance lingered around Kanika. He recognized the same scent from the lad's hair the night before.

When Giri opened the tent, gritty morning light filtered in. The lad sat very still in the corner, his arms wrapped tightly around his knees, like prey caught in a hunter's net. If he truly was related to the princess, his plain, ordinary clothes betrayed no hint of it. Giri caught the furtive glance the boy exchanged with Kanika and realized there was more to the story than what she had told him. Still, he had no interest in uncovering the lad's secrets.

Kanika rushed to the boy and pressed her hand to his forehead. "You're warm. I was worried when you didn't come home last night," she said, her concern evident as she hovered over him.

The boy exhaled nervously, his gaze shifting to Giri with an acute ache in his eyes—an unspoken appeal that Giri couldn't quite decipher. A sudden worry churned in Giri's stomach. What if sending the boy with the princess put him in harm's way? He silently chastised himself for not speaking with the boy in private before allowing Kanika into the tent.

"You are welcome to stay here," Giri said, watching the boy carefully for any signs of distress. To his surprise, the boy's lips twitched, almost forming a smile, before he swiftly shook his head.

Pushing his cousin away gently, the boy rose to his feet unsteadily. Kanika immediately wrapped an arm around his waist to steady him. Leaning on her, the boy pressed his palms together and inclined his head toward Giri.

Giri understood the boy's silent expression of gratitude even before Kanika said, "He is thanking you."

He nodded, his eyes sweeping over both of them. Hesitating, he finally asked, "Did you lie to me about knowing Poet Ravi?" His gaze lingered on the boy, who shrank back under its weight.

"No," Kanika replied firmly. "He does know the poet. We both do."

Giri decided to test their claim. He pulled a palm leaf scroll from the cloth tied around his waist. "Here is a message for the poet," he said, handing the scroll to the boy, whose eyes sparkled with sudden excitement. Giri then extracted two copper coins from a pouch and placed them on the boy's palm. "If you bring me the poet's reply, I will give you two more coins."

The boy's face brightened like a clear, cloudless sky. He tucked the scroll carefully into the folds of his dhoti and left the tent with his cousin. Giri followed them outside, the air thick with the scent of rotting leaves and fresh mud.

A few feet away, the boy turned to look at him, his lips curling into a faint smile. Then he continued on, leaning on his cousin for support. Every few paces, they paused to rest, making slow progress toward a palanquin resting on the ground. Giri watched intently, not looking away until they climbed into the palanquin and the curtains fell, blocking them from his view.

The boy will be safe, Giri thought. Around him, the day came alive: the thud of an axe splitting wood, the cascade of bells from the anklets of dancers practicing their moves, the rhythmic strikes of a musician tuning his animal-skin drum. *He must be safe.*

5

SURYAVATI

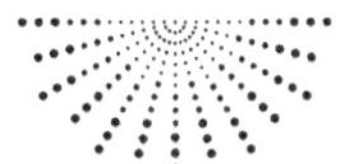

She leaned back against the smooth wood of her carriage, letting the rocking motion soothe her. Giri had a message for the poet. A warmth spread through her stomach, almost like happiness. She closed her eyes, recalling the sensation of his warm hands around hers.

"Suri, why did you stay here last night? And what was that about you falling ill?"

Suri gestured that she was feeling fine now.

"You can't be better so soon! You leaned on me and stopped to rest every chance you got—"

Suri responded with a soft smile, hoping to ease her cousin's concern.

"Were you pretending?" Kanika asked, her voice rising in surprise.

Suri nodded, a content smile spreading across her face. She hadn't intended to deceive, but perhaps she had wanted a few extra moments to linger and feel his gaze on her. Her fingers brushed the scroll hidden at her waist.

"Suri, read what he wrote," Kanika said suddenly.

Suri opened her eyes and glanced at her cousin. A teasing

19

smile played on Kanika's lips. Overcome by sudden shyness, Suri shook her head. She wasn't ready to share his words with anyone. Not yet.

The palace buzzed with early morning activity as the men set the palanquin down in a narrow alley. Servants carrying bundles of firewood moved toward the kitchen, and vendors pushed carts brimming with fresh fruits and vegetables. The sweet aroma of the produce filled the air as Suri stepped out.

"If we use the servants' entry and stay very quiet, we can reach your chambers before the queen notices," Kanika said, guiding her through a side door. They entered a narrow hallway and turned left. Maids sweeping the floor paused as they passed, their gazes recognizing Kanika's royal attire. At the end of the hall, a small staircase spiraled upward, beckoning them onward.

As they reached the top of the stairs, a sharp voice stopped them in their tracks. "In here. Now." Queen Urmila, Suri's mother, stood outside her chambers, hands on her hips. Despite the weariness etched on her face, her regal bearing remained unshaken.

Her mother waited until the door closed firmly behind them before speaking again. "How could you?" she asked, her tone deceptively calm, like the eerie stillness before a storm.

Suri flushed, lowering her head. The silence that followed was heavy and uncomfortable.

"We just went to see a play, Aunt Urmila," Kanika said in a nervous whisper, her voice tinged with guilt. Suri felt a pang of remorse for dragging her cousin into her deception and shot her an apologetic glance.

"Is that why she's wearing her brother's clothes?" her mother asked sharply, her accusatory tone pricking like a thorn. "I want an answer."

"She wanted to talk to the actors without revealing her identity," Kanika replied, her words coming quickly, as if hoping to defuse the tension.

Without intending to, Suri touched the palm scroll hidden in the folds of cloth tied around her waist.

Her mother noticed. "What do you have there?" she demanded.

Suri knew she looked sorrowful as she shook her head. Her mother's face darkened as she drew closer and held out her hand.

With trembling fingers, Suri pulled out the scroll and placed it in her mother's grasp. What ill luck. Why had she waited to read the message?

Her mother squinted at the writing. "Blinded by love, I go to the place where nothing stirs." She looked up from the palm leaf. "What is this?"

Suri stared blankly, her mind scrambling to understand the meaning of the words.

Once again, Kanika came to her rescue. "That's just a poem Suri wrote."

Her mother, born a princess and raised to guard her emotions, exhaled as if she could hardly bear to look at her. "You need to act like a princess of seventeen, old enough to marry and have children of your own." Her eyes softened as she stepped closer and gripped Suri's palm. "My child," she said in a low whisper, "don't make this harder than it is."

Suri knew her mother cared for her in her own way, but at that moment, all she felt was rage at her mother's lack of empathy. She bit back a deranged laugh that threatened to escape. What could possibly be harder than life as a mute princess?

As her mother's figure retreated, Suri thought bitterly, *She truly has no idea how I feel.*

Before she could sink further into self-pity, Kanika interrupted her despondent thoughts. "What do his words mean?"

Suri stared at the floor, her mind churning. Then, like a spark igniting in the darkness, understanding dawned on her. She grasped the meaning behind the playwright's message.

6

GIRIDHAR

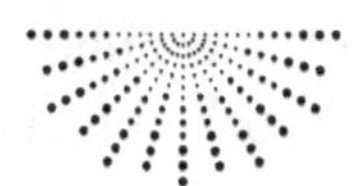

Blinded by love, I go to the place where nothing stirs.

Those were the words Giri had written on the palm scroll, his starting verses for a poem. If the lad knew the poet, he would send back the next few lines of the poem. Giri did not hold out much hope for that, though it would thrill him to correspond with another mind that melded with his. A soft, silky breeze swirled around him, laden with the heavy perfume of summer.

"Master," a woman called.

Giri turned to see a young woman about his age. He noticed her bare forehead and the absence of any jewels on her body—a young widow, then.

"What can I do for you?" he asked gently, the memory of his own mother, widowed when he was only seven, surfacing in his mind. Upon his father's death, his older brother had ascended the throne at the tender age of ten and had ruled for the past twelve years.

"I am looking for work, Master," the woman said.

22

Actors and musicians were a superstitious lot. They would consider a widow, especially one so young, an ill omen. "There is not much work here for you, but if you go to the cook, he will give you food." He drew a copper coin from his pouch and offered it to her.

Instead of accepting it, she timidly grabbed his hand. "I can sing and dance. Please give me a small role. I will work hard," she said desperately, her eyes pooling with tears.

Giri gently pulled his hand from her grasp and stepped back. His traveling troupe consisted entirely of men, with the exception of a few wives who accompanied their husbands. "There is no work for women here," he said, trying to keep his tone soft. Still, she shrank back from him, tears streaming down her cheeks.

A bitter smile transformed her plain face. "I am no old maid to wither like this." He said nothing, though he silently agreed with her sentiment. Then, in an instant, her shoulders slumped, and the anger drained from her. "Please," she uttered, as if that single word had sapped all her energy. That one word sickened him, for he could offer her nothing more than the coins in his pouch.

She refused his coins and walked away, leaving a trail of sadness behind her.

The breeze vanished, and the sun beat down on his head as if berating him while he made his way toward the actors gathered in a small group. During their rehearsal, he hoped to see the widow watching their performance, but she had disappeared.

That afternoon, the sky stretched wide, glowing like a rug of molten gold. Giri walked toward the stream, which glittered like diamonds. Smooth river stones lay scattered on the bank. Mooka paced beside him, his nose to the ground. Suddenly, he lifted his head and started barking.

Giri heard a sharp cry downstream and ran around a clump

of trees, emerging onto a sandy bank. A dark object floated up for a moment before submerging. Without hesitation, Giri dove in.

He swam through the murky water and spotted a long, dark, rope-like shape. A moment later, he realized it was braided hair. Grasping the waist of the person it belonged to, he pulled them up toward the surface. As they broke through the water, he recognized the young widow—her eyes dark and empty. She clung to him, her body pressed against his.

He let the current carry them downstream as he kept them both above water. Soon, he grabbed hold of some tree roots and pulled them both out. He laid her on the ground, gasping for air.

She rolled onto her side, coughing up river water. After heaving dry air, she rose with her hands pressed to the ground. Her chest rose and fell rapidly as she gazed at the horizon with empty eyes. Slowly, her breathing returned to a normal cadence.

He watched her carefully to ensure she was unhurt. As he hovered over her, she shrieked, "Why did you save me? I would rather be dead than live another day." She let out a heartbroken wail, and he could only watch her helplessly.

"Don't cry," he muttered feebly, ashamed of his inability to protect her. Reluctantly, he placed his hand on her head. She flung her arms around his neck and buried her face against his chest.

She sobbed hard, her grief pouring out, and he felt his own eyes misting. He held her tightly and rubbed her back, unsure of how to comfort her.

When he loosened his grip on her, she pleaded, "Don't leave me," the anger gone from her voice. Her arms wound tightly around his waist, and he felt her heart hammering against his chest. Her head, warm and heavy, rested on his shoulder, his breath stirring the tendrils of her hair. He stroked her soft tresses, and she tipped her neck back, gazing at him with warm, dark eyes.

"I'm sorry," he murmured, wishing he could do more to aid her.

She sniffed once, tears pooling in her eyes, and then leaned in and kissed him, her lips soft against his.

25

7

SURYAVATI

She sat gazing at the blank palm leaf resting on the table, her fingers holding the ink-tipped feather.

Blinded by love, I go
To the place where nothing stirs

Those were Giri's verses. He was testing to see if she actually knew the poet. A smile played on her lips. She knew the poet very well. She bent her head and started completing his poem.

Charging through the brush, although
In fear my heart murmurs.

Still smiling, Suri blew on the ink while her mind worked furiously. She wanted to hand over the scroll to Giri herself and watch his reaction as he read her verses. But her mother would be observing her every move like an eagle. She spent the day on edge, gulping down rice in the evening and pretending it was a normal day.

She lay awake at night, staring at the ceiling, trying to figure

26

out what to do. Suri decided not to entangle her cousin further in her mess. A gnawing idea came to her, and she sat up in bed, rubbing her eyes.

She opened her trunk quietly and pulled out her brother's clothes. She had stockpiled his discarded outfits, and they had come in handy over the last few days. After dressing in his attire, she moved to the open window like a ghost and gazed at the stars spilled across the sky. A soft breeze whispered through the room, carrying the scent of jasmine.

With nimble grace, she slipped one leg over the windowsill and onto the sturdy branch of the tree that stood sentinel just beyond. The rough bark scraped against her palms as she lowered herself down the tree's gnarled trunk. In the hushed darkness, she descended, her heart beating in time with the rhythm of the night. Finally, her bare feet touched the dew-kissed grass below, and she disappeared into the embrace of the shadows.

Floating like a cloud, she moved soundlessly through the palace gardens, arriving at a hidden gate by memory. She pushed it open quietly and slipped outside the walls. Walking through a patch of trees, she moved more slowly than usual, the lingering effects of her fever still gripping her. One of the tree roots caught her toes, and she stumbled, throwing her hands out to grab onto something. Her fingers closed around a trunk, and she held on to regain her balance.

A meadow opened up ahead, vast and misty, while a dark hill rose to her right. Wet brushes slapped against her arms as she slowed her pace.

She was close to the tomb of the fallen warrior. He had fought in a battle during her grandfather's reign on these very grounds. She recalled the murmured tales whispered through the castle halls—how enemies had cut off his head, yet his body continued to fight, wielding the sword with unerring precision.

Since then, it was said, he roamed the meadows, keeping watch over her kingdom.

In the daylight, the story had brought her comfort. In the dark, she feared encountering his headless form—dead but still not at peace.

She emerged from the trees and saw the crumbling tomb before her, its stones jutting out of the soil like a skeleton. Years of rain and wind had eroded most of the walls. She felt like a trespasser and wished her cousin, Kanika, were with her. She trod carefully, like an unwelcome guest. Old leaves crunched beneath her feet, and she fought the urge to bolt.

She did not believe in ghosts. All she had to do was cross the meadow and find the playwright. Despite her brave thoughts, a tremor ran through her body. Clenching her fists, she moved through the grass, staying quiet to avoid waking any sleeping spirits. Her heart pounded in her chest, betraying her dread.

The dim starlight cast dark shadows around her, and she felt as if someone were watching her. Her heart skipped a beat. She didn't dare turn around to check.

Thump. At the sound, she nearly jumped out of her skin. Her body shook as she froze. The night around her fell silent. Then, she saw him—a man, a headless man. The hair on her neck stood on end.

Thump. She took off running like a frightened deer. Her arms scraped against the thick brush. A rock jutted out, and she twisted to avoid it, but not in time. She went right over it and landed on her stomach, gasping for breath. She inhaled the cool night air—perhaps for the last time.

Something seized her neck, and she screamed, her voice echoing through the darkness like an unearthly wail.

8

GIRIDHAR

The touch of her warm lips sparked a sharp desire in Giri. He wanted to slip his hands into her thick hair, kiss her exposed neck, and lose himself in her sweet scent.

Mooka, dancing around them, decided to join the action and began licking his face, abruptly ending his imprudent thoughts. Giri reminded himself of who he was—the Crown Prince, not at liberty to share himself with any girl, especially a young widow. With great difficulty, he pulled away, gulping air to calm his wild wishes.

She grinned at the dog and gently pushed the animal away. When she leaned toward him again, he turned aside.

"Sister," he called, halting her movement.

Her face flushed deeply as she stepped back. "I'm sorry. I don't know what came over me."

Giri understood her plight. Despite her youth, society imposed harsh expectations on widows, forbidding them from remarrying and condemning them to a lifetime of mourning. He knew this all too well—his own mother was a widow. She had endured years of solitude, a loneliness he deeply sympathized with but was powerless to ease.

"He never bedded me properly before his death," she murmured, avoiding his gaze. Giri assumed she meant her late husband.

Giri himself had never bedded anyone in his life. The one girl he had kissed at fifteen had disappeared from court, likely because his brother had deemed the match unsuitable. Even then, in the height of his youthful foolishness, Giri hadn't possessed the courage to confront his brother. His voice grew thin whenever he attempted to contradict him. His brother—also his king—had taken his father's place in his life, demanding obedience. Disagreeing with him on anything made Giri deeply uncomfortable.

A loud sigh brought him back to the present.

Giri could do nothing about the widow's physical needs. However, he could ease her financial strain.

He stood and waited for her to rise. "Who do you live with?"

"My brother," she whispered, her head bowed. "I am a burden on him. He has too many mouths to feed."

"I cannot offer you any work with the drama troupe," he said, watching her deflate. "Tomorrow is market day. Come see me then. I can buy you a milking cow and her calf. You can support yourself by selling milk and yogurt."

"Cow?" Her head rose. "That would require a lot of coins." Her eyes narrowed into slits. "Are you jesting?"

Coins—he had plenty, more than enough to buy everyone in the village a cow. "I have saved some for a rainy day," he said instead.

That night, as stars hid behind the clouds, he walked aimlessly, letting the darkness offer him respite from his relentless yearning. The young widow had brought his own loneliness to the forefront. He craved warmth and comfort but dared not seek them in a stranger's embrace. The play, while bringing him some measure of fulfillment, still exposed a chasm in his life.

Beyond his physical desires, he hungered for intellectual companionship.

Had his father lived, his brother might have grown into a friend with whom he could share his fears and fancies. But his brother had a kingdom to rule and often lamented that Giri wasted his time reading poetry. So, he had to content himself with actors, who cared more about their lines than any reflection of his tale.

He picked up a fallen branch from his path, its dry wood snapping with a sharp *crack* as he tossed it aside.

Brooding darkly, he did not notice the figure ahead until Mooka, pacing beside him, barked. The human figure broke into a clumsy run, as though being chased by an army of hunters. It appeared to be a girl. Why was she out alone this late at night? Worried, Giri hurried toward her.

Before he reached her, she fell flat on her stomach. He saw no sign of any predators on her tail. As he drew nearer, the clouds parted, and in the dim light, he noticed the figure was dressed in boy's clothes. Giri had mistaken the slender frame for a girl's.

He grabbed the boy's neck to lift him, and a chilling scream made Giri nearly shrink back.

When the boy shifted to face him, Giri recognized him. "It's okay, lad. I mean you no harm," he said in a soothing voice.

The boy's howl dwindled, and his large, fearful eyes gazed at Giri intently.

"What are you doing here?" Giri asked, holding out his hand for the boy to grasp. There was something delicate about his features that gave him a vulnerable appearance. Giri's anxious imagination wondered if the boy was a prisoner at the palace who had decided to run away. The lad grabbed his hand, and Giri noticed the softness of his palm—strange for a palace-raised boy. Perhaps he had an illness that prevented him from undergoing weapons training.

"Is everything okay?" Giri asked gently, considering offering him shelter if the boy was in danger.

The lad nodded slowly, a subdued, flowery scent wafting from him, reminding Giri of jasmine. Then, still looking at Giri, he pulled a palm leaf from the cloth fold tied around his waist and extended it toward him.

Giri accepted the scroll and inspected it. He could faintly make out words on it but couldn't decipher them. A sudden thought struck him.

"Is this the Poet Ravi's reply to my message?" he asked eagerly.

The lad nodded while bending down to scratch under Mooka's neck.

"I need light to read it," said Giri, marching back to his camp, excitement coursing through his body. The lad followed with Mooka at his heels. Giri had longed for friendship with a like-minded man. He imagined going back and forth over the merits of a phrase while crafting their next play. Joy, of the kind he had never experienced before, heightened his senses.

As they crossed a road, he heard the sound of hooves. Immediately, the lad tensed and hid behind him, letting out an uneven breath. Giri, who knew all too well about hiding from trouble, recalled his earlier thoughts about the lad being in danger. His actions confirmed that suspicion. For an insane moment, Giri felt the urge to fold the lad into his arms and comfort him. He shook his head to clear his mind. The time spent with the young widow had clouded his thoughts. The lad did not need coddling. What he needed was someone to train him in the use of weapons to defend himself.

Giri halted and waited for the riders to pass. Two horses slowed as they approached. Giri stood tall, arms on his hips, providing sufficient cover for the boy. Behind him, he heard the lad's ragged breathing.

Before Giri could ensure the boy didn't disappear in panic,

one of the riders addressed him. "Why are you out this late at night?" The man pulled the reins and stopped beside them. Giri sensed, rather than saw, the man's hand tighten around the hilt of his sword.

In that moment, Giri realized his mistake. He had acted like a prince, not a playwright.

9

SURYAVATI

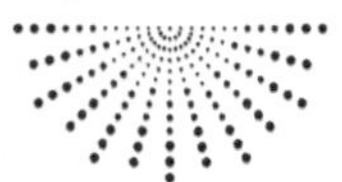

Suri recognized the commander on his horse, a man known for his violence. It made him a feared leader, and she realized she would have to reveal herself if he unsheathed his weapon. She did not relish the prospect, and her body quivered in opposition to the idea. She clenched her fist and readied herself by taking a deep breath.

Before she could move out of the playwright's shadow, he spoke in a voice her stablemaster used with a wild horse. "Apologies, master. Our dog ran off into the night. My brother and I went searching for it." He slumped his shoulders and adopted a subservient posture.

The commander, who liked to hunt, found this obedience robbed him of a fight. He grunted, kicked his horse, and vanished into the dark, with the other man following closely behind.

After watching the backs of the riders, Giri turned to her. "Come. I am eager to read the message." His calm tone surprised her; she would have thought a playwright would fear an encounter with one of their notorious soldiers.

He led them to a campfire and plopped down beside it.

Gesturing for her to sit next to him, he tilted the palm leaf to catch the light from the embers. The flames danced as the wind shifted, carrying the smell of burnt wood. Her heart raced like a deer on the run as she sank down, her eyes fixed intently on his face, hungry for his approval.

His lips moved slowly, and she sensed him reading her verse. She thought her heart would burst out of her chest. Then his lips curled up, and he wrapped a hand around her shoulder, pulling her closer. She worried he could hear her thumping heart. The idea of bringing him the poem had seemed so easy in her mind. Now, with the heat from his arm warming her skin, she wanted to tip her chin up and kiss his lips. She imagined the feel of his soft lips on her skin and scolded herself for such foolhardy notions. She was a princess, not a common maid, to fall for a playwright.

He began reading the poem aloud, including his own beginning.

Blinded by love, I go
To the place where nothing stirs
Charging through the brush, although
In fear my heart murmurs.

A sigh escaped him as he gazed into the fire, a lock of his hair falling over his forehead. She resisted the urge to tuck it behind his ear. If she had any speech left, she would have questioned him about the poem. Cursing the childhood illness that had left her mute, she tugged his arm and raised her brows.

"You have bestowed an immense favor on me by delivering this poem. I wish I could shower you with gold and gems, but you'll have to settle for a smaller token of my appreciation," the playwright said, his eyes sparkling in the firelight.

It sounded like he liked the two lines she had written. A

warm glow traveled from her stomach to her face, and she felt as if she had swallowed a star.

"Wait here. I will return with my response to Poet Ravi," he said, standing up. She choked up as she realized he was writing to her. She was the poet. A part of her was afraid of his reaction if he found out. But even that did not temper her elation.

Alone by the fire, Suri hugged her knees to her chest, all worries about her mother dissipating like the smoke from the flames, leaving only the joy of sharing her love for poetry with Giri. The wind had stopped, giving the night a pleasant stillness. She did not know how long she remained suspended in this state, only raising her head at the sound of approaching footsteps.

"It is late. You are welcome to sleep here tonight and return home tomorrow," Giri said as he came near, his eyes filled with concern.

Though touched by his worry, she shook her head. She could not risk her mother's wrath again.

"I will escort you back then," he said, gazing at her. Realizing he was waiting for her to stand, she rose reluctantly, miming a palm scroll with her hands.

"I have my verses," Giri said, holding up a thin leaf. His eyes narrowed as he asked, "Do you know how to read?"

She shook her head again. The accumulating lies bothered her, but it was better for him to think her unlettered than to guess her identity.

As they strolled through the meadow, Giri pulled out a small knife. "I don't know what you are afraid of, but I know you are scared of something. Take this knife and keep it on your person at all times. It might come in handy." He extended his arm to hand her the weapon.

She took the blade from him, unable to meet his gaze. He had guessed her emotions correctly. She felt as if his perceptive eyes pierced through her lies to uncover the truth. She could not risk him finding out how his mere touch caused her heart to race.

She halted and made a stop gesture with her hands. He understood her. "You no longer want my company," he said.

She wanted—needed—his company. But that path led to heartbreak. So she nodded. Then, without waiting for his response, she strode away.

As Suri entered the palace grounds through the hidden gate, the queen stood on the other side with her hands on her hips, the moonlight coating her in a ghastly pale light.

10

GIRIDHAR

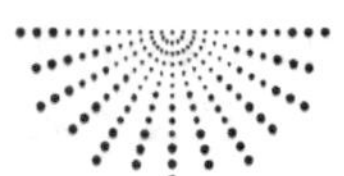

A smile played on Giri's face as he rested his head on the worn mat. He wanted to meet the poet and talk to him for days about the magic of his woven words. For now, Giri would settle for exchanging verses with him. Though the poem taking shape was darker in tone, pleasant dreams of sunshine and flowers filled his head as sleep claimed his mind.

The next day, as he watched the actors recite the lines he had written, Sangu approached him. "The young widow is here."

She was early. Giri realized the widow did not trust him to keep his promise of buying her a cow. He could not blame her doubts—he was a stranger to her, after all. Giri sensed Sangu lingering beside him, waiting for a response.

"I am going to the market with her to buy a cow."

Sangu drew in a breath. "I don't have to remind you that a widow—"

"You don't," Giri interrupted, cutting his guard off. He knew he had no future with a widow, whatever her wealth. But that should not prevent him from helping her. As a future king, he considered it his duty, though she was not a subject of his. "I am only buying her a cow."

As the sun rose overhead, Giri set out with the young woman. She avoided looking at him, knotting and unknotting her fingers.

After waiting for her to spill out whatever caused her distress, Giri looked down at her. "Go ahead. Tell me what is bothering you."

Her eyes met his tentatively, then dropped away like a child drawing their fingers back from a fire. Giri felt a surge of inadequacy course through his body. Instead of facing his brother's wrath, he had buried himself among actors, avoiding reality. Why did he think he could help others when he was a coward running from his own life?

Before the voice inside him tore through his rib cage, she murmured, "I have only one thing to offer you in return for the cow. You can come to me—"

He knew what she offered him—herself. Precious though it was, he could never accept her and wanted to spare her the humiliation of his rejection. "What is your name?" he asked, hurt lodging in his throat.

Confusion flashed across her face before she answered. "Vasantha."

"Vasantha, I am partial to freshly churned butter," he said with an awkward smile.

She swallowed, her eyes dark. "Butter?"

"Fresh butter," he agreed, his smile deepening as the clouds overhead drifted apart.

She nodded while quickly wiping the corner of her eye with her finger, squeezing his heart. They wandered through the market in silence, the buzz of chatter engulfing them as the breeze carried in the smell of pungent peppers.

She halted suddenly, her face crumpling. "You don't have to buy me a cow."

Giri looked at her worry-pinched lips. "Vasantha, don't fret about it."

"Did you steal from the temple coffers? How can you afford this?"

"I would never steal from a Goddess. But princes are fair game," he jested lightly.

She crossed her arms and stared at him.

"A nobleman gave me a pearl necklace for a play I staged," Giri lied easily.

"Why would you spend it on me? I don't deserve your kindness." Her eyes welled up.

Giri swallowed his guilt about not doing more for her. "By saving your life, I claimed you as my sister. I cannot think of a better use for the jewelry than helping you," he said, hoping to ease her heart.

"You are a strange man," she said in a thick voice. There was no joy in her tone, only resignation about facing a bleak future.

They passed dusty stalls, looking for cows. Giri knew nothing about them, but luckily, Vasantha did. She had tended her father's cows and knew enough about them to barter. As they approached several sellers, she whispered, "Don't mention the pearl necklace. Let me get us a good bargain first."

Vasantha found a calf growing fat on her mother's milk and stroked her neck. "How much for the mother and her baby?"

While she haggled with the farmer, Giri's gaze circled the surroundings. That was when he spotted him—his brother's spy.

SURYAVATI

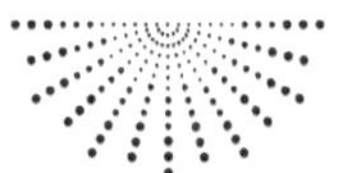

Suri faced her mother, feeling like a goat led to slaughter.

Her mother's voice pierced her heart. "You have shown me that you cannot be trusted. I am disappointed in you." She paused, rubbing her wrist, and the agony on her face was too much for Suri. "You leave me no other choice, child. Nanmaran will guard you day and night. If you leave the palace again without my permission, I will marry you off on the next auspicious day. A husband's command cannot be disobeyed like a mother's."

Usually, the king and the crown prince were assigned guards dedicated solely to protecting them, while she, like other family members, was guarded by the city guard. It was easier to give the slip to the city guard—they rotated and didn't know her well. A dedicated guard would be much harder to escape. Suri swallowed her rage and took a breath to bring herself under control. She nodded without looking up, lest her mother see the resentment in her eyes.

In the quiet of her room, she adjusted the cotton wick of a

brass lamp so the light burned brighter. She pulled out the scroll with hands that trembled in excitement, as if this was what she lived for, and read Giri's new verse. She smiled despite the dark words. He must have heard her cry of fear while stumbling through the old tomb. He was a quick thinker. She pulled out his opening verse and read the poem in its entirety.

> *Blinded by love, I go*
> *To the place where nothing stirs*
> *Charging through the brush, although*
> *In fear my heart murmurs.*

> *I hear a sharp howl of pain*
> *Piercing the deep quietness*

She knew what the next two lines should be. Reaching for the feather pen and a scroll, she wrote them. With a lightness in her heart, she curled up in bed, looking forward to his response.

The next day, Nanmaran followed her like a shadow, though both knew no dangers lurked behind the pillars of the castle. Suri wanted to rattle the golden cage that kept her in and find a way to escape. Still, she knew her mother would not give her another chance.

As she walked through the palace garden, a strange thought took hold in her mind. Whenever she touched Giri, unfamiliar sensations coursed through her body, making her desperate for more. Was this how it felt to touch any man? She glanced back at Nanmaran, walking two feet behind her. He appeared to be similar in age to the playwright.

Making an impulsive decision, Suri pretended to miss a step and skidded across the ground. Before she tripped face-first, Nanmaran grasped her elbow, steadying her. She could feel his calloused palm on her skin, but no sparks rose at that spot. No heat rushed to her throat. Her heart continued to beat at the same steady pace.

Nanmaran relaxed his hold. "Are you okay, my lady?"

She inclined her head and resumed her stroll. What should she make of this? Why was she drawn to Giri as if every part of her needed him—like a flower longing for warm sunshine?

She heard footsteps behind them and whipped around.

"Suri," called Kanika as she looked from her face to Nanmaran's. "I come bearing news."

Kanika approached her through the garden in a daze of sunshine, her hair shining like dark gems.

Suri signaled for the guard to wait, and Nanmaran bowed his head.

The cousins walked a few feet away, around flower beds spilling their heady fragrances. Suri raised her eyebrows, facing her cousin expectantly.

"I heard the playwright is leaving town," Kanika said in her sweet, clear voice, shocking her.

She felt a weakness in her knees and a dizziness in her head. Kanika wrapped her arm around her, led her to a stone bench, and sat beside her.

Many questions rushed through Suri's head. What had caused this change? When would he leave? Could she keep him in Jaisalpur forever? It was as if she had yearned for him all her life and now could not bear the thought of his departure. Suri shivered and drew the end of her sari around her shoulders, glancing at Kanika, waiting to hear more.

"I heard it from a maid. Her brother is a musician with the troupe. They are traveling to another city sooner than planned."

Suri buried her face in her hands, troubled by her swirling emotions for a near stranger. Kanika made no other comment while gently rubbing her back.

Her cousin's supportive gesture reminded Suri of her needs.

She realized Giri was a man who loved her poetry—a rarity in her grim world. She longed for their kinship of minds and did not consider this a vanity.

She jumped up, determined to find a way to keep Giri in Jaisalpur. Forever and ever.

12

GIRIDHAR

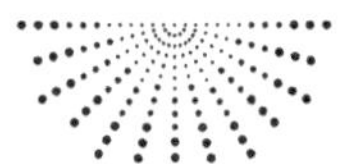

*H*iding from his brother was one thing. Disobeying an order from his king was treasonous, and Giri knew only one way out of it—not to let his brother find him. When he saw the spy, he knew he had to leave Jaisalpur before the spy spotted him. Giri longed to stay and make Poet Ravi's acquaintance, but he valued his freedom too much to risk it.

Once Giri made up his mind, things moved quickly. The troupe provided him with cover, and thankfully, they agreed to travel to another city. Not only did they agree, but they also seemed eager to move elsewhere. One final farewell, and then Giri could leave Jaisalpur behind.

Before dawn, Giri flung a shawl around his head, slipped out of his tent, and peered into the mist-filled air. He assumed his brother's man kept nocturnal hours and would not stumble upon him. Mooka lifted his head from under a tree.

"Stay," Giri whispered. Making very little sound, he walked toward the village, ensuring no one followed him.

"I am looking for Vasantha," he told an elderly woman strolling alone on the streets. She paused for a moment to gaze at him, then pointed the way.

He found himself along vegetable beds, pale in the darkness. Walking down the garden path to a shed, he heard water splashing inside. Peeking in, he saw Vasantha filling a barrel with water, the cows still lying on the ground, not ready for daytime.

Giri stepped forward, and Vasantha turned, holding a clay pot in her hands.

Her gaunt face brightened at the sight of him. "It is too early for fresh butter," she teased.

He smiled half-heartedly, worried about leaving her alone. "How are the animals doing?"

"I sold milk to the cloth merchant yesterday, and he agreed to give me six yards of cotton as payment for a fortnight of milk. It will be my first new sari since my wedding sari." Her voice broke, and she bowed her head.

The world outside lightened. "Do you have enough to eat?"

She nodded while picking up a broom to clean the tiny shed.

"I am leaving Jaisalpur," he said flatly, not wanting to betray his worries for her.

"For long?" she asked hesitantly, turning to glance at him, her smile gone. She had the look of a girl who rarely heard kind words anymore.

Giri nodded, inspecting a callus on the palm of his hand. He might never return to Jaisalpur, but he could not reveal that to her.

"Will you take me with you?" Her shoulders slumped, her eyes dark with fear. Her voice tore at his heart, and he wished he could cover his ears to block her plea. To distract himself, he picked at the hard skin on his palm with a stubby fingernail.

"Ever since my husband was stolen from me, I have been afraid. Afraid I would never know the comfort of a full belly. Afraid of dying a lonely woman. I am nobody here. No one would miss me," she said in a very low voice.

Giri sighed, suppressing his desire to put his arms around

her shoulders and embrace her, to offer her his protection. Instead, he shook his head grimly. "I will miss you, but I cannot take you with me, Sister."

She turned away from him and moved toward a cow. "You are young and strong." She gave a mirthless laugh and knelt down.

Pity for her stirred in his heart. Her world was hard and would remain so. She wanted him to love her, but that was beyond his power. In the dim light, he pulled out his coin pouch and held it to her. At least he could keep her hunger away. "Save this for a rainy day."

Her dark eyes narrowed to slits. "Go away," she whispered, gazing at the thatched roof.

Giri saw her weep silently and accepted her reproach. He dropped the pouch on the ground and strode away, no comforting voice calling him back. He had not made her any promises, yet guilt pooled in his stomach.

He heard the splash of water from women drawing water from the village well. Vasantha had no enemies, but she had no friends either.

Giri tried to put the young widow out of his mind and think about his future. For a brief moment, he longed to see the kind face of his mother, her soft hand resting on his head. His mother was alone, just like the young widow, and needed him, for his brother hardly spared any time for her. He knew he had to return to Nidhapur soon, but he wanted to push that day for a fortnight or two. Guilt rose again, this time for abandoning his dear mother, who loved him.

Lost in thought, Giri only partially noticed a man hanging around their tents, surveying his surroundings. When his eyes landed on Giri, he strode forward to meet him. For an instant, panic gripped Giri. Had the spy found him after all? But as the man came nearer, Giri realized this was not his brother's man.

"Prince Vikaran asked me to fetch you," the man stated.

Giri knew Prince Vikaran was the brother of King Vibudha of Jaisalpur. Why would he want to see him?

13

SURYAVATI

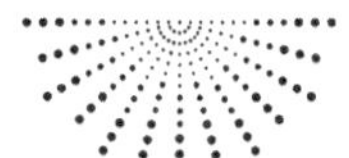

*H*er room was dark, lit only by a single brass lamp, casting long shadows on the walls. Suri pulled open the heavy curtains and blinked as bright light flooded in. Yet, it failed to warm her insides, chilled by the thought of losing the playwright—the only man who truly appreciated her poetry.

The colorful tapestries hanging on every wall of her room seemed to come to life, mocking her despair. Lotus flowers bloomed in a delicate pink shade on one of them, while the water underneath glistened a pristine blue.

The carved wooden door to her room swung open.

"He is here," said Kanika as she marched in, closing the door behind her.

Suri signed with her hand to confirm the man's identity.

Kanika nodded in answer. "It is the playwright, Giri."

Impatience coursed through Suri as she tugged Kanika's arm and pulled her toward the door.

Kanika stood frozen like a boulder. "Your uncle is meeting him behind closed doors. He's not going anywhere. Let's wait until he's done, and you can talk to your uncle later."

Suri shook her head. She wanted to catch a glimpse of Giri as he left. More importantly, if her uncle failed to keep him in Jaisalpur, she was willing to reveal her secret to make him stay. She hoped it wouldn't come to that. Only Kanika and her brother knew her identity as the poet, and she did not relish the thought of her mother finding out.

Kanika grinned mischievously. "You have the same look in your eyes that my brother did when he talked of his now-wife." Then her cousin frowned. "It's not the same, though. There was no reason my brother couldn't wed the princess. But a mere playwright is beneath you in status and wealth. Suri, set aside any feelings you have for the man. It will end in heartbreak."

Suri grimaced, clenching her hands into tight fists. Her cousin had it wrong. She only desired his friendship, for they shared a love for writing.

"Suri," called her brother, Prince Abhayan, as if her earlier thoughts about him had made him appear at her door. At fourteen, he was a lanky boy, with only his silk clothes marking him as the crown prince. A jewel around his neck—an emerald— winked in the light, and his thin golden crown sat askew on his black, curly hair. With piercing dark eyes, he stood gazing from his sister to his cousin.

"What mad plot are the two of you hatching?" he asked, his eyebrows drawn together, eyes fixed on his sister.

"Your sister has invited the playwright to the castle. With your uncle's help, she hopes to convince him to stage a play here. More importantly, she hopes he uses her poems for inspiration and incorporates them."

Abhayan smiled mischievously. "If he uses her poems, the play would be a sad, dreadful affair. We will have boats ready to rescue the crowd as the floor is flooded with the tears of the audience."

Kanika tittered while Suri flushed. As she swiped at her

brother, he ducked with a grin. "Write a poem about the bravery of soldiers ready to die on a battlefield."

"How is that any better than her tragic poems? And why do you think anyone desires to witness the re-enactment of battlefield glory? Folks attend plays to escape the grim visages of dying soldiers and grievous wounds. Suri, write about a girl falling in love," Kanika insisted brightly, a twinkle in her eyes.

Abhayan rolled his eyes at his cousin. "I would rather watch the tearful tales of Suri."

A knock sounded on her door, and Abhayan yelled, "Enter," before she could react. She glared at her little brother as Nanmaran opened the door.

"My lady, your uncle is waiting for you."

Without waiting for her brother and cousin, Suri followed him, her pulse racing. As they approached the smaller hall used for more intimate meetings, she could sense Giri's presence behind the thick wooden doors. Nanmaran glanced over his shoulder to make sure she was ready, then pushed open one of the doors.

14

GIRIDHAR

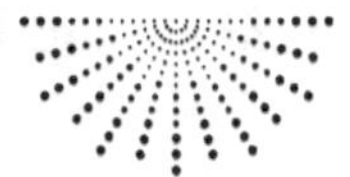

Sangu, his guard, appeared by his side as if carried by the wind.

"I am heading to the castle to meet Prince Vikaran," Giri answered the unasked question.

Sangu raised his eyebrows in surprise. "I can accompany you—"

"My orders were to fetch only the playwright," said the prince's man in a tone that brooked no argument.

"Watch Mooka," Giri said to his guard, knowing he would track him to the palace.

Prince Vikaran's man had come on foot, and Giri walked behind him, passing small houses set back from the earth roads. The chances of encountering someone who knew him as Prince Giridhar were higher at the castle than in a tent surrounded by actors. If a past acquaintance broke his cover, he would have no choice but to return home. He did not relish that option.

As they passed a pasture with grazing cows, Giri saw two towers rising dark against the morning sun, built with gray stones as thick as boulders. A forest grew against one side of the exterior castle walls, home to boars and wolves. A small track ran from the king's road to the mighty woods, and a deer moved quietly in the shadows. For an instant, Giri wanted to run into the trees and hide. He squashed that foolish notion. It would not take long for an arrow to find its mark on his body if he tried to flee. Better to hear what Prince Vikaran wanted from him.

At the fort entrance, the gates were shut. A shout came from one of the soldiers guarding the entry, followed by a gruff response from his companion. Then a little door cut into the massive wood swung open. Taking a breath, Giri bent his head and stepped into the castle grounds, feeling trapped by the long walls surrounding him.

Giri noticed the stables to his right, the rumble of hooves echoing from within. Before him stood a grand palace, a flight of stone steps leading to a pair of great double doors. His companion marched up the stairs to the arched doorway. The door, as thick as a tree trunk, stood open, allowing light to filter in through windows set high on the wall.

His companion called for a soldier, who stepped out of the shadows. "Here is the playwright. Take him to Prince Vikaran immediately."

"Follow me," said the soldier, leading him through a dark corridor. Mounted torches shed more smoke than light, staining the walls behind them with black soot. Giri trailed behind the man, climbing a narrow staircase until the soldier stopped and said, "Here," before knocking on a massive wooden door. It swung open.

Weak morning light filtered through a window overlooking the castle gardens. A long table of rosewood dominated the center of the room. It reminded him of the hall in his palace, which he used for smaller gatherings, and an overwhelming guilt surged in his heart for hiding from his brother. He had lost his dignity in one morning because of his stupidity in kidnapping a princess. He took in the scene in one rapid scan to mask his self-loathing. Beside the table, a man of middle age and medium height stood in the shadows, reading a scroll. His rich outfit of silk and gold informed Giri of his royal stature.

"Go on," the soldier said.

When Giri took two strides forward, the door shut behind him. The prince straightened and glanced at him. "Are you the playwright?" he asked.

Giri hesitated for the briefest moment before bowing, his palms pressed together in respectful greeting. He wanted to deny the title, but he sensed that the prince's question carried layers he couldn't yet fathom.

"I was expecting someone much older. You are merely a boy," the prince said in distaste. Giri wondered why the prince had invited a stranger.

"I have a little skill in writing plays," Giri said.

"In all of Jaisalpur, there is talk of a new playwright who came from nowhere and weaves magic on stage with his stories," the prince said with a disbelieving smile.

"I weave no magic, but I am the new playwright. What can I do for you, my lord?" asked Giri.

"You will stay here and write a play about our king. It is—"

Giri shook his head, momentarily forgetting he was masquerading as a playwright and not a prince himself. "My lord, I have already made plans to leave Jaisalpur."

"Change your plans," barked the prince. "You will leave when I say, and not before."

"My kinsman will be looking for me."

"I will have my men fetch him. He can stay with you at the palace."

"And if I refuse?" Giri asked in a gentle tone so the prince could not take offense.

"You cannot refuse unless you want to be hanged as a traitor." The prince smiled wickedly. Giri knew of no way to refuse the prince without revealing his own identity. He was not ready to traverse that path yet. "My lord, I consent to write a play about the king. I would thank you if you can find me a quiet corner, safe from interruptions, until I am done."

The prince nodded, measuring him. "Serve me well in this one thing, and I shall reward you richly."

Giri bowed again respectfully. "I am your faithful servant." He decided to use this time wisely and make Poet Ravi's acquaintance. "I do have a small request, my lord. I wish to work with Poet Ravi on this creation."

"Poet Ravi? I have never heard of him."

Giri nearly mentioned Princess Kanika's name but bit his tongue. It never did any good for an untitled young man to mention the name of an unwed princess. That's all he was at the moment. "I know how to get in touch with the poet, if you permit, my lord."

The prince shrugged as if he did not care how the play came together. "Open the door," he commanded.

When Giri did as commanded, a lad came running in. "Fetch the man's kin from the village. Give them a room near the servants' quarters. They will stay in the palace, working on a play about our king." Giri would be away from men who might recognize him in the servants' quarters, and he was thankful for that.

As the lad signaled for Giri to follow him, the prince said, "Help him find Poet Ravi."

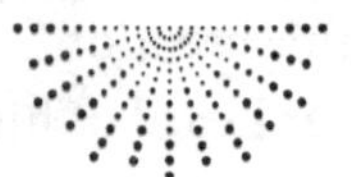

When the door opened, Suri hesitated outside, her gaze searching for Giri. Her eyes landed on her uncle, who sat at the head of the table. On hearing the door swing open, he looked up from his seat.

"Come in, Suri," he said, waving her in.

Barely hiding her confusing mix of emotions—disappointment and relief at not finding the playwright flooding her in equal measure—she stepped in. She could still sense a lingering trace of Giri's presence in the room, a scent that reminded her of the warmth of the sun.

"I know your love of poems and tales, so I did what you requested of me. I commanded Giri to create a play about your father."

Suri felt a lightness that seemed to lift her up and float her among the clouds. Her uncle, who truly cared for her, had not failed her. Giri would stay. She would have more time with him. If she inspected her joy more closely, she would realize she was not thinking of Poet Ravi at that moment. The warmth that spread through her limbs whispered the desires of a girl—of finding a way for them to be together.

Her uncle continued in a voice that had lost some of its earlier tenderness. "But now, I want you to listen to my command. You cannot contact the playwright for any reason. While I trust you, I don't trust any young man capable of telling stories that melt your heart. You stay away from him. If not, I will banish him from this kingdom. Am I clear?"

Suri flushed under her uncle's gaze. She nodded timidly while looking at the floor, lest he notice the glint in her eyes. He had said nothing about Poet Ravi reaching out to the playwright. Poet Ravi would collaborate with Giri. The thought made her glow like pearls set amidst dark hair.

Seeing her downcast eyes, her uncle chuckled. "Don't fret, my dear niece. I will not stop you from watching the play when it is ready. Leave now. I have to attend to important work."

Noiselessly, she left the room, the stone floors cold beneath her feet.

Nanmaran waited outside. "The queen wants you, my lady. Better make haste."

Suri shook off her dreamy contentment and fled across the hall to her mother's chambers.

She cleared her throat as she opened the door. Her mother sat straight in her chair, gazing absently at a scroll in her hand. She waved Suri to a chair near her, where she could watch Suri's face as she spoke.

Suri took her seat and glanced at her mother deferentially.

"A girl like you should be wed and raising children," her mother said.

Suri could feel the warmth from earlier seeping out of her body.

"Once, I had great dreams for you, filled with crowns and thrones." Her mother squeezed her hand gently and sighed. "But I cannot send you far away, not when you are defenseless."

A mute, unable to voice her desires, Suri thought.

"I have looked among the men in Jaisalpur for a good man for you," her mother continued.

Suri knew she could not write her poems if she were bound to a man. She felt anger rising within her.

Her mother mistook her emotions. "I know you are shy about marriage, my child. But I have found you a fine young man who will care for you."

Suri kept her gaze on the floor as blood drummed softly in her ears.

"The young man is a friend of your cousin, Dushyant. Rangapani is twenty years old and the son of our general. He has risen in the ranks of our military through his bravery and will one day command the army for your brother."

Rangapani? Suri remembered him as a skinny boy who followed her cousin around like a shadow. At the thought of marrying him, she tensed like a deer spotting a tiger hiding in the brush.

Her mother touched her cheek. "Fear is normal, my child. But you need not be afraid. You will be no ordinary wife. Rangapani serves your father and knows his place. The boy will cherish you. You will never hear a cross word from him. Most importantly, you will remain in Jaisalpur, under my care."

Suri recoiled from her touch, rose abruptly, and went over to the window. Gray clouds cast the gardens below in dark shadows, reflecting her bitter mood. She would still be wed to a man she knew nothing about—a man who would be ordered to marry her and would obey, even if he disliked the mute princess. She longed to be out there when it rained, getting wet, rather than here with her mother.

Her father, King Vibudha, lumbered in without knocking. No crown rested on his mostly gray hair.

"You sent for me, Urmila?" he asked, out of breath from the short walk. He did not look at Suri.

"I have some news for you," her mother said, patting the chair beside her.

Her father stood hunched, his gray beard touching his chest. "I don't have time to wait." He never had any time for Suri—not to play with her as a child nor to ask about her well-being now. He had left her care entirely to his wife.

"I will be quick then. Suri has agreed to wed Rangapani," her mother said too brightly, rubbing her wrist.

Stunned silence followed as Suri felt her throat tighten. Had her mother mistaken her lack of tears for consent? She wished she could yell or tear her hair out. Her gaze shifted to her father, searching for any sign of resistance to the idea of his daughter— a princess—marrying a mere warrior. But he never glanced in her direction, not even to check her reaction to her mother's words. She could have been one of the bronze statues littered around the room, glowing dully, for all the attention he spared her.

"Rangapani is away on a mission for me. I expect him back in a day or two. I will announce the betrothal then," her father said promptly, throwing Suri into despair.

16

GIRIDHAR

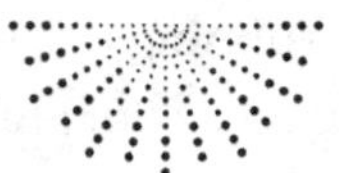

The skinny lad took him to a tiny room with an arrow-slit window, through which meager light filtered in, highlighting the sparse furnishings. A cot that would only fit a child stood against the wall with a worn blanket. Beside it rested a wooden chest, chipped and scuffed, as if it had been dragged roughly across the stone floors.

Giri looked around him. Dust swirled across the floor, and cobwebs covered the walls. The lad fetched him a broom and disappeared. Giri took it up with a grin. His mother would be wroth if she saw her precious son sweeping every corner of the room. Carefully, he collected the dust into a pile outside his door, leaving it there for the maid who cleaned the hallways to dispose of. He shook the thin blanket and folded it over the one solitary pillow.

As a room for a prince, it was pitiful. But as a room for a playwright, it was generous. A light wind traveled inside, carrying the smells of the garden outside.

The door opened, and Sangu peeped into the room. "There you are," he said awkwardly.

60

Giri raised his head and said nothing in front of the palace servant who had accompanied his guard.

Sangu looked around. "You have swept it," he said, surprised.

Giri nodded.

"I guess we are sharing this room. Who gets the cot?" his guard jested as he shut the door. Then he hurried to Giri's side and whispered in a voice that would not carry outside the room, "This room is not fit for a servant of your household, let alone a prince, my lord. Please reveal yourself to King Vibudha and command his horses to take us back home."

"Are you already tired of our simple ways?" Giri asked with a grin. "It is not time yet for us to return. Get me an audience with Princess Kanika so she can lead me to Poet Ravi." Giri longed to meet the poet and beg him, if necessary, to accompany him to Nidhapur.

Sangu glanced at his prince and nodded. While the guard departed to look for the princess, Giri wandered into the palace gardens, avoiding the pond and flower beds frequented by the royals. He found a young peepal tree, its trunk only as large as his thighs, its branches casting a web of shadows on the ground. He bent at the waist, carefully moving beneath the canopy, his head lowered to avoid the gnarled branches. When he reached the base of the trunk, he sank to the ground. The rough bark pressed against his back as he leaned on the tree with his legs stretched out in front, letting his mind wander.

The wind whispered in his ears, masking the sounds from the castle. His mind wandered from facing the wrath of his brother to the widow he was unable to help. It leaped from the words of Poet Ravi to the silence of the mute boy who had led him to the poet. But as he reined in his thoughts to the play he needed to craft, no tales flooded his imagination.

Soon, Giri understood the reason for this drought. He knew nothing of significance about King Vibudha, the star of his play. He knew of no battles the king had waged that would be worthy of immortalization in a play, nor did he know of great temple towers the king had built. Giri could take the barest thread and weave a carpet out of it, but he needed a silk thread first.

At the sound of rustling leaves, he looked up to see Sangu stoop under the canopy. His guard knelt in front of him. "There is a dance at the Durga temple this evening. The princesses are expected to attend."

Giri smiled. Sitting in the audience, he could pick up a tale or two about the king. Or he could send a message to Poet Ravi to write a poem about the ruler. This evening could provide the spark he needed.

To avoid detection by any spies, Sangu and Giri set out separately, with Giri leaving first. He watched the lamps being lit as he strolled through the hallways and exited the main palace through a side door. Trusting his guard to follow him, Giri stayed in the shadows of the buildings as he made his way to the temple.

Giri ignored the vendors hawking flower garlands outside the temple courtyard and made his way in. A small crowd thronged inside, vying for a standing spot on the gravel ground around the large hall encompassed by stone pillars. He scanned the hall, spotting a makeshift stage. Musicians stood to one side, tuning their instruments. A servant spread a silk carpet on the floor in front of the stage. Giri saw no royals yet to occupy their places on that carpet. He chose a spot between two pillars with an obscured view of the stage but a clear view of the royals.

As Giri waited for Princess Kanika, his eyes roamed the carvings on the pillar in front of him. Carved out of the rock, a serpent's sinuous body coiled around a large sphere. Its scales seemed to ripple and shimmer, winding tightly around Mother Earth. Above, its majestic hood flared protectively over the earth like a celestial umbrella.

As he marveled at the craftsmanship, he heard a noise from the entrance and spun around. Four men lowered a palanquin to the ground. A slender hand, lined with gold bangles, parted the ornate curtain. Standing beneath the pillar, Giri watched the girl who emerged gracefully, her delicate silhouette glowing against the evening sun, strangely captivated by her movement. Her fingers gripped the frame of the palanquin as her feet touched the ground, the folds of her sari cascading around her like a waterfall of silk. As she straightened, she scanned the surroundings, her eyes meeting his—widening in shock—before she looked away.

For a brief moment, his world seemed to fall away, and then a curious thought emerged. He knew her, though he had no recollection of ever meeting this girl.

He gazed at her as she climbed the stone steps and made her way to the carpet. He briefly glanced at the middle-aged woman who accompanied her. The golden crown sparkling on her head revealed her identity as Queen Urmila. Princess Kanika strolled behind these two women, her face brightening upon seeing him. With a bow, he acknowledged the princess, playing his part as the humble playwright.

His eyes returned to the girl, who lowered herself onto the carpet, adjusting the folds of her sari with the grace of a dancer. As if pulled by his unspoken desire, she turned her head and looked at him, her face a mixture of elation and dread. Giri was struck most by her eyes, which seemed to be pools of the black sea that tugged at something deep in his chest. He knew he was in danger of losing his way in them.

Sangu appeared by his side and saw the glance they exchanged. "That is Princess Suryavati." With a grin at his prince, he added, "Maybe something good will come from this quest, after all."

17

SURYAVATI

female dancer, dressed as Lord Krishna, leaped onto the stage with a peacock feather as her crown and a wooden flute tucked into her waist. Radha, his beloved, had waited long for him to arrive and beautifully expressed her torn emotions by rushing toward him with open arms, then spinning around in anger. Suri's mind wandered from the lovers' tiff playing out on stage to the man standing hidden between the pillars.

She could sense his eyes on her and worried he would recognize her as the mute boy he had tended to in sickness.

"The playwright is here," Kanika whispered into her ear, her face erupting into a grin. "Watching you like a hawk. Maybe he's wondering why the princess looks so familiar."

Suri glared at her cousin behind her mother's back.

"Is there a message the poet wants to pass along?" teased Kanika.

The scroll tucked into her sari folds with her next verses pressed against her waist. She did not want someone else to give them to Giri. She wanted to watch him read the lines, to observe the way his mouth curled around the words.

The dancers approaching them at the end of their performance pulled her back to the present. She greeted them with a polite smile.

"You transported me to Brindavan with your performance," the queen said as she handed them a pouch of silver coins.

Bowing deeply, the performers accepted their reward.

The queen rose to talk to the temple priests, while Suri stood hesitantly, wondering how to approach Giri. Being mute had never felt like a barrier until that moment when she could not whisper in Kanika's ear.

"He is coming," her cousin said, her eyes looking past Suri's shoulder.

Suri stiffened immediately, dread surging in her throat. She did not want him to recognize her.

"My lady," Giri said, his voice brushing her ears.

Kanika dipped her head in acknowledgment, while Suri stood with her back to the man, unable to move.

"Forgive my imprudence, but I hope you will pass a message to Poet Ravi," he said, as she watched her cousin's eyes sparkle with merriment.

Kanika sneaked a peek at her and then gazed past her. Ignoring his request, she asked, "What brings you to the castle?"

"Prince Vikaran has tasked me with creating a play celebrating our king, my lady." She wondered what story he would choose from her father's life. He had fought in a battle as a young prince, when her grandfather still ruled the kingdom. "I need the poet's help to bring this to life." Suri brightened at the thought of them leaning against a wall, heads close together, arguing over the scenes and shaping the tale. Then the dream shattered like a coconut dropped on a hard floor. She could never reveal her identity as the poet. Even if she did, how would she, a person who could not vocalize her thoughts, work with Giri? The best she could do was write a poem for the play. She would be content with that, she thought, to still the voices whispering otherwise.

"The poet is elusive. I will pass on your message to him," said Kanika, still grinning like an idiot. If she didn't stop, Kanika would reveal all her secrets. Suri cleared her throat and took a step forward, moving farther away from him.

"Apologies for the interruption, Princess Suryavati," said Giri in a cold tone. Suri was well aware that her behavior could come across as rude to Giri, but she made no effort to acknowledge his presence. Better for him to consider her discourteous than for him to find out she was the poet.

When she returned to her room, she ordered her maid to bring a tub for a bath. Servants carried pots of hot water and filled the tub to the brim. When the servants left her, she shut the door on Nanmaran, standing guard outside. She removed her clothes hurriedly and changed into her brother's old garments. Using her hands, she splashed the water, hoping it sounded like her stepping into the tub.

Then, tucking her scroll into her waist, she opened the window very slowly and slid down the tree. Gradually, she crept into the dark, staying in the shadows. A light wind rustled the leaves, masking her tiny sounds. After making sure no one followed, she relaxed her shoulders and nearly bumped into someone.

A sharp yelp was followed by two people leaping apart as Suri tried to blend into the background. One of the figures, a girl, vanished into the night. The boy pushed his hair back and straightened, halting Suri. Abhayan?

Instead of retreating, she moved forward and faced him with her hands on her hips. He saw through her disguise immediately. "Suri?" her brother stammered. "What are you doing here? Are those my clothes?"

She continued to glare at him. Did he not know the folly of fooling with a girl?

"It was nothing," he muttered, bowing his head. "Don't say anything about this to Mother, and I'll pretend I didn't see you strolling outside at night." With that, he strode away without a backward glance.

She sighed. She would deal with him in the morning. She continued to Giri's quarters and knocked on his door.

Giri opened the door, holding an oil lamp in one hand. As the light fell on her face, he whispered, "Princess?" All warmth fled her body, replaced by a fear that he knew her secret. Peeking outside, he looked both ways before pulling her in and shutting the door behind her.

Then the corners of his mouth lifted into a smile, lighting up his eyes and soaking the corners of her heart in overwhelming brightness.

18

GIRIDHAR

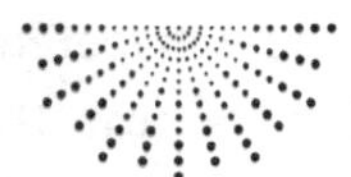

*O*nce the dance ended, Giri approached Princess Kanika to ask her to pass on a message to Poet Ravi. As he neared the princess, his mind went blank, much to his astonishment. The presence of Princess Suryavati had distracted him. It was a very strange feeling, as if merely breathing the same air as her had intoxicated him.

Princess Suryavati, on the other hand, completely ignored him, not even acknowledging his presence. Somehow, a part of his mind took over and carried on a conversation with Princess Kanika, while the rest of it ached for Princess Suryavati to spin around and gaze at him. Instead, she cleared her throat and stepped away.

Brought back to his senses, he remembered he had passed himself off as a playwright, while she was the princess of this kingdom. "Apologies for the interruption, Princess Suryavati," he said humbly, hoping for a glance. She departed without uttering a word to him.

Standing alone, he watched her lustrous hair flowing down in abundance to her waist. "What blunder did I commit to earn her silence?" he muttered, wondering why he felt this pull toward a girl he hardly knew.

Sangu heard him as he came closer. "She lost her ability to speak due to an illness in childhood," he said in a quiet voice. "I just learned about it this afternoon, while talking to a maid."

Mute? Her lips, her eyes, the tip of her nose floated into his mind along with visions of the mute boy. He forgot to breathe as he realized the mute boy who had slept in his tent was the princess. He was not the only one masquerading in humble clothes. He knew why he disguised himself—to stay hidden from his brother. Why did she come to him as a boy? Not only a boy but a boy who knew Poet Ravi. The thing he had missed earlier landed on his head like a boulder. She was Poet Ravi. That seemed the only reason for her disguise.

That night, he paced his room, lost in thought. He couldn't decide his next steps. He still wished to work with Poet Ravi, but if his suspicions were correct, it wouldn't be simple to collaborate with the princess. He suspected she wanted to remain hidden. If royal families were wary of a playwright prince, they would abhor a poet princess even more. Revealing her passion would only bring her harm. The sparse cot offered no comfort, so he decided to go to the garden.

As he pulled an upper garment on, a knock sounded on his door. Sangu had disappeared to learn the secrets of the palace, and he did not expect his guard to return till dawn. Wondering who sought him at this time, he opened the door. The mute boy stood outside. Though dressed in plain clothes, her graceful movements and confident demeanor proclaimed her status as clearly as if she were dressed in silk.

"Princess?" he asked, and the princess turned aghast, recoiling like a startled deer. He took that as confirmation of her identity. Making sure she was alone, he tugged her into his room and shut the door.

Despite his misgivings, a moment of pure joy, not coated by worry, surged through him as he faced the poet. The princess seemed frozen in shock, and his smile dissipated in a rush. Before he could react, she pulled a knife from the folds of her garment—one he had gifted to the mute boy—pointed it toward him, and growled.

"I am not going to hurt you," he said, watching her and waiting to see if the tension in her face dissipated. His reassurance appeared to calm her, and her face emptied of all emotion, though he knew a shock of this nature would take time to subside.

"Why are you here, my lady?" he asked, astonished by her courage in seeking him.

She removed a scroll tucked into her waist and handed it to him. He placed the oil lamp on the wooden chest, read the lines quietly, and then narrated the poem crafted by them from memory, turning to gaze at her.

Blinded by love, I go
To the place where nothing stirs
Charging through the brush, although
In fear my heart murmurs.

I hear a sharp howl of pain
Piercing the deep quietness
Cry of someone in chain
While I search around restless.

Silence followed, her breathing filling his ears, tense and eager. She watched him as closely as he watched her, while her face remained a stoic mask. A tension hung between them, so heavy it pressed against his chest. At that moment, he knew he had fallen for this brave girl who wrote poetry that melted his heart. Two armies fought a fierce battle in his head: one wanted him to court the princess, the other to befriend the poet. He could not decide which side to take. As a playwright, he faced steep consequences for courting a princess, so that path would have to wait until he was ready to drop his impersonation. In the meantime, befriending the poet allowed him to develop a friendship with her, a rare opportunity he did not want to miss.

"Will you collaborate on the play with me?" he asked. The wind seeping in stirred up the sultry air.

Her eyes smiled as she nodded. Imagining working with her filled his heart with a strange sensation, one he could not classify.

She gestured toward herself with her right hand, imploring him silently, and he understood her even without any words being uttered.

"I will guard your secret," he replied. "However, you visiting me is not safe, my lady. Let me escort you partway to your chambers, and you can show me a secure place for us to meet."

They walked along the dimly lit halls, and he was aware of every movement of her slender body. He watched the shadow cast by her on the floor, her feet stepping soundlessly, his heart hungry and full of that strange emotion that he now recognized as hope.

When they got outside, a faint moon hung in the sky, and Giri could smell a flowery scent emanating from her. He strode, impatient to get to her hidden spot, a tingling sensation climbing up his back.

She led them into thick trees through which little light escaped. He could barely see his hands, let alone her. "My lady, I cannot see in this darkness," he whispered, not wanting to lose sight of her. Her hand, warm and soft, grasped his, and he knew he would walk to the ends of the world holding it.

As they walked past the palace pond, the croaking of frogs could be heard, a breeze bringing in the smell of wet mud. She guided them to a cluster of about six or seven trees growing close to each other, their deep roots ancient and formidable.

Letting go of him, she approached the large tree in the

middle. As she reached her hand toward the tree, he heard a gentle hiss. Forgetting she had good hearing, he leaped into the air, grabbing her by the waist and pulling her back. Something slipped out of a hole in that tree.

19

SURYAVATI

Giri's hand wrapped around her waist like a silk sari. She could hear his pounding heart against her back, her own heart beating in harmony with his. She had heard the hiss of a snake earlier, but before she could react, Giri had pulled her away. She barely noticed the tiny snake slithering down the tree—it must have made the hole its home. All her attention focused on his warm breath coating the back of her neck. She was not prepared for the assault on her senses from his nearness. She was drawn to him like a moth to a flame, though she knew the danger of the fire.

Giri dropped his hand and took a step back. Cold air rushed to fill the space vacated by him, and a sudden loss clutched her stomach. Her mother had revealed in many different ways that Suri was not a desirable match for any man. Since she was old enough to grasp the meaning of marriage, Suri understood that only her royal status prevented her from remaining a spinster. A man would only marry her because of her wealth and connections.

An intense ache spread through her limbs from the yearning churning in her stomach. She almost threw herself at Giri, ready to lay bare her passion, until she realized with chilling despair that he knew her true identity. He might pretend to reciprocate her feelings because he saw the princess, not the mute poet. No one wanted to court the mute girl who wrote strange poems. She needed to remember that.

Giri cleared his throat. "Do we leave messages for each other in that hole, my lady?" he asked. His voice embraced her like the wind, and she imagined his fingers tracing her skin.

She nodded brusquely, trying hard to contain her overflowing emotions. A lone tear slid down her cheek, and she brushed it away before he saw it.

"My lady?" His voice caressed her. She stiffened her shoulders, frustrated that she could not just say what she wanted to convey.

Giri shifted to face her, moonlight draping him in silver. He gazed at her intently, his look sweeping over her like a brush of silk. "Am I—May I—Is everything all right with you?" His tone seemed filled with care, but that could have been just her longing coloring his words.

Suri nodded again and dipped her head in farewell. Leaving Giri standing amid the mighty trees, she walked back to her chamber. Her mind preoccupied, she let her memory guide her, reaching the door that led inside the palace. She pushed the right spot, and the door swung open.

Suri glided through the dark hallways, eager to change back into a sari and climb into her bed before her mother or her guard came looking for her. Suddenly, she heard footsteps echoing down the corridor. Instinctively, she ducked into a nearby room, pressing her back against the cool stone wall, barely daring to breathe. She listened, straining to hear any clue about who might be approaching, as her heart pounded in her chest.

The footsteps grew louder, and soon a figure entered the room. Suri's breath caught in her throat, and she shrank deeper into the shadows. The figure moved with purpose, seemingly unaware of her presence. Stealthily, Suri crept behind a curtain, hoping they would leave soon. Instead, another set of footsteps approached, and a second person entered the room, closing the door firmly behind them.

The first person spoke, their voice low and urgent. "Are you sure it is wise to marry Suri to Rangapani?"

Suri's eyes widened as she recognized the voice—it was her uncle. She leaned forward slightly, trying to catch a glimpse of him without revealing herself. The second person stepped closer to her uncle, and in the dim light, she could make out their silhouette but not their features. Then the second person spoke, and Suri's heart sank—it was her mother.

"What other options do I have?" her mother replied, her tone equally urgent.

Suri's heart leaped out of her body. Why were they meeting in secrecy? She longed to step forward and demand answers, but she knew revealing herself now could jeopardize everything.

"Rangapani is not her peer in wealth or wit," said her uncle, warming her heart.

Suri's mind raced. Would her mother agree with him? She held her breath, hoping to remain undetected long enough to learn more.

Her mother sighed, her voice heavy with resignation. "I know, but someone inferior to her will treat her with respect. She is voiceless, Vikaran. I cannot risk sending her to a strange land, married to a powerful man who might treat her poorly."

Suri's heart ached at the fear in her mother's voice.

Her uncle placed his hands on her mother's shoulder. "You are underestimating her, Urmi. Suri deserves a man who understands her. Rangapani is not that man."

Her mother responded with a hint of frustration. "She will never find a man who sees her as an equal."

"You found someone who cherishes you," her uncle said in a strange voice.

"Don't bring us into this," her mother replied.

What were they talking about? Suri remained hidden, listening intently, hoping to piece together the puzzle from the shadows.

A sliver of light appeared under the door, signaling that someone was outside. Her uncle and mother immediately quieted, their conversation cutting off abruptly. After a moment, the light under the door disappeared, and the room was once again plunged into darkness.

"I am leaving," her mother whispered urgently. Without another word, she hurried toward the door. She paused for a moment to open it, casting a cautious glance around the hallway before slipping out. Her uncle followed closely behind, softly shutting the door after them.

Suri remained pressed against the wall, her heart racing. She waited until she could no longer hear their footsteps before allowing herself to relax slightly. What was the reason for this strange meeting in the middle of the night?

2 0

GIRIDHAR

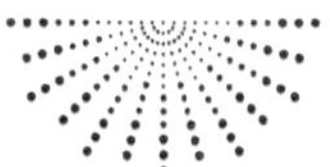

Giri stood amidst the towering trees, troubled for the princess. She was in distress, and he had let her depart without a word of solace. As the night air enveloped him, the next verses of their poem came to him.

He hastened to his chamber, drew the lone oil lamp close, and wrote with fervor. Not waiting for dawn, he made his way back to the tree. He tapped the hollow with a stick to check for serpents, then dropped the palm scroll within.

Sleep eluded him as he tossed and turned on his thin bed, the image of Princess Suryavati etched in his mind. When he had imagined Poet Ravi as a man, he had dreamed of a friendship based on their shared love of poetry. Now his heart craved more than friendship. He envisioned a lifetime bond forged with a girl who wrote poetry, someone who shared his passion. But she was not just any girl—she was a princess, an ideal match for him. His insides warmed as if he had drunk nectar. In the past, he had always considered marriage a necessary burden, an act that would bring him little joy. He had resigned himself to that life.

Now, his mind conjured a different world, one even beyond

77

his dreams—a union with a girl who would understand his need for creating stories, a true companion. His mind raced ahead in a dreamy state, but then, abruptly, it was as if a boulder had dropped on his head. He had forgotten one key characteristic of the princess—she was mute. His brother and mother would never approve of him marrying a princess who never uttered a word, especially if he were to ascend the throne after his brother.

The power of royalty rested on the stories they wove—tales of divine incarnations, invincibility, and superiority over the common populace. That image had to be preserved, even at great cost. A mute girl shattered the illusion of their extraordinariness. Without that myth, why would the common man be willing to pay levies, serve in an army, or die for their monarchs?

All the joy from earlier drained away, leaving him dejected, as if he had woken up from a dream filled with colors into a dark reality. When Sangu knocked on the door before dawn, he threw off the sheet and rose.

After opening the door for his guard, Giri shut it behind him. "Did you discover all the secrets of this place?"

"I made a few good friends who offered me some gossip. Apparently, Princess Suryavati is marrying Rangapani, son of the Jaisalpur general." Sangu stretched his hands overhead and yawned, not realizing the impact of his words on his prince.

Giri rubbed his dry eyes—another reason for him to forget Princess Suryavati. "I am heading to the river for a bath."

Leaving his guard to get some rest, Giri strolled outside. Faint daylight edged in through the windows like smoke creeping under a door, providing meager light. With shadows for company, he walked to the river, worrying about staying in Jaisalpur.

The water, calm and translucent, mocked his fears. He removed his dhoti and placed it under a tree. As soon as he plunged into the water, his worries dissolved, leaving him weightless. He swam across the narrow river, gazing at the pebbles resting at the bottom, wondering how far they had traveled from their mountain homes.

The solitude gave him peace to rearrange his thoughts. Just yesterday, he had been eager to work with Poet Ravi to create a masterpiece. Why should he abandon that plan upon learning that Poet Ravi was a woman? As the sky brightened, he decided to stay and finish the play.

As he rose, water dripping from his limbs, a sweeping gust of wind swirled around him. Marching to his clothes, he pushed aside the whisper in his head that the true reason he wished to remain in Jaisalpur was his attraction to the princess. Drying himself, he draped his dhoti around his waist and legs.

If the princess was getting married soon, he had only a short time to work with her to create the play. He knew nothing about its subject and needed to rectify that. Fortunately, he had a way to do so while also feeding his body.

Familiar with the layout of palaces, he had no trouble finding the communal kitchen. After loading his plate with a simple rice and lentil dish, he found a quiet corner and sat on the floor. The warm, spicy aroma of the food filled the room with a comforting atmosphere. Head bowed, he ate slowly, his ears tuned to the conversations around him—the voices of servants, warriors, and courtiers blending into a lively hum.

It did not take him long to notice a recurring theme—Prince Vikaran, the brother of the king, was mentioned more often than King Vibudha.

"He has returned, then?" one man remarked, stroking his beard. "Prince Vikaran has come back from the flood-hit regions."

"That is a rare sight," said the man beside him, shaking his head. "Our prince hardly steps beyond the palace walls, yet few know how much he labors for the people."

"Indeed," another joined in, leaning forward. "I heard he's been working with farmers on a new irrigation plan—one that will bring them steady water while keeping the river from turning against them. He wished to see the flooded lands with his own eyes, to be certain his designs would hold."

Giri finished his meal in thoughtful silence, wondering how he would write a play about a king overshadowed by his brother.

Giri walked back to his room, pondering his next steps, when an older man accosted him.

"Are you the new playwright?" the man asked in a belligerent tone.

Giri looked him over. He wore a thin gold chain around his neck, and his black and grey hair was tied back. The man looked like a courtier of some importance. Giri knew he was not a prince here in Jaisalpur, so he acted accordingly.

"I am Giri, and many question if I can call myself a playwright," Giri said with a self-effacing smile.

The other man did not return his smile. Instead, he glared at Giri. "I am the Royal Poet of Jaisalpur. How come I have never heard of you before?" His stern expression cast a shadow over the brightening hall.

Sensing this was not a casual visit, Giri straightened his shoulders. "I lived in Garthapuri before I arrived here," he answered. He had become proficient at these half-truths. He did stay in Garthapuri for a few days, courting Princess Lalitha. That ended in disaster, and he fled the kingdom. Too ashamed to return home, he came here.

The Royal Poet took a step closer. "You are new, as I suspected. As the Royal Poet of Jaisalpur, I must ensure that all literary works adhere to our traditions. You will show me each scene as you craft it."

Giri felt a strong desire to protect his creative process.

"Royal Poet, I will happily share my work once it is complete," he said, keeping his voice steady.

The Royal Poet's eyes flashed with irritation. "You may believe you are creating a masterpiece, but it needs my approval to see the light of day. Is that clear?"

Giri swallowed his response, not wanting to create a powerful enemy. Instead, he nodded meekly.

The Royal Poet smirked. "Good. See that you remember it." With that, he turned on his heel and left in the opposite direction.

SURYAVATI

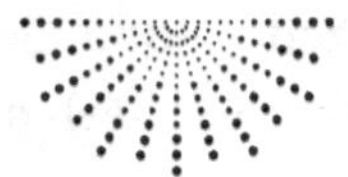

Suri lay still on her bed, watching the moon travel across the sky, her thoughts drifting to her mother and her uncle. She could not help but wonder why they had met in the middle of the night. She knew her mother consulted her uncle on important matters because her father never had the patience for her. Suri was no different in that regard. She had turned to her uncle to bring the playwright to the palace rather than ask her father. Even if her father had cared enough to listen, he would have rejected her. A worrying thought lay in the recesses of her mind; she tried to grasp it, but it evaded her.

Was it only that morning her mother had proposed her marriage to Rangapani? Suri had barely any time to contemplate it, but hearing her uncle's opposition cheered her. With him on her side, she might find a way to wriggle out of the marriage. Like the female poet Avvaiyar, who had lived two centuries ago, she wished she could remain a spinster and continue writing poems.

A gentle night breeze carried to her the feelings she had when Giri's arms had wrapped around her. She sighed, knowing the futility of her yearning. To stop her insistent thoughts, she slowed her breath, and it began to work. She fell into a fitful sleep as the sun rose in splendor, dreaming of the warm embrace of Giri.

Deep in her sleep, she woke suddenly, a noise penetrating her sleepy haze. Hearing a servant yell outside, she tugged her silk sheets to her chin, curled up, and drifted back into slumber.

Then, she heard it clearly—the sound of anklets. Kanika, her cousin, swept into the room. "The sun has been up for hours, yet here you are, still nestled in bed," she mocked.

Suri groaned softly, nestling deeper into her pillow.

Kanika moved to the window, throwing open the shutters to let in the full light of morning. "A glorious day is unfolding, and there is no time to waste. Tell me, what message does the poet wish to pass on to the playwright today?" she asked, her eyes gleaming with curiosity and mischief.

Suri's cheeks flushed with a mix of embarrassment and irritation. She wanted to keep her clandestine meeting with Giri hidden, but Kanika, who knew her so well, would guess something was amiss if she acted strangely. She sighed, swinging her legs over the side of the bed.

Kanika raised an eyebrow, a playful smile tugging at the corners of her mouth. "You know how these walls have ears, and tongues wag freely in the palace. If you have a message for him, it's better I deliver it discreetly than have some nosy maid or guard see you with him and start rumors."

Suri hesitated, longing to see Giri that day. She decided to keep her connection with him hidden from her cousin and nodded reluctantly. She would check the hole in the tree later that night to see if he had left a message for her.

She sat at her table and pulled a dry palm leaf toward her. Like a lightning strike, a sudden thought struck her. She hurriedly wrote, "Let us tell the tale of the King and Queen of Jaisalpur, starting with their wedding."

Since seeing her mother last night, Suri realized she had

underestimated her mother and her role in the welfare of their kingdom. She was suddenly eager to learn more about her. She recalled the quiet strength in her mother's eyes, even when her father disregarded her wishes. There was a grace to her that Suri had overlooked. Since her mother had placed many obstacles in her path, Suri had treated her as a hindrance to overcome. She had never truly desired to understand her.

Suri's quill moved swiftly across the palm leaf, asking Giri to meet with her mother. In the back of her mind, the thought of crafting this story with Giri brought a secret smile to her lips. She handed the scroll to her cousin.

Kanika's expression softened slightly as she read the message. "Be careful, Suri. Don't let your heart get tangled in this treacherous place."

Suri could not bear the pity in her cousin's eyes and yearned to scream. She did not want to be treated like a delicate clay sculpture that would break at the slightest touch. Instead, she managed a small smile, trying not to be angry at Kanika's genuine concern.

With a nod, Kanika left the room, closing the door behind her. Suri stood and moved to the window, gazing out at the sprawling palace grounds below. The morning light bathed everything in a golden hue, and before she had a moment to reflect, her mother entered the room.

"Rangapani is a good boy and will take care of you," her mother said without any preamble. "Marrying him will allow you to remain in Jaisalpur," she added, approaching Suri.

A wave of nausea hit Suri at the thought of marrying this stranger. The room seemed to spin, the walls closing in around her. She struggled to maintain her composure, but the effort was too great. Her mother touched her shoulder gently, and it was as if the last thread of her strength snapped. Suri collapsed into her mother's arms, hot tears pooling in her eyes and spilling down her cheeks.

Her mother's arms wrapped around her, holding her tightly. She began to rub Suri's back in slow, soothing circles. "I would not let any harm come to you," she murmured, her voice soft and comforting.

Suri pulled back slightly, looking up into her mother's eyes. Her mother sighed, her own eyes glistening with unshed tears. Suri remembered her earlier desire to learn more about her mother. She rubbed her eyes and walked to a plate of rice she kept on her table. On the rice, she wrote,

Tell me about your marriage.

Her mother's eyes softened. "In our world, choices are often made for us."

2 2

GIRIDHAR

With the Royal Poet's warning ringing in his head, Giri strolled through the palace gardens. He had no ideas for a story, not even a single grain. The more he learned about King Vibudha, the less inclined he was to portray him as the central character in his tale.

The sound of footsteps caused him to halt.

"I ran into Princess Kanika. She recognized me from yesterday and remembered seeing me with you. She asked me to tell you that she wants to meet with you," Sangu said, coming to a stop beside him.

Giri wondered why Princess Suryavati's cousin wanted to see him. Did she know about their clandestine meeting last night? He decided that it was not his secret to reveal.

Sangu led the way through some banana trees. A few purple banana flowers greeted them as bees buzzed around the ripe banana clusters. As Giri pushed a long banana leaf out of his way, he saw a cascade of silk. Princess Kanika turned to face him as he approached her. He bowed his head, playing his role as the humble playwright.

"I brought you Poet Ravi's message. He will disappear if you

86

attempt to find him. Send any message through me," she said, arching an eyebrow and handing him a palm leaf scroll. With a curt nod, she disappeared.

Giri realized that Princess Kanika did not know he had already found the poet. Leaving Sangu, he found a quiet spot under a neem tree and read Princess Suryavati's message.

"Every man has a shadow. King Vibudha's shadow is Queen Urmila. Let us shed some light on him so the shadow grows."

A smile spread across Giri's face. Princess Suryavati wished to tell her mother's tale. He pondered how he might gain an audience with the queen. Perhaps he could entreat Prince Vikaran to arrange a meeting.

Presently, a guard approached him once more with further tidings. "Poet Giri?"

Giri nodded and rose.

"The queen has summoned you to her presence."

Giri assumed the princess had arranged this meeting with her mother and wondered if her mother knew her secret. His knowledge of the royal duties of a princess led him to believe that the princess safeguarded her secret like a crow guarding its nest.

The guard stood patiently beside the tree, his posture straight and expression impassive, waiting for Giri to emerge from under the vast tree. Giri followed him through winding corridors, his mind racing with anticipation. They arrived at a modestly adorned door, which the guard opened before motioning for Giri to enter.

As Giri stepped inside, he observed the room before him. It was not the queen's private chamber but rather a space likely designated for meetings with individuals such as himself. The small hall was decorated with understated elegance. A few ornate wooden chairs, carved with intricate patterns, were arranged around the room. In the center of the floor lay a large rug depicting a tranquil pond filled with lotus blossoms, its colors rich and vivid. Sunlight streamed in through a large window, spilling light across the room and illuminating the majestic flowers on the rug.

Giri gazed out the window, momentarily lost in thought as he admired the view. The gentle hum of the palace garden reached his ears, mixing with the distant chatter of courtiers. Suddenly, he heard the soft rustle of silk and the light patter of footsteps approaching.

Turning his head, Giri saw Princess Suryavati enter the room behind her mother. Suryavati's eyes met his briefly, and the princess paused, holding herself like a bow stretched taut. He noticed a flicker of misgiving pass across her face. His instinct had told him that the queen did not know of her daughter's life as a poet, and he guessed the princess worried that he might betray her identity.

Giri, masquerading as a playwright and not as the prince he truly was, understood her concern. He inclined his head slightly to reassure her, while the princess scanned his face intently. Whatever Suryavati saw convinced her of his loyalty, and she relaxed her shoulders, the tension that had gripped her moments before beginning to ease.

Her mother approached the center of the room, unaware of the silent exchange between her daughter and him. "Welcome, Playwright Giri," the queen said. "I trust you find your stay at the palace to your liking?"

Giri bowed deeply. "My stay has been most comfortable. I am honored to be here." He kept his voice steady and composed, doing his utmost not to glance at her daughter, though his eyes longed to feast on her face. He hoped his demeanor would reassure Suryavati that her trust was not misplaced.

The queen took a seat on one of the ornate chairs, while Suryavati stood slightly behind her. "We are pleased to have such a talented playwright in our court. My brother-in-law has spoken highly of your work. My daughter wishes for me to recount the story of my marriage so that you may weave it into the tale of our king."

Anticipation filled Giri as he nodded, his demeanor respectful and attentive. "My lady, I am keenly aware of the significance this story holds, and I will ensure that its telling is worthy of your legacy."

For a while, silence reigned in the room as the queen stared outside, her right thumb pressing against her left wrist absently. "In my youth," the queen began, her expression unreadable, "my sister Neelavati had a Swayamvara. It was a grand event, as our parents had expected her to choose King Vibudha, who had no heirs from his previous marriage."

The queen paused, her eyes momentarily distant as she recalled the past. "But instead of fulfilling their expectations, Neelavati chose King Lambhodara, a man known for his indulgence and wayward ways, unworthy of my sister's love and devotion. Her choice shocked everyone and led to her estrangement from our family."

Giri listened intently, his gaze fixed on the queen, knowing he was hearing the tale of King Dushyant's parents. When his wife had died, Lambhodara had returned to his drunken ways, neglecting his duties as a king and a father. It fell upon Queen Urmila to rescue her sister's children and raise them as her own, ensuring they did not suffer the consequences of their father's actions. In one way, Dushyant had resembled his father. Dushyant won the hand of Princess Lalitha at her Swayamvara, sending Giri into his exile.

"At the time of my sister's marriage, I was not yet of age," the queen continued, her voice growing stronger. "But as the years passed and I came of age, my parents arranged my marriage to King Vibudha, fulfilling the alliance they had long desired."

The room was silent, the weight of the queen's story hanging heavily in the air. Giri knew King Vibudha was in the sixth decade of his life. There likely existed at least two decades of age difference between him and his queen. This union, like most royal alliances, was no merger of their hearts.

Suryavati placed a comforting hand on her mother's shoulder, as if she understood her mother's pain. Giri wondered if Suryavati dreaded her impending nuptials with Rangapani. The queen sat straight, not acknowledging her daughter's gesture.

"I broke the curse while fulfilling my duty by providing the king with two heirs," the queen continued after a few moments, sounding more like a warrior recounting a battle victory than a loving wife. "That is the story of my marriage and the legacy of my family," the queen concluded, her voice losing its earlier calmness. "I have other urgent matters to attend to," she said, her composure now visibly shaken.

The queen departed in haste. Before Suryavati followed her, she thrust a torn parchment into his hand. "*Tonight*," it read.

23

SURYAVATI

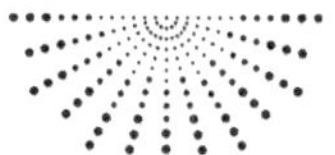

The day passed torturously slowly for Suri, who waited eagerly for the sun to bid farewell to the earth. Giri had not betrayed her confidence, and that alone caused her heart to flutter. When the moon rose, she slid down the tree outside her window and made her way to the cluster of trees she had shown Giri. After making sure no snake resided in the hole, she plunged her hand into it and drew out a palm leaf.

She strode to a clearing, eager to read the next two lines in the poem. She tilted the leaf to catch the moonlight.

I hear her pitiful moan
But I cannot tell from where

Her heart nearly stopped as she read his lines again, her fingers tracing the letters. She did not realize she was crying for help until the meaning of his verse sank in. But a mere playwright could not save her from her marriage to Rangapani. Maybe her mother was right. By marrying Rangapani, she could continue to live in Jaisalpur, under her mother's protection. No,

91

she did not want that life. She would be a bird in a golden cage, her wings clipped, with no poetry to feed her heart and mind.

She heard the crunch of leaves and turned to see Giri walking toward her. He paused in the clearing, the moonlight coating him in silver light, making him shimmer like a warrior come to rescue her. He bowed to her, but Suri sensed no deference in his posture. As he moved closer, she realized that while he was courteous, there was no submissiveness in his manner. Did he view himself as her peer because of their mutual love of poetry? It would be a mistake to allow a commoner to get close to her heart.

She straightened her shoulders, crossed her arms, and glared at him. A mistake. She noticed the tiny droplets of mist on his hair and a faint smell of the river on his person. She stood riveted, forgetting her manners.

An owl swooped out of the trees and flew past their heads. He glanced up at the bird and then back at her. She realized she was still staring at him, as if she wanted to devour him. She took a step back, and her foot caught in a protruding root, causing her to falter. Giri reached out and caught her elbow, steadying her. His touch sent a frenzy of emotions through her body.

Frustrated with her traitorous body, Suri shook off his hand, trying to calm her heart. Instead, she lost her balance and nearly tumbled to the ground. This time, Giri's arm slipped around her waist, pulling her close to him to keep her from falling. She gazed up, ready to glare at him, only to find a playful smile on his face. He truly looked at her—something people rarely did, afraid to see her defect reflected in her eyes. But not him. He seemed to see all of her. The warmth in his eyes melted her defenses. Steady on her feet, she heard the beating of his heart, which matched her frenetic pace.

Abruptly, Giri dropped his arm and took a step back, and she nearly threw herself at him, feeling the loss of warmth immediately. His voice halted her.

"My lady," Giri said in a soft voice, "I have an idea for the opening of our play." He stared at the top of the trees as if he expected the idea to drift down from the leaves. She wondered if he was purposely avoiding her gaze.

She could not let her heart rule her mind and ruin their relationship. If he left, she would have no one to share her love of words. She nodded encouragingly for him to continue.

"We can start with a girl portraying Queen Urmila discussing the virtues of King Vibudha with her mother." She pondered if her father had any worthy virtues. He had not harmed her mother or her—maybe that counted.

Giri paused, still staring at the trees. She wished she had her voice to inquire what marvels he beheld among the branches. As if reading her mind, he turned to glance at her, his face losing all its earlier playfulness.

He bent his head and chuckled nervously. "What do you think of my opening?"

Suri dropped to the ground, her fingers tracing the cool sand as she tried to capture her thoughts. But the moonlight was too faint, the words barely visible in the dim glow. She heard Giri's footsteps approach and looked up.

"Write on my hand," he suggested softly, extending his palm toward her.

She hesitated, her breath catching as memories of her earlier reaction to his touch resurfaced. The warmth of his arm around her waist, the way it had sent her heart into a frenzied dance— she wasn't sure she could handle that again. But she nodded, trying to steady herself, and took his hand in hers.

Carefully, she began to write, her fingers moving over his skin with delicate precision. The contact was electric, sending a shiver through her as she formed each letter.

Describe her virtues to my father.

She spelled out the words on his palm.

As she finished, she looked up at him, her gaze lingering on his face, trying to gauge his reaction. She saw immediate understanding on his face.

"You have good instincts for storytelling," he said, wonder suffusing his voice.

You are surprised because I am a woman?

Giri turned to her and bowed. "I meant no disrespect, my lady. I know no man who is your equal."

They stood beneath the night sky, Giri speaking with fervor as he discussed the play, while Suri scribbled her thoughts on his arm. Soon, before she finished her sentences, Giri nodded his understanding, their thoughts blending into one. In that moment, her entire world seemed to shrink to just this—this man, and the shared passion for stories that bound them together. In the world of make-believe, rules that one accepted in real life did not apply, and that made Suri free.

Isn't the story filled with hardships and heartaches?

"Good stories are filled with joy. Great ones are filled with pain we endure and overcome," he said.

They would have stood there all night, Suri holding his hand, if not for the tiny drops of water showering down.

At first, it was just a light drizzle, misting their faces and making the world around them shimmer. She glanced up, feeling the rain's gentle touch on her skin, and her grip on his hand tightened slightly.

Within moments, the drizzle turned into a steady rain,

soaking through their clothes and sending ripples through the puddles forming at their feet. The earthy scent of wet soil filled the air, mingling with the freshness of the rain. Suri's hair clung to her face as she laughed softly, the sound mingling with the patter of raindrops. Giri looked at her as though seeing her for the first time, his gaze deep and searching.

24

GIRIDHAR

The beautiful princess in front of him had bewitched him completely with story ideas even before the rain fell on her lustrous locks and drifted down to her neck. His eyes traced the path of the water with hunger, longing to touch the hollow in her throat, where a drop of water sparkled.

Suryavati's fingers around his arm tightened, and then she laughed with pure joy, turning her face up. Lightning brightened the sky, illuminating a curl of her hair nestled along her neck, tantalizing him to touch it—to feel the silky waves.

A loud thunder followed, and he felt her shiver. Instinctively, he draped his free arm around her shoulders and pulled her close. He felt her warm breath on his neck as she reached out and moved the hair falling over his forehead.

Giri dropped his gaze to her moist lips as they parted invitingly. His heart quickened as the princess leaned toward him. Her fingers circled his neck and tugged him lower. Her face was mere fingernail-length away from his. He felt the blood rising to his face. With no resistance left in him, he kissed her lips softly, while his hand circled her tender waist.

The entire world disappeared, and only the scent of her wet

96

skin remained. Her fingers clutched his hair in a possessive manner, sending tremors through his stomach.

The howl of a fox brought him back to reality. Her parents had picked a match for her, and he was still role-playing as a playwright. With regret, he lifted his head. Suryavati still held his face with both hands, her body pressed into his. Her scent disoriented him, and he clenched his fist to stay in control. She saw him as he wished to be seen and understood the depth of his heart. Yet, his mind reminded him that she didn't know his full story—the one where he was a prince. Can love truly flourish in soil built on lies?

"It is getting late, my lady. Please allow me to escort you back." He shifted uneasily, feeling the wet leaves crunch under him.

Suryavati swayed for a moment like a drunken soldier, and he resisted the temptation to wrap her in his arms. Then she laughed bitterly and stepped back.

Without looking at him, she gestured for him to stay and ambled away.

The rain vanished with her, and a cool breeze encased him in the scent of the earth. With a sigh, he squeezed the water from his clothes. He scanned the surroundings, but she had disappeared from view. He imagined her moving through the darkness, her chest heaving, breathing in the moist air. Slowly, he made his way back. Her touch had awakened something in him, and a tumult of confusion and desire coursed through him.

Alone in his room, he remembered her warm lips against his. He fell asleep thinking of her.

Thump.

Giri smelled horses and stiffened. Had Sangu returned from the stables? He opened his eyes.

A slight figure sat on his wooden chest, dressed in silk clothes. He blinked, and the figure came into focus—a boy. A simple gold crown rested on his head. The boy watched him intently, his arm resting limply on his thighs.

"My sister has taken a liking to you." The boy's lips bowed in distaste. His sister? He must be Prince Abhayan. "She has such poor judgment," he continued in a mature manner that clashed with his boyish looks.

Giri's mouth was parched; he was unbearably thirsty. He ran a hand over his face and swung his legs to the floor. He wanted to swat the prince's head for waking him up. He breathed in, then out. Reluctantly, he rose and bowed.

"My lord, had you sent word, I would have come to you myself," he rasped, his voice hoarse and dry.

The prince tilted his head, regarding him like a wooden toy.

"I beg your forgiveness. I need a drink of water," he said and walked to the clay pot. The room was silent as he lifted the pot to his dry lips. The cool water slid down his throat and coiled softly into his stomach. He set the vessel down and wiped his mouth.

The gangly prince continued to gaze at him, his eyes glinting with intelligence.

"You mentioned your sister," said Giri, infusing deference into his voice to avoid raising any suspicions in the young prince's mind about his relationship with her. Yet even Giri himself was unsure of what the princess truly meant to him.

"I am visiting a nearby flood-affected village with my father. My sister wants me to take you along so you can learn more about our king." The prince narrowed his eyes contemplatively, reminding Giri of his uncle, Prince Vikaran. "Have you met the king yet?"

Giri shook his head.

"He is not someone you should face on an empty stomach. Come eat with me," the prince said and rose, shaking his clothes lightly.

Giri's mouth watered as he pictured the rich food served to a prince. That was one of the few things he missed during his self-imposed exile. The other was riding horses. Maybe today, both of his longings would be satisfied.

He followed the prince to his chambers. Two large elephant tusks from an adult male, mounted on the wall, shimmered in the sunlight, catching his eye.

The prince followed his gaze. "That beast was sacrificed to protect me." His mouth twisted. "After the birth of my sickly siblings, my father killed—rather, forced his men to murder—this king of the forest." He did not take his eyes away from the pure ivory. "Since I am healthy, I guess the sacrifice worked." He did not look in the least pleased with the outcome.

25
SURYAVATI

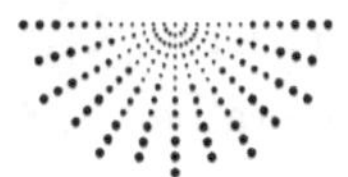

Suri touched her lips and sighed. Of all the people in the world, she had to kiss a man who lived in a make-believe world. In this world of imagination, with his feather dipped in ink, he could make a princess fall in love with a commoner. Suri could write a poem about their eternal love too.

In the real world, her mother had chosen Rangapani as her future husband. She lay on her bed and stared at the stars twinkling in the night sky. In the faint light, she could make out the arched windows near the top of the main palace tower. In her mind's eye, she saw the wooden frames intricately decorated with carvings of two elephant heads, their trunks meeting at the apex of the arch. Her family hailed from a long line of kings who ruled Jaisalpur from this ancient, storied castle. With her legacy, a match with a commoner—not even a warrior, but a mere playwright—was unthinkable.

The words for the next two lines in the poem she wrote with Giri floated into her head. Tossing the silk sheets aside, she rose and walked to her table. Kindling the cotton wick, she waited for the light to burn brightly. Then, she pulled a palm leaf toward her.

While I go up the hill alone
All I hear are cries in the air.

There would be no happy ending in this poem. Letting the ink dry, she returned to her bed. When sleep claimed her, her dreams returned to her shared kiss with the playwright, his warm hands encircling her waist.

A cold hand touched her forehead, and Suri's eyes fluttered open. Instead of her mother's usual stern face, Suri saw a gentleness in her eyes as she leaned over her daughter. For a moment, Suri imagined her mother learning about her dream. Though her mother appeared to be in a good mood, the woman who had taught her about the noble blood of their family and recounted the history of their glory would surely admonish Suri for her weakness.

"Rise, child," the queen said gently. "We are visiting the temple this morning."

This was no dream. Gazing at her mother, Suri suddenly understood her role. Her brother, the last blossom at the tip of their noble tree, needed her help. Her mother had wanted to set her on the right path, to pass on her courage and strength. But she had luxuriated in her life of ease and learned nothing of use. She had indulged in her love of literature, and look where that had gotten her. She had nearly brought shame to the family name with her actions. Locking away the memories of Giri, she rubbed her eyes. She would do everything in her power to serve and protect her kingdom.

She gestured with her hands to indicate she would get ready, slipping out of bed.

Her mother departed, leaving instructions for her to meet

her at the palace entrance. Suri dressed hurriedly. She had one remaining task before she could completely forget Giri. With her palm scroll tucked into the folds of her sari, she marched to her brother's chamber. The guard opened the door and let her in.

She found Abhayan asleep, his head nestled among his pillows. His sleeping face had the same serenity as their older brother, Mahabahu, who had always read poems to her. Mahabahu had died nearly nine years ago, when she was eight and Abhayan was only five. For the sake of their dead brother, Abhayan should learn to become hard and sharp instead of how he was now—pampered and soft. She made a fist and punched Abhayan on his chest.

The boy woke up with a howl and reached for his sword. Suri glided out of his reach in case he swung his sword before seeing her.

With a weapon in his hand, Abhayan looked up. "Sister," he uttered the word as a curse. "I nearly cut off your head! I didn't even hear your anklets—they usually sound like temple bells." He dropped the blade back onto his bed and suppressed a yawn.

She had stopped wearing anklets because of the disguises she often donned. It was easier not to wear them at all than to remember to remove them whenever she masqueraded as a boy. She sat on the edge of the bed and grabbed his hand.

Give this to the playwright.

She wrote on his hand with her finger.

"Are you still writing your silly poems?" Abhayan reached out with his long arm and draped it around her shoulder.

She pulled away from his embrace and swatted his head with one hand while holding out the scroll with the other.

Abhayan grinned as he accepted the palm leaf. His smile was a replica of their mother's smile, on the rare occasion she smiled.

Take him with you when you go out with Father. Giri is writing a play about him.

"He is writing a play about our father? About how the old man has grown soft and fat from complacency?"

She swatted his head again.

"Don't worry. I will behave like a proper prince once I have woken up," he said, leaning back on his pillow and stretching out his legs, positioning one over the other.

As a boy, Abhayan had shown hints of brilliance—he could read and write before he had turned five. But then, their brother died, and Abhayan professed a disdain for their customs, questioning everything his gurus taught. The teachers soon ran out of patience and complained to their mother. Their father never had any patience for his children. Suri knew her mother prayed every day to her goddess to set her babies on the right path. Suri had had enough of his lazy and foolish ways.

You are all we have. Remember that.

Abhayan frowned, reminding her of their uncle deep in thought. She tousled his hair and left to find her mother.

At the palace entrance, her mother stood beside a wooden palanquin, the silk curtains fluttering in the wind, with four bearers standing a few feet away. What caught Suri's attention was the young man beside her mother, his shoulders broad and his chest bulging over his waist.

"Rangapani arrived last night and will escort us to the temple," her mother said, turning on her charming smile. Her eyes looked nothing like the warm eyes of her son, and in that instant, all of Suri's goodwill toward her mother evaporated, replaced by stubbornness.

GIRIDHAR

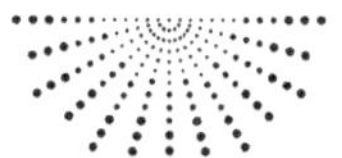

G iri arrived in the dark stables with the prince. The smell of horses, hay, and dung swirled in the air, taking him back to Nidhapur.

"Have you ridden before?" asked the prince, rubbing the mane of a brown stallion.

Giri nodded like a woodpecker pecking a tree trunk. A stable boy handed him the reins of a mare. Giri wished he had brought a cube of jaggery as his hand gently rubbed the bridge of its nose. The animal snorted softly, its warm breath misting the air.

The king arrived with his brother, deep in conversation. They both wore the same hard expression, but the resemblance ended there. Prince Vikaran, though younger, carried more gray hair than his brother. The king towered over him by nearly a foot. A faint scar on his jawline proclaimed him no stranger to battles. The king had grown softer with age, his belly a little fuller and pressing against his upper garment, stretching the fabric, but one could still see signs of the hard edges of the past. Giri knew which brother spent his days scribing inside the castle and who rode around the kingdom.

Prince Vikaran's face grew serious as he whispered into his

brother's ear. The king shook his head impatiently and waved him away. Giri realized that Prince Vikaran would not be joining them on this journey. With the help of two men, the king climbed into his saddle. The young prince jumped into his and gestured for Giri to follow.

With practiced ease, Giri grabbed the saddle's horn and swung himself up, settling into the seat.

A dozen soldiers joined them, and the king rode in their midst, leading the way. Giri rode alongside the prince, trailing the king. The crowd parted effortlessly before them, like waves parting for a ship, as they traveled outside the fort.

One of the soldiers carried a long silk banner embroidered with a male elephant, the symbol of Jaisalpur, its trunk held high and its two long tusks gleaming in the sun. King Vibudha understood the necessity of visibly reminding the population of the king's authority and might. His lower body was wrapped in a shimmering silk dhoti, and his crown, a marvelous wonder of gold and glittering gems, shone like the full moon on a cloudless night.

The young prince appeared bored as they rode in silence, the boy not having learned the art of keeping his face emotionless.

"Does Prince Vikaran have any children?" asked Giri. As a younger son himself, he was curious about the relationship between the brothers.

"My uncle? No, he has no children. His wife died a few years ago, and he never remarried." Giri wondered if Prince Vikaran had put off marriage on his own or if King Vibudha had refused to give his consent to prevent any rivals for his son.

Fallen trees, flooded homes, and little water creeks everywhere highlighted the flood damage. While only a light rain had fallen on the palace and its surroundings a few days ago, the same raincloud had caused a swollen river to wreak havoc in this village. When they arrived at the village's main square, local officials and dignitaries gathered to welcome their group. Giri dismounted and blended into the shadows to observe the proceedings.

The villagers had scrounged up local delicacies even in their difficult circumstances and proffered them to the king. The granite temple at the center of the village had withstood the flood, but the same could not be said for the mud houses. Some of the walls had been repaired, the fresh clay standing in stark contrast to the weathered, older sections.

An argument nearby attracted his attention, and Giri edged closer. A middle-aged woman, dressed in a clean cotton sari, begged a soldier. "My youngest son was only eight. He has been missing since the river overflowed and flooded our village. Now you are taking my eldest away. Who will help me drain the fields, harvest what remains, and plant for the new season?"

The soldier, who had probably arrived immediately after the flood to help with recovery, brushed away the woman's pleading impatiently. "I think this story of your youngest is a fabrication to get out of doing your fair share to help rebuild the village."

"I am telling the truth. You can ask any of my neighbors," said the woman, her face trembling with sorrow.

It brought to Giri's mind the face of his own mother. She must be worried for his safety. His confidence in his decision to remain in exile evaporated. How could he let his mother suffer when a word from him could bring her peace? How many people in his kingdom needed his help while he wasted his time here?

The prince had sauntered up to him. "The woman has lost one of her sons in the flood. She wants the other to stay and help her with the harvest," Giri narrated. He wanted to slap the soldier for berating a grieving woman, but this situation called for finesse, not force.

Prince Abhayan eyed the soldier and the woman.

"Flattery does wonders," Giri whispered.

Prince Abhayan raised his eyebrows.

"One does not become a playwright without understanding human nature," explained Giri.

"Soldier, I've heard great things about your recovery work here." The prince was all smiles as he approached the man. "Why don't you show me?"

Giri realized he had underestimated the young prince.

The soldier bowed to the prince while the pleading woman fell at his feet.

"Who do we have here?" asked the prince, helping the woman rise to her feet.

"My—" she started.

"She was just thanking the king for helping us rebuild her house," the soldier interrupted. The woman stood frozen, her mouth open, probably too surprised to speak.

"Who is the boy?" asked Giri. He wanted to ensure the soldier let the boy stay with his mother.

"Her son, who is helping his mother harvest her field," the soldier answered again.

Understanding that the soldier would not take him away in front of the prince, the woman's son shook her by the shoulder. "Ma, let's get going."

The woman seemed to waken from a dream and bowed to the prince. "You are wise and kind." She followed her son.

"You are a good man for helping her," the prince praised the soldier, while Giri stole a glance at the woman, blinking his suddenly warm eyes.

27

SURYAVATI

hile her mother talked to the temple priest, Suri made her way outside the inner sanctum. The morning sun coated everything in gold, and she ran down the cool stone steps to the sandy courtyard. The warm sand crunched under her feet as she circled the sanctum. Rangapani followed her at a distance.

Suri longed for speech so she could talk to the man her mother had chosen for her. Would he move to the king's palace after their wedding? He currently lived within the fort, in the nobles' quarters, as the son of the general. Most royal women kept their own rooms even after marriage. She would hate to share her room with an unknown man, so she hoped to keep to the same tradition.

Suri stopped to adjust her bangles, glancing at Rangapani from the corner of her eye. His face was unreadable. She decided to find a way to converse with the man. She walked to a neem tree in the courtyard and waited for Rangapani.

When he came under the tree's canopy, she gestured for him to break a branch. His eyes widened in surprise, but he obliged.

She stripped the leaves from the branch and used one end to write in the sand.

Did you watch the play?

Rangapani came closer, and her mind involuntarily compared him to Giri, who appeared more hardy and determined. Though not as physically imposing as Rangapani, Giri somehow seemed far less delicate. Unaware of her musings, Rangapani began to read her writing. His face grew blank for a moment before clearing.

"No, my lady," he said, too loudly. *I am not deaf,* she wished she could say.

"I was away on an errand. But some of my friends did watch it. From their whining about the tragic ending, I don't seem to have missed much. I have little use for poetry. My interest lies in history and military strategy." He smiled at her encouragingly, as though she were slow to understand.

Suri tried hard not to frown. The man clearly had no idea she was the one who wrote the poem that inspired the play. Why would he, when she had kept it a secret from almost everyone? Still, why would her mother choose a man like Rangapani for her if she truly cared about her daughter's happiness? Her mother knew of her love for poetry, even if she didn't understand the depth of her passion. When her brother rose to the throne, Rangapani would support him ably. Was that reason enough for her to marry him? The wind carried a cotton seed in the air. Watching the seed drift, she imagined soaring high into the air like the puffy seed and flying far away. That would not be possible, tethered to a man like Rangapani.

Rangapani faced her and became serious. "Why watch a play about failures and disappointments? I will make sure our life together is filled with sweetness, not bitterness." She remembered Giri's words from the night before about the play they crafted: 'Great stories are filled with pain we endure and overcome.' That applied to real life, too. *Without enduring pain and suffering, one cannot truly treasure happiness*, she thought. At that instant, she was grateful for her lack of speech. Otherwise, she would have spoken those words aloud and sent the young man running from her—which wouldn't have been such a bad thing, except he would likely run straight to her mother.

When they climbed into the palanquin, her mother turned to her. "What do you think of him?"

Suri shrugged her shoulders and looked away. She would not lie, so she welcomed being mute, at least on these occasions. Her mother sighed.

What could she say that would make her mother happy? That he was not ugly? That growing old alone seemed preferable, even if it meant staying with her mother forever?

When she retreated to her bedroom, her cousin, Kanika, arrived at her door.

"Did you scare him off?"

Suppressing a smile, Suri shook her head.

Kanika collapsed on a chair. "Did you tell him about your secret admiration for the playwright?"

Suri's smile grew into a laugh. Kanika did not know the whole story yet. If she knew Suri had kissed the playwright, she would consider them betrothed.

"You keep this up, and soon you will be exchanging garlands with Rangapani."

That caused her joy to vanish. She pulled the plate filled with dry rice kernels to write.

Once my mother's mind is made up, it cannot be changed. I have resigned myself—

"No, I won't have you give up so easily," protested Kanika. "I will send a message to my brother, to learn more about your suitor."

Rangapani grew up with her cousin, Dushyant—King Dushyant now. After their mother's death, Dushyant, along with his two sisters, spent their childhood at this castle. She had grown to love him as her elder brother, and he read her earlier poems with patience. If he thought Rangapani ill-suited for her, she wanted to know.

Suri nodded to give her consent.

That night, lying in bed, she remembered how Giri had pulled her closer as lightning streaked across the sky. She imagined the feel of his lips against hers. Almost immediately, her mother's stern face drifted into her vision, mocking her weakness. An intense pain rose in her stomach as she shut her eyes to block these images. She had not gone to see the playwright that night. What more could her mother want from her?

Though she wanted to forget him, her mind had its own will. It wondered how the playwright fared with her brother. She didn't have to wait long to find out, as her brother arrived at her doorstep the next morning.

GIRIDHAR

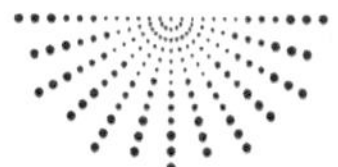

The sun disappeared behind the horizon as Giri made his way back to the fort. The king rode ahead with his retinue, while Prince Abhayan and Giri followed behind with three soldiers. A few yards away, a bark sounded from the bushes. Giri looked around and spotted two bright eyes hidden among the leaves.

"Mooka!" Giri exclaimed, hopping off his horse. The dog bolted toward him, licking his face and neck, its tail wagging furiously.

The prince dismounted. "Is this your dog?"

"Yes, my lord," Giri replied with a grin, rubbing behind Mooka's ears. The dog's tail wagged like a woman fanning her cooking fire.

The prince stepped closer, and Mooka cautiously approached, sniffing the air.

"Please, let him sniff your hand," Giri suggested.

The prince extended his hand, and Mooka sniffed it for a few moments before trotting back to Giri.

"Bring him to the castle," the prince ordered, climbing back into his saddle.

Giri scooped the dog into his arms and brought him closer to the horse. The dog gave a tentative bark, glancing between Giri and the horse. His mare snorted softly, her ears flicking as she eyed the dog with mild curiosity. Then she lowered her head slightly, her warm breath ruffling the fur on Mooka's back. The dog flinched but didn't retreat, his tail wagging cautiously now.

"That's it," Giri encouraged. "You'll be friends in no time."

He swung himself into the saddle, settling comfortably before reaching down to scoop up Mooka. The dog squirmed slightly but stilled as Giri set him gently in front of him on the saddle.

"Stay," Giri commanded firmly, holding Mooka steady as the mare shifted beneath them. He wrapped an arm loosely around the dog's chest for support and clicked his tongue to urge the mare forward.

At the stable, Mooka went around sniffing the horses. Most of the larger beasts ignored the small animal at their feet. Giri brushed his horse and led it to a pot of water.

"Prince Abhayan," greeted a voice.

"Rangapani, I was not expecting you back so soon," said the prince.

Rangapani? Giri remembered his guard mentioning that Princess Suryavati was promised to the general's son, a man named Rangapani. He moved toward the prince to catch a glimpse of the man. With broad shoulders and a thick neck, the man resembled a buffalo. If Giri had paused to examine his negative perception, he would have realized it stemmed from jealousy.

The prince noticed him and beckoned him closer. "Rangapani, Playwright Giri and I are headed back to the castle to eat our evening meal. Would you care to join us?" The man barely glanced in Giri's direction as he dipped his head.

Giri was close enough to catch a hint of sandalwood on

Rangapani and became conscious of reeking like a muddy dog. He had held Mooka in his arms, so it was no surprise that he smelled like he had rolled in mud. For a man who normally did not spend any time thinking about his appearance, Giri hesitated to join the princess's suitor in his present condition.

"My lord, I beg your forgiveness. I am not fit for a royal audience in my present condition," Giri said, gesturing to himself. "If you will excuse my absence, I would like to take a dip in the river with my dog."

Prince Abhayan inhaled deeply and laughed. "You and me both. We smell no different from men who have traveled all day. You are a playwright with different sensibilities than warriors. I don't mind the smell of the road. Leave the dog with a stable hand and join me."

Giri accompanied the prince grudgingly. While he and his men had chased some bandits, he had gone for days without a bath. Neither he nor any of the men in his company had worried about their appearance then. Now, in the presence of the man set to marry Princess Suryavati, his unkempt appearance felt less like armor.

He made his way to the prince's chamber like a man walking on sharp pebbles. When the prince invited him to sit at his table, he sensed a measure of condescension in Rangapani's surprise at the invitation.

"I have not seen your play, Giri," said Rangapani, uttering Giri's first name as an implicit dismissal of his talent. "I find stories constructed in the air, with no foundation in reality, illogical. I am a simple man with a sword in my hand, fighting real enemies." His tone mocked storytelling as a vain pursuit.

Giri understood the veiled criticism but simply bowed his head. As a playwright, he wrote without concern for pleasing others, a luxury not available to him as a prince. However, he worried for Princess Suryavati. She was a rare princess who wrote poetry about water dripping down the leaves in spring and the stars spinning in the skies overhead. Rangapani would smother her very being.

"Sometimes, we all need to escape from our realities," Prince Abhayan stated. Giri understood a kindred heart troubled by the burdens of the crown. He also saw a brother's concern in his eyes as he regarded his sister's suitor.

"Escape reality? Prince Abhayan, as your future brother-in-law, it is my duty to think of what's best for you. You have the blood of our royal line. You will be commanding our armies with grace. When they put you on the throne, you have to dwell in reality."

Giri had never wanted to punch someone in their smug face more than at that moment. He had known men like Rangapani —men who craved power, who attributed every victory to their own genius and bravery.

"Let us then pray for the long life of our king, so I can ignore reality for now," said the young prince with a smile.

Rangapani stared at the prince with his dark eyes, his cheeks puffing as if weighing whether to retort. Then, like boiling milk spilling over, he said, "Forgive me, my lord. I forget your age. You should not neglect to have fun at this age."

Prince Abhayan's eyes narrowed at the insult, but only for a fleeting instant. He laughed loudly. "Let us play a game of dice after dinner. That would be a welcome diversion."

Carrying two silver trays laden with food, a servant entered the room. He walked around the table, placing the first plate of steaming rice and spicy stew in front of the prince. When the servant approached Rangapani, he stumbled. Some of the hot stew spilled onto Rangapani's lap, and he leaped to his feet with a shout.

"You clumsy oaf," he shouted, drawing his sword. "I will chop your ear off."

"I will have no blood spilled in my room," said the prince, his gaze cold. Rangapani refused to meet it and stared at the table.

"Sit, brother," added the prince more warmly. "Let us enjoy the meal."

Giri thanked the servant as he placed a plate in front of him, and the man bowed gratefully.

Rangapani lowered himself onto his seat, his face red as vermillion.

After the plates were cleared, Prince Abhayan said, "Playwright Giri, come and help me set up the game."

While handing the silk cloth board to Giri, Prince Abhayan whispered, "Help me defeat him."

"Nothing would make me happier. And he would deserve it. But, my lord, do you want to earn his loyalty or his enraged enmity?" Giri asked.

Prince Abhayan gave him a meaningful look. "You are a wise man," he finally muttered.

Giri was trained in military strategy and tactics. He had run drills with his army and assembled his men in battle formations. He played the game of dice with the same discipline. Prince Abhayan, though young, was diligent in his moves. Rangapani never suspected that they had teamed up to defeat him.

When Rangapani was soundly defeated, Prince Abhayan grasped his arm with warmth. "Rangapani, I know what happened. You lost to me on purpose." Rangapani appeared stiff and awkward. "Don't be embarrassed. You are a true friend. I will remember your loyal gesture."

After Rangapani departed, the prince held Giri back. "I have something for you from my sister," he said, handing him a scroll. For some reason, Giri felt as though he had been subjected to some unspoken trial by the prince and had emerged having earned his favor.

2 9

SURYAVATI

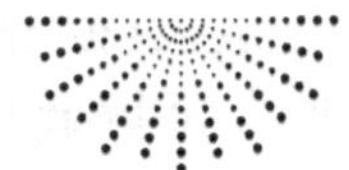

*A*bhayan dropped into a chair, swinging his legs idly, with his arms folded leisurely behind his head.

Suri put her hands on her hips, ready to give him a withering look. "You look like our mother when she is about to berate me," Abhayan said with a smile.

Tell me what happened, Suri gestured, not falling for her brother's charm.

Abhayan sat up straight, and his face grew serious. "Everyone always tells us our parents want what is best for us. I am not so sure anymore, especially after watching Rangapani."

Suri felt a wave of tenderness for her young brother. She patted his shoulder.

"Well, our family is a mess. Our father could care less about us, while mother insists on helping us but does the exact opposite of what we need. Only our uncle actually listens to what we want." Her brother shook his head. "Yet they say blood is thicker than water!"

I do care for you, she gestured, pointing at herself.

"I don't know," Abhayan said, looking at her with a teasing smile. "You are only good at ordering me around."

118

She gave Abhayan a gentle nudge, so he would quit stalling and tell her what happened.

Her brother's face turned grave. "As a playwright, I knew Giri had fine feelings in his heart. Along with beauty and grace, I found him quite hardy and tough."

She saw a sincere glint in his eyes and no whimsy.

"There is more courage and wit in Giri's little toe than in the entire body of Rangapani. Giri understands my loneliness in a crowd of people I would one day command. I want him as my friend."

Her brother glanced at her, suspicion in his eyes. "Were you meeting him the night I found you strolling?" He looked sheepish when she shot him a glare, knowing all too well she had caught him fooling around with a girl that very night.

"Don't be mad at me. You're not the only one stifled by palace life. Besides," he said with a knowing smirk, "your eyes have already answered my question. You did meet Giri that night."

He paused for a moment, his voice softening. "It would be easier if I could think of him as my brother. I wish I could elevate him somehow, make him worthy of you."

She listened carefully, while her heart felt so full she thought it might burst. She had not dared to dream of even a kind husband and healthy children. Watching her mother suffer, she had settled for a roof over her head and warm food in her stomach. But Giri awoke something in her. She felt like he understood her and saw her as more than a princess, one who knew that she wrote poetry about the emptiness in her heart. Her brother's words kindled hope in her mind, yearning for more than survival.

"I will invite both Rangapani and Giri to join me at the temple dance tonight," Abhayan said as he rose. "May the divine goddess guide you, my sister."

After Abhayan departed, Suri sat on the floor, with her head on her knees. Though Giri was a playwright, she suspected he would not hand out lines for his wife to say and show her gestures to make. Such a wife would be happy. It was a cosmic injustice that a man like him had not been born into nobility.

Kanika arrived at her door. "I dispatched a lengthy missive to my brother, informing him that I shall remain here until your wedding. I also made mention of your fortunate suitor, Rangapani, and requested that he extend his congratulations to his friend on such good fortune. My brother is certain to reply with his thoughts on the union."

Suri gave only half an ear to her cousin's words as she fastened her gold earrings, her mind instead dwelling on seeing Giri again since their shared kiss.

When they walked into the main temple hall, a loud male voice hailed her. "Suryavati!"

Suri turned to see who would be calling her by name and saw Rangapani beckoning her. He stood there with an air of smugness, as though he already possessed her, his posture oozing an unearned sense of ownership. It took all her grace to appear demure while her insides seethed with rage. How dare he use her given name before they were even betrothed?

"Your neck has turned red. Should I hand you my knife to stab the man?" asked Kanika as they walked toward Rangapani. Despite the surge of anger, a small smile crept onto her lips at the thought.

She bowed her head, avoiding the sight of the fool's face. Marriage to him would be insufferable—unless he traveled as frequently as her father did. She noticed her brother's feet—or rather, his foot, as he shifted his weight from one to the other, fidgeting as if he couldn't stay still. Then her gaze fell on two feet planted firmly on the ground. Giri?

She glanced up from the feet, tracing her gaze along the legs clad in a simple cotton dhoti, past his bare midriff, to his shoulders draped in a shawl, and finally fixed her eyes on the side of

Giri's face. He was glaring at Rangapani's back, as though trying to burn a hole into the man's head with his eyes.

"You are not the only one mad at Rangapani," whispered Kanika.

Suri stole another glance at Giri and met his dark eyes. There was no trace of the fury she expected, but instead, they held an intense, unreadable emotion that made her heart quicken. His gaze lingered on her lips for just a moment, and in that instant, the memory of his warm lips pressed against hers flooded back. She wished she were an ordinary girl in love with another ordinary man, but her royal blood made that dream impossible.

"I will sit next to Rangapani and whisper all your good qualities in his ear, Suri," said Kanika with a teasing smile as she placed herself between Suri's brother and her suitor. Thanking her in her mind, Suri moved to her brother's right side.

"Let me introduce my sister, Princess Suryavati," Abhayan said to the playwright, as if unaware that they needed no introduction.

"I had the fortune of meeting the esteemed princess with the queen earlier," said Giri as he bowed his head. His face betrayed no hint of the bond they shared, a connection stretching back to the day she first encountered him, disguised as nothing more than a young errand boy.

While she sat next to her brother, Giri positioned himself behind the royal siblings.

Suri could hear Kanika's lively chatter with Rangapani, though his responses were limited to single words. The musicians, having gathered at the side of the stage, began tuning their instruments, their melodies slowly blending into the air, creating a soft undertone that signaled the beginning of the evening's performance.

"Playwright Giri, do you have a response to the scroll's message?" Abhayan asked, glancing over his shoulder at Giri.

Suri's heart skipped a beat as she realized which scroll Abhayan was referring to—it was hers.

Giri hesitated for a brief moment, his gaze meeting hers before he replied, "Here is my response, my lord." He slid a palm leaf toward Abhayan with a steady hand.

Suri watched, her heart pounding, as her brother accepted the scroll. Giri's calm demeanor betrayed nothing, but she knew that every word on that palm leaf carried a hidden message meant for her. Abhayan unfolded it, scanning the text briefly before nodding.

"I see," he said, his tone neutral. Then, without further comment, he placed the scroll on her lap.

Suri could barely breathe, her fingers trembling slightly as they hovered over the palm leaf, wondering what words Giri had crafted for her.

GIRIDHAR

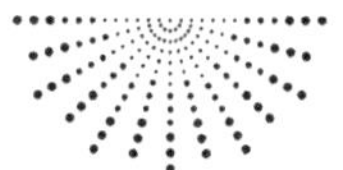

*G*iri wished he could see the lively, dark eyes of the princess—eyes that said so much, making up for her lack of speech. Instead, he had to content himself with observing her side profile.

Her words in the poem they crafted together read:

While I go up the hill alone
All I hear are cries in the air.

He had heard the hopelessness in them. When he first met her, she reminded him of a flower rooted in the soil but forever reaching for the skies. But something—likely Rangapani—had crushed her spirit. Before their kiss, his words would have been different. But now, he was determined to fight for her. Though she was mute, she had shown incredible ingenuity—meeting him in disguise, convincing her uncle to patronize his play, persuading her mother to share her story, and even getting her brother to learn more about him. Now, that was a girl worth fighting for. A tiny voice in his head argued that he didn't truly know how she would treat her subjects, but the memory of how she felt in his hands quickly silenced those concerns.

He watched her slowly open the scroll and read his verses:

I am determined to find her place
Crawling around the shrubs blind.

Her fingers trembled as she folded the scroll and tucked it into her waist.

Three dancers leaped onto the stage, spinning gracefully as the music swelled. While the princess's eyes followed their movements, Giri's gaze lingered on her. Her long hair, intricately bundled, exposed the bare expanse of her back, with her sari draped elegantly over one shoulder. The single strip of cloth tied around her chest left a delicate knot at the center of her mid-back, and for a fleeting moment, the sight of it tempted him more than he cared to admit.

As if the princess had read his mind, a shiver ran through her back. Then, she shook her brother's shoulder and pointed with her right index finger. Following her gaze, Giri spotted the dancer she was watching. Was the dancer limping? Something had injured her foot.

Prince Abhayan noticed it as well and beckoned a servant. "Check if the dancer is well," he commanded, concern flickering in his voice.

Princess Suryavati gestured swiftly with her hands, her expression urgent. Giri understood she was asking for the dance to be stopped.

"Stop the dance if she's hurt," the prince added, interpreting his sister's silent plea.

Giri watched as the servant approached the stage. The lead dancer immediately halted the performance, helping the injured dancer off the stage. While someone tended to the wounded dancer, the lead dancer approached their group.

"Apologies, my lady, my lord," she said, bowing deeply. "One of my dancer's anklet bells fell to the floor, and she stepped on it, pricking her foot. We will resume the performance shortly."

Princess Suryavati gestured with her hands, inquiring about the dancer's condition.

"She will be fine, my lady," the lead dancer reassured, her voice soft.

The prince spoke up, his tone firm but considerate. "You may cut the performance short. We wouldn't want her to injure herself further."

The injured dancer remained offstage while the other two gracefully completed their routine, bringing the performance to a close. As Prince Abhayan approached the musicians to greet them, Princess Suryavati quietly made her way toward the injured dancer, her expression filled with concern. Though she spoke no words, her fingers moved gracefully, like a puppeteer commanding invisible strings, as she conversed in her silent language. Watching her, something stirred deep within Giri—a mixture of admiration, awe, and a growing sense of connection to the princess.

As the moon slowly ascended over the palace towers, Giri made his way toward the cluster of trees. An ethereal moth glided nearby, its silvery wings shimmering in the moonlight, casting fleeting shadows as it fluttered through the still night air. He did not know if the princess would come that night, though he longed to see her.

She arrived, her eyes shining like crown jewels, her hair cascading around her shoulders, inspiring him to compare her to a goddess, the very epitome of beauty and grace. But he could not deny that she looked unhappy.

"My lady," he bowed.

She grabbed his hand and wrote *mistake*. He knew she meant their shared kiss.

"No, my lady. Something that feels so right cannot be a mistake." Yet, his heart whispered a bitter truth: his mother and brother would never support their union. Without their blessing, their love was doomed before it even began.

I am a princess. Princesses accept their fate.

"Would you be happy as Rangapani's wife?" Giri had wished he would be valued for what he could write, not just for how well he fought. Rangapani did not seem like a man who would value her for how well she thought. He would treat her as an ornament.

Still holding his hand, she wrote,

What other choice do I have?

He studied her profile, etched with sadness, and his stomach twisted into a tight knot. The urge to blurt out the words—*marry me*—was almost overwhelming, but he restrained himself. He was bound by circumstances, and he knew he could not make such a bold offer yet. Instead, he softened his voice, his gaze unwavering as he said, "I am certain a path will open for you."

Outwardly calm, inwardly turmoil brewed within him. He knew what he desired, and it felt right to be bound to this girl who had claimed a place in his heart. Could he trust his feelings not to lead him astray? Would he regret not having fought for her if his mother and brother opposed their union? The answer to that question came readily, and he knew what he had to do. He would send his trusted guard to his mother, seeking her blessing to marry this princess—the girl who had captured both his heart and his admiration. He would not give her up without a fight. His wilted hope began to grow roots, steady and unyielding.

Princess Suryavati leaned into him, her closeness setting his bones humming with the rhythm of her heartbeat. Then, as if gathering resolve, she released his hand. Her expression remained serene on the surface, but her eyes betrayed the storm of emotions churning within.

With deliberate grace, she placed a scroll in his palm, its weight far heavier than its delicate form suggested. Without a backward glance, she turned and glided away, leaving him anchored in place.

SURYAVATI

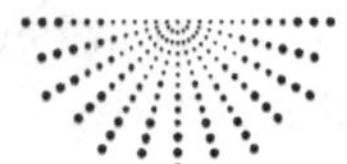

Suri closed her eyes and savored his voice. It was like drinking warm milk flavored with honey on a cold, wet night. *I am sure a path will open for you*, he had said. His voice wrapped around her like a soft silk sari. She could fall asleep to his words and dream miraculous dreams. He almost made her believe.

With great reluctance, she pushed him out of her mind. She was a princess, a symbol to behold. There was no way for her to marry a common man. She only wished she had been a little less obvious with her desires.

Her brother visited her a few days later. "Giri is holding his first rehearsal. Come watch the play with me."

Suri had avoided Giri since their last encounter, and he had made no attempt to deliver the next set of verses for their poem. Yet the allure of his play tugged at her, curiosity and longing intertwined. In the scroll she had sent him, she had included a poem for him to use in his play. She hesitated, but the temptation to see his work was too strong. With a single nod, she accepted her brother's invitation, her heart already anticipating the moment.

Afraid of her feelings, Suri dragged her cousin Kanika along.

"Am I rooting for Giri or Rangapani?" Kanika whispered, her eyes darting curiously toward Suri.

Suri slowed her pace for a moment but quickly resumed walking, though the brief hesitation was telling.

"Don't tell me you're settling for that idiot," Kanika muttered, her voice laced with disbelief.

Suri's lips tightened, but she let the conversation hang in the air. They arrived in the open courtyard, where the actors milled about, rehearsing their lines and adjusting costumes. The buzz of excitement filled the air.

Her brother, Abhayan, waved at them from the shade of a neem tree, and Suri's eyes immediately narrowed as she spotted Rangapani standing next to him. Curse the man, she thought, for attaching himself to her brother like a leech.

Kanika nudged her, noticing the shift in her expression. "Well, this just got more interesting," she whispered with a smirk.

Suri suppressed a groan, forcing herself to walk forward despite her growing irritation.

Her eyes sought Giri. He stood among a small group of actors, his presence commanding without effort. As she watched, he spoke to a young woman on stage.

"You are the princess of this land," he said, his voice calm and reassuring, yet guiding the young actress with confidence. "Your grace and beauty reflect your kingdom and its ideals. Shoulders straight, eyes cast down, a smile on your face."

Suri froze, a flicker of surprise running through her. Those were the very words she had whispered to herself earlier, preparing for the duties of her own station. She hadn't expected to hear them again, let alone from him.

For a moment, the noise of the courtyard faded, and all she could hear was Giri's voice. They were more alike than she realized.

Suri watched the young actress portraying her mother move across the stage, her steps hesitant and lacking the regal poise her mother was known for. It was, after all, only the first day of rehearsal. With time, she would improve, but for now, the portrayal felt unsatisfactory.

Then, the girl stood on stage and uttered the words from her poem.

Waiting for spring to come,
When my flowers bloom,
Bursts of fragrance pierce the sky,
And coat the entire palace with their perfume.

He had used her poem in his play. It was the poem of a young girl who still believed in the impossible, and in writing it, she had imagined her mother as a girl with dreams of her own. As she reflected on this, she saw Giri approaching their group. He bowed to her brother.

"Strange, watching my parents' story come to life," Abhayan said, his tone neutral but his eyes betraying a mix of curiosity and nostalgia.

Suri glanced at Giri, wondering what thoughts ran through his mind as he brought their family's history to the stage.

"I hope to create a fitting tribute to honor their achievements."

Rangapani snorted loudly.

Kanika, ever sharp-tongued, glanced at Rangapani. "Tell me, Rangapani, how many stories have you written?"

Rangapani scowled. "Writing stories is no skill for a warrior. It's child's play."

Giri smiled, his eyes glinting with pride. "My work as a playwright has touched many hearts. It takes courage to put your heart into something and share it with the world." He glanced at Suri and added with a slight smile, "A different kind of courage, perhaps, but one I'm glad to possess." Suri pondered whether the compliment was intended for her.

Rangapani sneered, his lip curling in disgust. "Courage? For scribbling words and prancing on stage like a fool? That's the work of weak men, not warriors. A real man swings a sword, not a quill. You should wear a sari and line your eyes with kajal," he jeered, his voice heavy with disdain.

Suri couldn't help but notice the irony of him equating poetry with women when she herself was unable to pursue such a passion openly.

Giri shrugged, a playful smile still tugging at his lips. "I look pretty good as a girl. I played one for a few days in my last play."

Kanika chuckled, unable to contain her amusement, despite the stern look Suri shot her way.

"Have you no sense of shame?" roared Rangapani.

"Shame? Why would I feel bad about being compared to a woman?" Giri said calmly.

Suri watched the exchange, her heart pounding. Giri's calm confidence seemed to deflect Rangapani's scorn like a shield, leaving Rangapani's anger hanging in the air like a broken arrow.

"Women are weak and in need of a man's protection. Only a coward will drape himself in a woman's sari," shouted Rangapani.

Suri cringed at his insult. Kanika nearly spoke up, but Suri silenced her with a look.

"I have seen the bravery of women firsthand," Giri answered. He was not shouting, but his voice could be heard clearly. "When the men are at war, the women farm our lands and feed us. I know many women who exceed me in courage, so being compared to a woman is no insult. I consider it an honor."

Not many men would agree that a woman's courage was equal to a man's. How she wished she was not a princess but an ordinary girl who could follow her true feelings.

Giri made her heart flutter and her breath quicken in ways she had believed only existed in the minds of poets like her. What she enjoyed most was listening to him. Giri, though not born noble, seemed to understand how hard it was to meet the heavy expectations of others. He had treated her honorably, guarding her secret. Most importantly, he had respected her creative talent and treated her as an equal.

Even her impatient brother watched Giri quietly, a rare flicker of intrigue crossing his face.

Rangapani began to speak, but Abhayan silenced him with a raised hand. "Playwright Giri, if you write as well as you speak, this will surely be a great play."

Rangapani turned the color of vermilion as he pressed his lips together.

Suri dragged Kanika away from the scene, not wanting to antagonize Rangapani any further.

As they stepped away from the bustling courtyard, Kanika leaned closer to Suri, her eyes sparkling with mischief.

"Did you see the way Giri held his own against Rangapani?" she said, a teasing grin spreading across her face. "I dare say he could charm even the most hardened warrior with his words."

Suri felt her cheeks flush at the thought, but she tried to dismiss it with a roll of her eyes.

Kanika playfully nudged her shoulder. "You cannot fool me! I saw the way you looked at him when he spoke. There's a spark in your eyes, my dear cousin."

Suri knew the danger of entangling her emotions with Giri; that path was strewn with misery. What pained her most was that she truly liked him, especially because he did not see her as a mere diversion, as most men did. Though she was noble, she wasn't sure if she was worthy of an honorable man like him.

3 2
GIRIDHAR

Giri shook his head, snapping himself out of the dreamlike state he often fell into around Princess Suryavati. Her flowery scent still lingered in the air, intoxicating his senses. For a moment, when he gazed into her eyes, it had felt as though time had stopped, and all he wanted was to sit with her for hours, just watching her. But was it right to feel this way for a woman promised to another? A pang of jealousy shot through him at the thought of Rangapani, who didn't deserve her—not with his quick temper and fragile pride.

The words of her verses in the poem they wrote together remained etched in his mind:

I can never see any face
Maybe it is all in my mind.

He considered them the words of a girl dismissing her true feelings. Even the poem she had written for his play, though seemingly hopeful on the surface, spoke of a girl in suspension —waiting for a spring that might never come. Giri understood the weight of obligation that rested on her shoulders. He shared her burden, striving to live up to the image others had of him, suppressing his own desires. Their shared love for poetry had drawn them together, but they had much more in common than just their passion for verse. He had never felt as close to another person. He knew he wanted to spend the rest of his life with the girl who could touch his soul with her writing.

All this time, he had yielded to society's belief that her muteness was a curse. Yet, as a storyteller, he could craft a different narrative—one where her silence was not a curse but a blessing. It had taken her voice yet filled her with words. Why should it matter if she couldn't speak to mere mortals when her poetry allowed her to converse with the gods? With ears finely tuned to the suffering of others, she would serve the people of Nidhapur with grace and wisdom as their queen.

Giri believed in propriety, and his intentions toward the princess were honorable. He would send his trusted guard, Sangu, to his mother to seek her blessing, and then he would approach King Vibudha himself to ask for Princess Suryavati's hand.

Giri and Sangu retreated to a quiet corner of the palace grounds to train. If anyone spotted them, Giri had a ready excuse prepared—he was learning to fight in order to write more realistic scenes for his play.

Swords drawn, Giri and Sangu spun around each other like two prowling tigers, their blades clashing in a rhythmic dance.

"I want you to deliver this message to my mother," Giri said, his voice steady as he parried Sangu's strike. "Tell her I seek her blessing to marry Princess Suryavati."

Sangu spun around, countering Giri's move. "My lord, while I'm glad the princess has captured your heart, I cannot leave you unprotected. Let us both travel back, and you can ask your mother's permission directly."

Giri sidestepped, deflecting Sangu's blade. "I have to remain here until the play is complete."

"My lord," Sangu started to protest.

Swords clashed as Giri raised his hand to halt Sangu mid-strike. "No one knows my real identity," he said, stepping back to deflect another blow. "I will be safe here. You'll go alone at dawn to Nidhapur."

His tone, like the sharp edge of his blade, left no room for argument. It was an order. Sangu nodded, though his stance remained tense, as they continued to circle each other.

Leaving the swords with Sangu to hide, Giri made his way back to the palace alone, his thoughts heavy with the weight of what lay ahead.

"Playwright Giri."

Giri halted at the voice and turned to see the Royal Poet approaching, his eyes cold. "I heard you invited the prince and princess to your rehearsal today for a play script I have yet to review."

"Apologies, Royal Poet," Giri replied, keeping his tone respectful. "Things moved rapidly, like floodwaters overflowing a riverbed. I will bring you the script tomorrow."

The Royal Poet's lips curled in a sneer. "I also heard about the poem you had the actress recite. Something about spring blooms—immature, like you. You're young and think your work will be lasting, but I cannot allow such mediocre words in this play."

The sting was meant for Giri, to demonstrate how much power the Royal Poet had over him. Unwittingly, the Royal Poet mocked the words of the princess herself—the very heartbeat of the land he served.

Having just decided to seek his mother's blessing to marry the princess, Giri had no patience for the man. "Do not speak ill of my poem," he said sharply.

"How dare you speak to me this way!" the Royal Poet howled.

"You are a weak old man, living off the glory of others," Giri mocked, fully aware he was making an enemy. But he would not tolerate anyone insulting Princess Suryavati's verse. Without waiting for the man to respond, Giri strode into the night.

His thoughts drifted to his mother. Unlike his father or brother, she had always supported his passion for writing plays. He recalled her defending him to his brother, invoking the legendary King Harsha, who had written three famous plays, including *Ratnavali*. When he first arrived in Jaisalpur, he had sent his mother a message assuring her of his safety, mentioning that he was traveling for a few fortnights and would return soon. He could almost picture her now, sitting cross-legged before her God Krishna idol, praying for his safe return. Giri knew the message he was sending with Sangu would bring her great joy.

His thoughts flew from his widowed mother to the young widow, Vasantha. He hadn't seen her since the day he had gone to bid her farewell, refusing her request to accompany him and, in doing so, breaking her heart. With little regard for her well-being, he had lived in the comfort of the palace, weaving stories and dreaming of distant worlds. Sangu would likely spend the night planning how to ensure Giri's safety during his absence. With this in mind, Giri decided it was time to pay Vasantha a visit.

Giri found Vasantha's house with ease, walking through the small vegetable beds toward the shed in the back. He had guessed correctly that, with her brother and his family crammed into the modest house, she would spend most of her time in the shed. A faint glow from a small lantern lit the inside, casting soft shadows on the rough walls. There, Vasantha was bent over, raking cow dung into neat piles. She worked quietly, gathering it to be dried in the sun and later used as fuel or fertilizer for the vegetable gardens.

After ensuring no one else was nearby, Giri softly called her name. "Vasantha."

She startled at the familiar voice, turning swiftly to face him. For a brief moment, her expression was one of disbelief. Then, with a surge of emotion, she rushed toward him, throwing her arms around his neck. "Playwright Giri, you came back for me."

Though he had never left Jaisalpur, Giri didn't correct her misunderstanding. Instead, he stood still, unsure of how to respond to the intensity of her affection, guilt stirring in his chest.

Giri patted Vasantha's back awkwardly. *Crunch.* A faint sound caught his attention. With Vasantha still clinging to him, he turned to glance behind him. In the dim light of the small lantern, a figure stood watching them. His heart skipped a beat when he recognized the figure—it was the beautiful boy. Princess Suryavati in her disguise.

Their eyes locked for a fleeting moment, and Giri's heart sank. He realized with a jolt how damning the scene must appear to her. To Suryavati, it must look like he was wrapped in the arms of a secret lover. His mind raced, trying to find a way to explain, but before he could untangle himself from Vasantha's embrace, the princess had already melted into the shadows, vanishing into the night.

A cold dread settled over him.

33

SURYAVATI

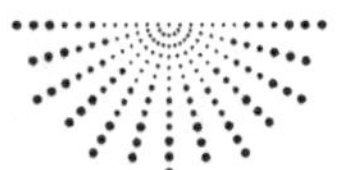

Suri struggled to breathe, her chest tightening as if an elephant had settled upon it. Strands of jealousy swirled within her, almost setting her on fire. How could she have been so naïve? She had allowed herself to trust the playwright, to dream of a life that seemed so far from her reality. In her mind, she had built a special connection with Giri, a bond forged through shared verses and stolen moments. She had kissed him—a kiss that felt like a profound act of intimacy, something she had never experienced before. But now, seeing him with another, she questioned everything.

Had that kiss meant anything to him? Or was it just another fleeting indulgence for a man who moved from one pretty face to another? She had heard the rumors, the whispers about the fickle nature of theatre folk—their lack of loyalty, their tendency to flit from village to village without care or commitment. Perhaps Giri was no different. He had betrayed her trust, leaving her feeling utterly drained and foolish. Suri could only blame herself for allowing her heart to be taken in so easily.

Her dreams of a life with him now felt like ashes.

As Suri replayed the scene in her mind—Giri entwined in the arms of another young girl—her hands trembled with a fury that surged through her. Yet, even in the midst of her rage, she could not suppress the truth that gnawed at her heart. Despite knowing the emptiness of his promises, despite the betrayal she had witnessed, she still cared for him.

Her feelings for him had been real, undeniable. She had taken something precious from within herself—her most vulnerable thoughts—and transformed them into poems she had shared willingly with him. And in return, Giri had shattered that gift. He had torn her words apart and scattered them like leaves in the wind. But the words did not matter anymore. What she truly longed for, what her heart ached for, was not the return of those scattered fragments of poetry.

She only wanted the man back—the man she had thought she knew.

Wiping her eyes with a rough swipe, Suri walked through the shadowed halls of the castle, her footsteps unsteady. The weight of her emotions bore down on her. Only when she reached her private corridor and saw Nanmaran's startled expression did she realize her blunder. The guard stood at attention outside her door, his eyes wide in shock.

"My lady!" Nanmaran gasped, his gaze darting between her disheveled appearance and the door he thought she was still resting behind.

Suri froze, her breath catching. She had slipped out through the window, climbing down the tree in a desperate escape, all while Nanmaran believed her soundly asleep in her bed. Now, standing before him with her face stained by unshed tears, dressed in a man's clothes, the evidence of her night out was unmistakable. Her tunic was rumpled, her hair unraveled from its topknot. The guard's eyes widened as he struggled to comprehend what had happened.

"My lady…" His voice softened, his confusion laced with concern.

Suri's mind raced, desperately searching for an explanation, but her heart throbbed painfully from the sight she had witnessed. Before her despair spiraled, she squared her shoulders and tilted her chin up, gesturing for him to open the door.

The guard hesitated, concern clear on his face, but he bowed his head. "Of course, my lady," he murmured, stepping aside to allow her passage.

Without another look, she strode past him, her composure fragile, uncertain if she could trust her guard—a man appointed by her mother. Surely, his loyalty lay with the queen, and he would no doubt report her outing. The very walls of the castle, once a comforting refuge, now felt like they were closing in, their familiarity suffocating.

Suri's thoughts churned as she entered her chambers, shutting the door behind her. She leaned against it, her heart a storm of betrayal and confusion, the image of Giri entwined with another searing through her mind. She had opened her heart and shared not just her poetry but her very soul. Now, the weight of that vulnerability felt unbearable.

But the guilt—oh, the guilt—was worse. She had betrayed her mother's trust, sneaking out in the dead of night, abandoning the path her mother had carefully laid for her. All for a man who had shattered her trust, leaving her with nothing but the bitter taste of regret. She had only wanted to meet Giri, to congratulate him on the play. But then, she had seen him speaking with the Royal Poet. Though too far to hear their words, she could see the Royal Poet's fury, his face flushed with rage as Giri walked away abruptly. Driven by some unknown urge, she had followed him, only to uncover his betrayal.

Suri's shame was so heavy that she couldn't lift her head. The weight of her actions pressed down on her, and the thought of facing her mother was unbearable. Yet she knew what she had to do. She would talk to her mother tomorrow at dawn and confess everything. She would tell her she would marry the man chosen for her, even if her heart bled in the process. At least that way, she could reclaim some semblance of honor after so much had been lost.

GIRIDHAR

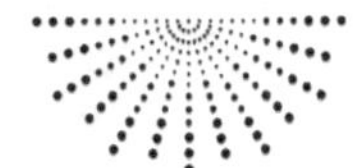

Vasantha watched him intently, her eyes following the direction of his gaze toward the disappearing figure of the princess, still disguised in a man's clothes.

"Who was that boy? And why does his presence cause you such pain?" she asked, her voice gentle but perceptive.

Giri stepped back, putting some space between them, and ran a hand through his hair. "That is a long story, best saved for another time," he said, his tone weary. With great effort, he pushed the princess from his thoughts, though her image lingered in his mind. "I came here to ask after you. How are you doing?" Giri asked, his voice softening.

Vasantha shrugged, her expression unreadable. "My limbs are intact. My cow gives me sufficient milk, and I've planted some vegetables. What more do I need?"

Giri observed her carefully, sensing the emptiness behind her words. He knew that survival alone was not enough to fill the void in one's heart, but he held his tongue because he had already rejected her overtures to become his companion more than once.

"Why did you come back?" Vasantha asked, her eyes bright, a tinge of hope coating her words.

Giri hesitated, knowing the truth would only bring disappointment. He didn't want to rekindle the flame of hope he had extinguished before. "Is it wrong for a brother to visit his sister and make sure she's doing okay?"

Her hopeful expression dimmed, and she turned away slightly. "My brother is in that house, tired of caring for his sister. I don't need to burden you with my worries too." The hurt in her eyes, caused by what could never come to pass, pained him, but Giri knew that saying anything now would only reopen old wounds.

"Did you come back for the coin purse you left me?" Vasantha continued, her voice steady as she moved to the back of the shed. She rummaged through an old pot and pulled out the small pouch of coins he had given her, holding it out to him.

"No," Giri replied softly, shaking his head. "Those are yours to spend."

Giri's gaze lingered on Vasantha as she tucked the coin pouch away. Her movements were slow, deliberate, as if they carried the weight of the emotions she refused to show. The silence between them felt thicker than any words that could be exchanged—full of regret, of what could never be.

"Take care of yourself," Giri finally said, his voice softer than before.

"Do not come back here," Vasantha replied, her tone cool but not unkind. There was an acceptance in her voice, a quiet resignation to the life she now led.

Giri nodded, though she wasn't looking at him. "I wish you strength, Sister," he said. Then, without another word, he turned and walked away, his heart heavier than when he had arrived. The night felt colder as he left the shed behind.

His thoughts oscillated between the young widow and the princess. He had purchased a cow and given coins to Vasantha, and though he longed to do more, he could never give her what she truly wanted. He cared for Vasantha, not out of romantic desire, but because he had witnessed his mother's loneliness after his father's death. What had haunted him as a child was not his mother's crying but her silences, as if her grief were beyond words. Time and her children had healed his mother's wound. Unlike his mother, Vasantha had no children to care for, making her solitude even more unbearable. But he could not fill that hole. If he were honest with himself, he saw her more as a friend—or a sister—someone he wanted to help. She stirred his compassion and his sense of duty, but he had never imagined a future with her, their lives intertwined.

Princess Suryavati, on the other hand, caused his heart to flutter. Looking into her eyes made time stop. He felt she was like him—struggling with the burden of being born noble, unable to chase her own dreams, always living for others. He knew he needed to talk to her and correct her misunderstanding of what she had witnessed between Vasantha and him.

His feet led him to where the theater troupe gathered after a play. At these gatherings, the actors and musicians told crude jokes and drank cheap coconut liquor that could burn a hole in one's stomach. Growing up, his father, and later his brother, had kept him away from the brew so he could focus on his studies and military training. But today, he longed for the coarse speech, the informal manners, and the throat-burning liquor.

When he arrived, the men hailed him like a long-lost friend. Someone placed a clay pot in his hand, and Giri gingerly took a sip—the taste was as bad as he remembered, but to his surprise, he found he enjoyed it.

"We were wondering if you found a girl to warm your bed and forgot about us," slurred one of the actors.

"Never mind him. He's just jealous because he only gets lucky once a year," jabbed another.

"It's that beard. If he tried to kiss anyone, he'd stab holes in their face," added a third.

For the first time in many days, Giri didn't feel alone. He felt like he belonged. It surprised him that he found this sense of belonging among actors and artists, drinking cheap liquor—men his brother would consider ordinary, who only played lords on stage. Giri was tired of hiding behind his mask. Didn't he deserve to relax, just a little?

As the sun rose, Giri stood unsteadily, surveying the sleeping men sprawled around him, empty cups scattered across the ground. His head throbbed, and he shut his eyes against the harsh morning light. Slowly, like trees gaining color as the night receded, the memories of yesterday crept back in. He had to find Princess Suryavati.

With that thought, he made his way back to the castle. Giri's head pounded with the aftermath of too much cheap liquor. His mouth was dry, and each step felt like his skull might split open. Still, the memory of Princess Suryavati—her eyes filled with hurt and betrayal—drove him forward. He needed to make amends, to explain what she had witnessed.

As Giri approached the palace gates, his steps faltered. The guards might recognize him and ask questions about his disheveled appearance. He had intended to wash himself in the river, but it was too late for that now. Prince Abhayan might have instructed the guards to keep an eye out for him, especially if the princess had gone to her brother with what she perceived as his betrayal.

Just then, an old woman shuffled past him, leaning heavily on her stick and struggling with a basket she carried.

A sudden thought struck him. "Let me help you, Ma," he offered, extending his hands toward the basket.

The old woman, her hair completely white but her eyes bright and piercing, handed it over with a grateful smile. As they walked together, she glanced up at him.

"Are you the playwright?" she asked in a trembling voice, surprising him.

Giri nodded cautiously, unsure how she knew him.

"Politics is also an art form," she said softly. "Your gift with words need not be used only for entertainment."

Her cryptic comment startled him, but before he could respond, they had reached the gates. As he had hoped, the guards waved them both through, along with the vendors bringing fresh produce and milk.

Once inside, the old woman held out her hands. "Find the girl who has occupied your mind," she said, as if she could read his thoughts. Then, she took back her basket with a nod and disappeared into the palace grounds, leaving Giri to ponder her words.

He made his way to his quarters, eager to clean himself up and change into fresh clothes before attempting to find Princess Suryavati again.

Spending only the briefest time in his room to wash and change, Giri hurried back outside. He wandered through the palace gardens, his thoughts focused entirely on how to gain an audience with Princess Suryavati. As he paced through the lush greenery, a familiar voice suddenly stopped him in his tracks.

"You are a cruel and manipulative man," Princess Kanika said, her eyes flashing with accusation. She stood before him, arms crossed, as though ready to judge him for all his misdeeds.

35
SURYAVATI

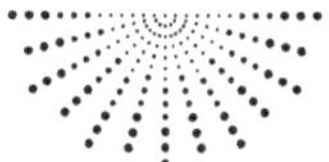

The birds in the palace garden welcomed the morning with their cheerful chirping, but Suri's world remained dark. Her decision last night to marry Rangapani suffocated her very breath. She had allowed Giri's words to seduce her heart. And what had she gained from her disguise and deceit to be close to him? Only memories filled with regret.

Suri slipped out of bed and moved toward the window, the morning light spilling softly across the room.

Her maid entered silently, offering a quick bow before setting to work. She fluffed the pillows, dusted the statues, and swept away the scattered remnants of yesterday.

"Leave," came a firmer voice—her mother's.

The maid froze for a moment, then hurried out, closing the door quietly behind her.

"Do you want to disgrace our family?" her mother asked, anger dripping from her voice.

Suri's face grew hot. She wanted to scream, to ask if her mother couldn't wait until the sun had risen before starting her insults.

"Listen to your heart, my daughter. You know my words are true. What caused you to leave your room unaccompanied?"

Suri turned away, doubt and guilt tugging at her mind like twin horses pulling a chariot. Her mother's presence only added dry wood to the fire burning inside her.

I bestowed my affections on one who did not deserve them, Suri wanted to say, her tear-filled eyes meeting her mother's gaze.

Her mother understood her without words. "My dear child, there are so few worthy of our love. The best you can hope for is one who will not trample your heart."

Suri bit her lip. For a time, when she had shared her verses with Giri, they had transported her to another realm, one filled with blooms and light.

"Rangapani will not set your heart on fire, but he will not burn your house down either," her mother said kindly.

Suri turned toward her mother and bowed in acceptance. As her mother left, Suri stared at her departing figure in silence.

Suri spent the day in her room, her mind clouded with gloomy thoughts. People were always watching her—the mute princess—reading meaning into the smallest gestures: how she held her hands, how she listened, how she sat. The constant performance drained her, and today she had no energy for concealing her tears. She chose to remain hidden, away from scrutinizing eyes.

But her solitude didn't last long. Her cousin, Kanika, soon came looking for her. With Kanika, Suri felt no pressure to hide or pretend, and her cousin always seemed to see through her evasions. Today was no different.

"You are profoundly sad," Kanika said, her eyes soft but probing. "I doubt Rangapani could evoke such deep emotions from you. This must be about the playwright. Did something happen between you two after the play rehearsal?"

Suri's lips trembled, betraying her inner turmoil. Kanika sat beside her, draping a comforting arm around her shoulders.

"Suri, tell me what I should do. I cannot bear to see you like this."

Though doubt gnawed at her insides, Suri wiped her eyes and shook her head. She could not ask her cousin to intervene in her affairs of the heart, especially when everything felt so unsettling.

Kanika stayed with her in silent support for a while, but before she left, she said firmly, "You are angry at Giri. If you won't tell me what happened, I'll get the answers directly from him."

As midday approached, a box arrived from Rangapani. Suri opened it with little interest, her mind still heavy. Inside, coral earrings glittered up at her. Though she possessed far more exquisite jewels, the meaning behind these was clear. When she wore the earrings, she would become his woman, bound to him in the eyes of everyone.

The thought weighed on her—not with joy or excitement, but with the suffocating finality of duty. Suri placed the jewels back in the box and shoved it into her armoire with little care. She then sat at her desk, staring at a blank palm leaf, an ink-dipped pen in her hand. Yet no poetic verses came flooding into her mind to spill onto the leaf; her thoughts were as parched and dry as desert sand.

Kanika entered the room with a scroll in hand, her face unreadable. "That man is as stubborn as you. He wouldn't tell me anything, only insisting that he needs to speak with you." She handed the scroll to Suri.

Hope flickered in Suri's heart. Were these the next two lines of the poem they had been composing together? Her fingers trembled as she unrolled the scroll. But the words she found were not poetry.

"I am guilty of deceit, but not for the act you witnessed."

Suri blinked, her heart thudding. What did he mean by this cryptic message? A sense of confusion washed over her, mingling with the anger and betrayal she still felt. Could there be something she didn't understand?

"The heart is a complicated thing, Suri," Kanika said wisely, her voice gentle but firm. "You're angry at Giri, and you have every right to be. But don't let that anger push you into the arms of someone like Rangapani just to find escape in convention." She paused, placing a hand on Suri's shoulder. "Give Giri a chance to explain himself before you make any decisions you'll regret."

Suri bit her lip, the weight of her cousin's words sinking in. She wanted to remain stubborn, to shield herself from more hurt, but Kanika's advice tugged at the part of her that still hoped. Was she truly ready to bind herself to a future with Rangapani just to avoid facing the pain Giri had caused?

Suri's heart sank as her mother entered the room, her head high. The door clicked shut behind her, and she greeted Kanika with a smile.

"My dear niece," her mother, Urmila, began, "after Suri's wedding, I'll start looking for a suitable husband for you. Since my sister's passing, I feel it's my duty to care for you and your sister."

Kanika smiled politely, but with a hint of defiance in her eyes. "Aunt Urmila, don't worry about me. I've already convinced my brother to arrange a Swayamvara, so I can choose my own husband, just like Queen Lalitha chose my brother."

At this, Urmila's face darkened, and she laughed bitterly. "Just make sure your sister isn't left to marry one of your discards."

The words pierced Suri deeply, as the painful story behind her mother's resentment resurfaced in her mind. Her grandparents had arranged a Swayamvara for Kanika's mother, Neelavati. But when Aunt Neelavati garlanded King Lambhodara instead of King Vibudha, as her parents had intended, Queen Urmila was left to marry King Vibudha, the unchosen one. Though her mother loved her niece and nephews, the bitterness of being a consolation bride still festered in her heart, casting a shadow over her relationships.

Suri cast a glance at Kanika, who remained composed despite the sharpness of her aunt's words. Her cousin's strength and calm demeanor were unshaken, but Suri herself felt trapped, the weight of her mother's expectations pressing heavily on her chest.

"Girls," Urmila continued, her tone softening ever so slightly, "join me for the evening meal. I've invited your father, brother, and uncle as well. Rangapani will be there too."

The mention of Rangapani sent a cold shiver down Suri's spine. The reality of her impending marriage to him seemed suffocating. She couldn't help but fear turning bitter like her mother, forced into a union she didn't desire.

Kanika gave her a knowing glance, her earlier words resonating once again in Suri's mind. *Don't retreat into conventionality...* Could she truly face Rangapani tonight, when her heart still yearned, in some part, for Giri?

Nodding mutely, Suri was unsure of what else to do. She felt herself being swept away in a relentless current of expectations and obligations, her own desires drowning beneath the weight of it all.

36

GIRIDHAR

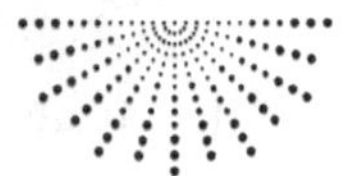

Giri followed Prince Abhayan into the royal quarters, his steps heavy with uncertainty. As they passed through the corridors, servants bowed their heads respectfully to the prince. A guard stepped forward, opening the door to one of the grand halls.

They stopped at the threshold.

There, sitting alone, was Princess Suryavati. The sight of her startled him—it had only been yesterday that they had last seen each other. But something was different now. She looked up, her eyes meeting his, and in that moment, he realized it: she had made a decision. She had chosen to marry Rangapani.

A wave of pain surged through Giri's body, surprising him with its intensity. Why did it hurt so much? He could have his pick of women—many far more beautiful, more graceful, more conventional. And yet none of them stirred his heart like Suryavati did. He wanted to compose poems with her, to weave stories that could make her laugh or cry. There was something about the connection they shared, the way their words blended together, that felt irreplaceable.

"Don't just stand there," the queen said, waving her son inside. Giri hesitated before stepping in, following Prince Abhayan. His steps faltered as his eyes scanned the room, taking in the others he hadn't noticed at first. His gaze landed on Rangapani, who was deep in conversation with the king. Rangapani's face twitched upon noticing Giri's presence.

"You've brought the playwright with you," the queen stated, her voice carrying a hint of curiosity.

Rangapani's expression darkened, but he said nothing, his eyes darting toward Giri with a flash of displeasure.

"He's hearing the legends of you and Father that live in people's minds," Abhayan explained. "I thought it best he see the real people for himself so there's some truth to his play."

"Our lives are too brief to waste worrying about our history," came a voice from the doorway. Prince Vikaran strode into the room, a feather still in his grasp as if he had been pulled away from his writing mid-sentence.

"Easy for you to say, Vikaran. He's not writing a play about you," the king remarked as he moved to the center of the room. "I don't want a thousand men thinking I'm some kind of tyrant."

"Don't worry, Brother," Vikaran said with a grin. "They're all terrified of us anyway—no one would dare speak such untruths."

The brothers burst into laughter, their shared joke filling the room, but Giri's mind drifted elsewhere. He noticed Princess Kanika moving toward Suryavati, glancing at him pointedly before sitting beside her cousin. Had Kanika passed along his message? Would Suryavati even want to hear his side of things? Giri felt a gnawing uncertainty, as if he were slowly fading into the background.

As they all sat to eat, servants bustled around, bringing dish after dish—plantain stir-fry, sesame rice, and mangoes soaked in honey. Yet Giri barely tasted any of it. His thoughts raced. He couldn't give up now. Once he secured his mother's blessing, he would reveal his heart to the princess.

But until then, he had to do something—anything—to stop Rangapani from claiming her hand in marriage.

Rangapani stared at him as if he could read Giri's mind. "To write about a king, it is not sufficient for Giri to merely sit down to a meal with us. He needs to hold a sword in his hand to understand what it feels like to wield a weapon," Rangapani declared, the challenge clear in his tone.

Giri looked at him steadily, unshaken. "I am not a complete novice when it comes to weapons of war," he said softly.

Rangapani's grin twisted. "Great, let us duel then. I promise not to kill you."

"I welcome it," Giri replied, his gaze shifting to Suryavati, who watched the exchange with wide eyes.

"Let us meet at sunrise," Rangapani said, his voice low and confident. Prince Abhayan watched them both, as if sensing the tension between them.

Giri spent the night restless, his mind a storm of guilt and regret. The hollow, lifeless gaze of Vasantha haunted him, a stark reminder of his failure to help her. Suryavati's image lingered too, their future together slipping further from his grasp with every moment he delayed sharing the truth.

As the first light of dawn crept through the shutters, he threw off the thin blanket in frustration, surrendering to his sleepless torment. It was only then, in the quiet stillness before the world stirred, that Rangapani's name surfaced in his thoughts like a boulder coming into view as the road turned.

Giri arrived early, surveying the weapons laid out before him. He couldn't use his own sword without revealing too much of his identity, so he carefully selected a blade that felt balanced in his hand. As he tested its weight, Rangapani strode in with a swagger, flanked by Prince Abhayan and the two princesses,

Suryavati and Kanika. The sight of Suryavati sent a pulse of heat through Giri, though he kept his expression neutral.

"If things get out of hand, I will put an end to this," Prince Abhayan warned, casting a sharp glance at both men.

Giri and Rangapani faced each other, swords raised. They circled, eyes locked, matching blow for blow. Each strike was calculated, yet Giri held back, careful not to fight at his full strength. Though he had often skipped lessons to read under a tree, his royal upbringing had still trained him far beyond what he intended to reveal today. Revealing his true skill would risk exposing his heritage—a secret he could not afford to unveil. Not yet, anyway.

Sweat dripped from their brows as the clash of swords echoed in the morning air. Giri swung his sword carelessly through the air, and Rangapani's shield rose to meet it with a loud clang. Rangapani was a trained warrior, and it took considerable effort on Giri's part to match him strike for strike while feigning less skill. The clouds whirled above them, the sun casting long shadows as they engaged in what felt like a dance, their movements both fierce and graceful.

The onlookers watched in tense silence, their eyes darting between the two men as the duel raged on. Giri forced himself to remain calm, his focus unwavering. Rangapani grew increasingly frustrated at his inability to overpower Giri easily. As Rangapani's breath became ragged and his movements sluggish, Giri seized the moment. With a powerful strike, his weapon crashed into Rangapani's shield, shattering it.

For a brief moment, Giri had the advantage. He could have pressed forward, but instead, he staggered back and lowered his weapon. It was enough to teach Rangapani some humility, but Giri did not want to push him over the edge.

"Enough," Prince Abhayan called, stepping forward. "You both fought well."

Rangapani's face flushed with humiliation as he sheathed his blade, his eyes burning with hatred as he glanced at Giri. Without a word, he stormed away, leaving a sour taste in the air.

But Giri felt no triumph. His eyes flickered briefly toward Princess Suryavati, but her expression remained unreadable.

37

SURYAVATI

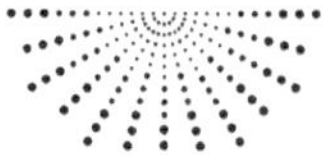

Suri watched Giri and then Rangapani as they spun around each other, their feet kicking up dust. She felt troubled and equally angry at these two young men. Images of Giri embracing the young woman flashed in Suryavati's mind. What explanation could he offer that she would believe? He must think her naïve to fall for his words. She knew Rangapani would show no genuine interest in her creative passions or her desire to continue writing. But her heart's desires seemed insignificant compared to the kingdom's needs. Her brother needed powerful allies like Rangapani when he ascended the throne.

As the duel dragged on and Giri held his ground, a stubborn part of her began to question whether her choice was truly between political obligation and following her heart. When Giri emerged victorious, she was surprised—not just by the outcome but by the joy that surged through her, though she kept it carefully concealed. Perhaps, with some guidance, Giri might prove capable of helping her brother rule the kingdom after all.

As she walked back with her brother, Suri noticed the

furrow in his brow. Tugging his elbow gently, she silently asked what was troubling him.

"There's something odd about Giri," Abhayan murmured, his gaze distant. "The way he fought—it wasn't the kind of skill you pick up on the streets or the stage. It was formal military training."

"Maybe he was a soldier in one of the neighboring kingdoms and abandoned that life for his love of theater," Kanika chimed in, her voice light.

"Maybe," Prince Abhayan replied, though his tone lacked conviction, a trace of suspicion lingering in his eyes.

Suri recalled Giri's cryptic message in the scroll: *I am guilty of deceit but not for the act you witnessed.*

Curiosity burned within her. What secret was he hiding from them all? She longed to uncover the truth, but sneaking out of her window was no longer an option—her mother had stationed a guard beneath it.

Determined, she decided to seek her brother's help. Yet she would have to tread carefully, not revealing the true reason behind her request, a door she wasn't yet ready to open, even to herself.

I need to talk to Giri about the play, Suri conveyed through a combination of gestures and writing on her brother's hand.

Abhayan's eyes narrowed slightly, suspicion flickering in his gaze. If he had been older, more perceptive like Kanika, he might have seen through her intent. But fortunately, he only said, "I will invite Giri to my chambers. You can join me there."

Suri nearly protested, wanting to meet Giri without her brother's presence, but she knew better than to push her luck. She could hardly ask Abhayan to leave them alone. Instead, she nodded, keeping her thoughts hidden.

Suri stared at the mirror in her room, her reflection staring back, mocking her. Mirrors always troubled her. They reflected her outer self—her beauty, her grace—but they hid the ugliness that lay deep within her, the silence that marked her muteness. Her throat tightened as she thought about it, her greatest flaw, the curse that separated her from others.

For too long, she had focused on her own desires, but now doubt began to gnaw at her. Why would Giri, a man of words, choose someone like her—a caged princess unable to speak? Her body tensed, and the room seemed to close in around her, growing darker with every thought. She stared at her throat in the mirror, feeling as though the silence suffocated her, deepening her isolation.

"Am I late?" Kanika asked, stepping into the room with a playful grin. Suri turned in surprise, her cousin's sudden appearance breaking through her cloud of doubts.

"What? Did you think I'd let you miss this chance to confront Giri?" Kanika teased, moving closer. "I'll keep Abhayan busy with a game of dice while you talk to him. No need to worry."

She gently took Suri's hands, gazing at her face. "You look beautiful, as if you're ready for your story to begin."

Suri smiled, touched by her cousin's poetic words.

When they entered her brother's chamber, Giri bowed his head respectfully, though his gaze lingered on Suryavati for a moment before he looked away. His presence stirred something deep within her—an unspoken tension that made her heart race. She maintained a stern expression, determined to show him she had not forgiven him. Yet, as her anger simmered, she worried it betrayed how much she truly cared about this man's actions.

"Abhayan, let's leave the crazy poets alone and play a game of dice," Kanika said with a mischievous smile, tugging Abhayan by the arm.

Abhayan hesitated, glancing between Suryavati and Giri, clearly uneasy about leaving them alone. But Kanika's persistence won out, and with a sigh, he allowed her to pull him toward the adjoining room.

The silence that followed their departure was heavy. Suryavati and Giri stood only a few feet apart, yet the distance between them felt vast.

Suri took her seat at a small table and gestured for Giri to sit across from her. He obliged, leaning back in his chair.

In the other room, Kanika spread out the silk dice game cloth on the floor, and Abhayan sat down across from her, though his gaze kept flicking toward his sister and Giri.

What did Abhayan think she could possibly do with both him and Kanika just a few feet away? Especially when she couldn't even whisper her thoughts aloud. Suri turned her focus to Giri. He showed no signs of strain from his earlier duel with Rangapani.

Giri met her gaze, and it appeared as if he was searching for something in her face.

"The young woman in the story," Giri said, "is not the man's lover. She is someone he cares about and wants to help. But there are no other connections."

Suryavati traced the word *Lies* on the table with her finger.

Giri shook his head. "The man saved the young widow's life and feels a duty to protect her. There is nothing more between us—them."

She kept her gaze on Giri, waiting for him to waver, to show even a flicker of guilt. But his expression remained steady, his eyes holding hers without faltering.

Does he care about someone else more deeply?

Heat crept up her cheeks at the thought, but she had to know.

"There is a princess," Giri whispered, his voice so soft it

barely reached her ears. "She has become as vital to him as the air he breathes."

Her heart constricted, and for a moment, Suri looked away, unsure how to process the overwhelming emotion rising within her. But his sincerity, the way he held her gaze, made her feel the weight of his words.

"Suryavati," he breathed her name as though it took all his strength, dropping the formality and sending a shiver through her entire body. "You are the one I want to share my stories with. My heart—it has only one desire. I'm not playing games with you. Will you marry me?"

Suri's gasp was loud, breaking the fragile tension in the room, and for an instant, she forgot everything else around them. Suri's heart raced at Giri's sudden, bold question. The world around her seemed to blur, and she found it difficult to breathe for a moment.

Giri quickly raised his voice, masking the intimate moment. "Yes, that's exactly the reaction the audience will have," he said, smiling broadly, as if they were simply discussing a scene in the play.

Kanika and Abhayan glanced at them briefly before returning to their game. "You moved your piece twice," Abhayan accused, his brow furrowing.

Kanika grinned mischievously. "Did I?"

Suri, heart racing, quickly wrote on the table,

Marry you? My mother will never agree to it.

"She will," Giri replied confidently.

How?

Her eyes searched his face for answers.

Giri leaned in, lowering his voice. "I—"

A sudden knock interrupted them.

"Prince Abhayan!"

Rangapani?

Abhayan stood swiftly and gestured toward Giri. "If he sees you here, Playwright, there will be trouble. Go hide in my bedroom. Sister, sit with Kanika."

Suri moved to sit next to her cousin while Giri slipped out of sight.

Once they had settled, Abhayan called out, "Let him in."

The door swung open, and Rangapani staggered inside, his face flushed and eyes wild.

3 8

GIRIDHAR

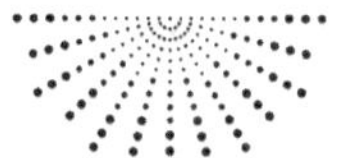

Curse that man. Like an ill omen, Rangapani had barged in just as Giri was about to ask Suryavati to meet him alone tonight. The urge to punch Rangapani in the face—maybe knock out a tooth or two—surged through Giri, but instead, he crouched behind a chest, staying hidden.

From his vantage point, he could see Suryavati sitting by the game board, her hands nervously twined together. Her long lashes cast delicate shadows on her cheeks, making her look like a beautiful, gilded sculpture. She hadn't refused his proposal, even though she knew him only as a mere playwright. That thought alone made his heart soar.

Rangapani's gaze flickered over Suryavati, his face betraying a whirlwind of emotions—shame, shock, and, finally, a mask of forced bravado. It was clear he still harbored resentment toward Giri for what he considered his defeat in the duel, despite Giri's restraint in not disarming him and merely shattering his shield.

"Suryavati, I'm glad to see you," he said, his voice oozing false confidence. "I let that playwright win this morning only because of my generous nature. He'd be useless without his fingers." He grinned, the expression twisting his features into something ugly.

"Yes, I was telling them the same. A mere playwright couldn't have possibly bested Jaisalpur's most feared warrior," Abhayan said, his tone smooth and disarming.

Rangapani's chest swelled with pride as he straightened his shoulders, eager to believe the prince's flattery. Giri wondered if the young prince suspected he was not who he claimed to be.

"You've arrived at the perfect time, my friend," Abhayan continued. "Would you mind escorting my sister and cousin back to their quarters?"

Without waiting for a response, Abhayan guided them all toward the door with practiced ease that belied his age, skillfully maneuvering them out of his chambers before Rangapani had a chance to linger further.

When the door clicked shut, Prince Abhayan wasted no time. He strode toward his bedroom and ordered, "You can come out, Playwright."

Giri rose from behind the chest, straightening himself and offering a nod. "Thank you for keeping me hidden."

The prince's expression remained stern. "I didn't do it for you," he replied, his voice edged with a protective tone. "I did it for my sister."

Abhayan's eyes bore into Giri's. His youth might have prevented him from fully unraveling the truth, but suspicion clouded his face. "I meant what I said earlier. You're not just a playwright. Where did you learn to fight like that?"

Giri couldn't afford to raise more doubts, especially with Rangapani lurking nearby, ready to exploit any weakness. He hesitated, his mind racing, then met Prince Abhayan's probing gaze. "I was trained alongside a prince," he said, carefully choosing his words.

It wasn't a lie, not entirely. He had trained alongside his brother, who was a prince at the time. But revealing the full truth now, before he could speak to Suryavati, was too risky. He couldn't afford to expose his royal heritage just yet—not until he knew where Suryavati stood and what her heart truly desired.

The prince's eyes narrowed, sensing something unsaid, but for now, he let it pass. "If you leave now, you can avoid detection by Rangapani," Prince Abhayan said, his tone firm. "Just remember, my parents want him to marry my sister."

The warning was unmistakable—a subtle reminder of the forces aligned against him. Giri bowed respectfully, holding back the emotions swirling within him. With a final glance at the prince, he turned and departed, knowing that his life would be empty without Suryavati in it. The thought of losing her gnawed at him, and he felt a surge of resolve. He was prepared to face not only Rangapani but even his brother's wrath if it meant winning her hand. Suryavati had become his every thought, his every breath, and no obstacle—royal or otherwise —could keep him from her.

As long as she accepted him once he revealed his deception.

The weight of that truth hung over him like a storm cloud. If Suryavati could forgive his hidden identity, there was hope. But if she couldn't—if she saw his actions as betrayal—then he would lose not only her trust but any chance at the life he now dreamed of. The risk was great, but Giri knew he had to take it. For her, he would risk everything.

He marched to the storage room where the costumes for the play were kept. After rummaging through the racks, he found a sari and a long black wig. He had portrayed a female character in his last play when the regular actor fell ill, so he was no stranger to the disguise. Luckily, he had shaved his mustache and beard for that role and had kept his face clean since. Wearing a sari with a beard would've been comical.

After a few clumsy attempts at draping the fabric, he managed something passable, hoping the cover of night would hide his errors. Dressed in his new guise, he set off to find Princess Kanika.

Fate seemed to favor him as he spotted Princess Kanika walking through the halls. She nearly passed him, not recognizing his disguise.

"My lady," he whispered.

She paused and turned, her eyes narrowing in confusion. He took a step closer, lowering his voice. "It is Giri. I need an audience with Princess Suryavati."

Kanika's eyes widened, and then a smile blossomed across her face as she looked him over. "I was just coming to find you," she said, clearly amused by his transformation. "This disguise will work perfectly."

Together, they approached Suryavati's chambers, and Giri's heart pounded in his chest.

The guard stationed outside, Nanmaran, glanced at him briefly before bowing respectfully to Kanika.

"Announce us, Nanmaran," Kanika said smoothly. "I've brought a maid to assist Suryavati with her hair."

Nanmaran knocked on the door, unsuspecting. When Princess Suryavati opened it slightly and peered out, the guard announced, "Princess Kanika is here to visit you, my lady."

Suryavati's eyes narrowed briefly as she noticed Kanika standing there with Giri in disguise. After a moment's hesitation, she stepped aside, allowing them both to enter.

Once the door closed behind them, Suryavati moved gracefully to the center of the room. The soft glow of a brass oil lamp illuminated her figure, casting a golden halo that made her seem almost ethereal. Giri swallowed, trying to contain the rush of emotions overwhelming him at that moment.

"I brought the playwright," Kanika said lightly, her tone playful, "so you can finish your conversation."

Without waiting for a reply, she gracefully wandered into the adjoining room, leaving them alone.

Suryavati's eyes widened in disbelief as she tried to see him through the disguise of a woman's clothes, the weight of their last conversation evident in her expression.

Giri stepped forward, gently taking her hands. When she didn't pull away, hope flickered within him.

"Will you marry me?" he repeated, his voice barely above a whisper.

He could see the tears shimmering in her eyes, but he held back his urge to embrace her.

Without a word, Suryavati led him to the table where a silver plate of rice lay. She dipped her finger in the grains and wrote carefully.

In my dreams, I will marry you. But this is real life.

"This dream can be real," Giri said, his voice filled with determination. "I am not just a playwright. Not entirely. I am a prince."

Her face froze, shock overtaking her. Then, without warning, her hand shot up and slapped him hard across the face, the sound ringing in the room.

39

SURYAVATI

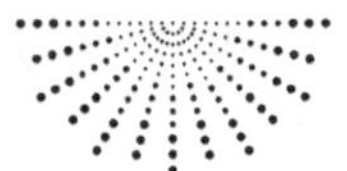

Silence hung in the room as Giri stood motionless, his cheek still burning red from the force of Suri's slap. Her chest tightened, a storm of emotions swirling inside her—rage, betrayal, confusion. A prince? The thought echoed in her mind. Why had he let her believe they were incompatible? Why had he left her to wrestle with the idea that their worlds could never align?

Kanika rushed in, sensing the tension. Her eyes flicked between the two of them, but Suri didn't acknowledge her cousin. Instead, she balled her fists, glaring at Giri with fury she couldn't contain.

Slowly, Giri spoke, his voice heavy with regret. "I deserve that—for my deceit." His words hung in the air, but the weight of more than one lie lingered between them. She glanced at him, realizing how ridiculous he looked in the sari. As if anyone could truly mistake his strong jawline and muscular arms for a woman's. The absurdity of the disguise only deepened his deception. If she weren't so angry, she might have noticed the poetic gesture—him donning a sari just to see her, as if he

168

would cross seven mountains and seas to fulfill her heart's desires.

But with anger swirling in her stomach, Suri had little room for poetry. She couldn't find it in her heart to trust him. How could she? What if this was all an elaborate con to manipulate her, a princess, into marriage? If she believed him—if she were naïve enough to fall for his words—he would gain access to her power, her wealth, everything. And she would become nothing more than a puppet on a string. Her chest heaved as fear clouded her mind.

Show me proof.

She wrote with her finger in the rice.

Without hesitation, Giri reached into his pouch and pulled out a ring—one that gleamed under the light. He handed it to her, and as she examined it, her eyes widened. The ring bore a fish emblem. Was that the royal emblem of Nidhapur? What was his connection to this royal symbol?

Her breath hitched as she stared at him, emotions swirling in her chest. Could he really be telling the truth? She glanced at the royal ring in her palm, feeling its weight, wondering if it had been stolen—or if Giri was truly who he claimed to be.

Without answers, she handed the ring back and traced the word *Why?* in the rice on the table.

Giri's gaze softened. "If a princess cannot be a poet, do you think a prince can be a playwright?" he asked gently.

The question struck her. She remembered her own disguise when they first met, how she had hidden as a boy to protect her passion for writing. She knew what it meant to conceal one's true self from the expectations of royalty.

His eyebrows were drawn together as he scanned her face. "I

did what I do best—fabricated a story to protect myself. Fiction felt safer than my truth."

Giri's words could have been hers, another bond tying them together.

Why not tell me?

"Blame my vanity. I wanted you to like me for myself, not because I was a prince. I wanted to be seen."

Like me, she thought.

Just then, Kanika moved closer, her expression full of curiosity. "What's going on?" she asked, looking between them.

Giri turned to her, his voice steady. "I've revealed the truth to Suryavati, and I will do the same for you—but it must stay between us." His tone was serious. "I am Prince Giridhar of Nidhapur. I've already sought my mother's blessing to ask for Suryavati's hand. Once I have it, I will reveal my identity to your parents."

Suryavati's heart raced as Giri's words sank in. *Prince Giridhar of Nidhapur*. She wanted to believe him, but the weight of his deception still pressed heavily on her. The memories of their time together—moments shared under the guise of mere playwright and princess—flashed before her. Their connection had felt real, but now she wondered if it had been built on half-truths.

Kanika's eyes widened, the shock clear on her face. She looked at Giri, then at Suryavati, slowly nodding as she began to understand the gravity of the situation. "You're a prince?" Kanika whispered, her voice barely audible.

Giri nodded solemnly.

Kanika's eyes lit up, and she turned to Suryavati with excitement. "That changes everything, Suri! You don't have to marry Rangapani," she said, her voice rising with enthusiasm.

But Suryavati's heart didn't mirror Kanika's joy. The confusion, the deceit, and the whirlwind of emotions left her feeling conflicted. She glanced at Giri, unsure whether to feel relieved, hopeful, or more guarded than ever. The sudden shift in her fate was as disorienting as it was promising.

Giri stepped closer and gently took Suri's hand in his, his lips curving into a worried frown. "I can invite Rangapani to another duel and prove my skill with a sword. Or perhaps I could regale you with stories of every neighboring kingdom and their history." His voice was soft, but the warmth of his touch made Suri's pulse quicken. She hoped the heat in her cheeks wasn't as obvious as it felt.

Kanika's voice cut through the moment. "If you are truly Giridhar of Nidhapur, then where were you two months ago?"

Giri released her hand, and she felt an immediate sense of loss. Before she could understand her feeling, Giri turned to Kanika, his expression darkening. "I was humiliated by your brother, King Dushyant," he admitted. "With my tail between my legs, I fled to Jaisalpur, too ashamed to return to Nidhapur and face my own brother. I wasn't brave enough to stand up to either of them." His words carried the weight of past failures.

Kanika's face softened, her doubts about his identity seemingly melting away. She must have asked the question to confirm what she already knew about Giridhar from her brother. But for Suri, the doubts were only beginning.

If he truly was the prince of Nidhapur, marrying him would mean leaving her home, her family, and everything familiar behind. She was voiceless even in her own land. Could she trust this man—a stranger who had hidden his true identity from the start—to protect her in a foreign kingdom? And the fears she had carried with her forever surfaced with force—her inadequacy as a mute princess, unable to perform her royal duties or give him an heir.

And then there was Rangapani. Marrying him would allow

her to stay home, surrounded by people and places she knew. Would that be the safer choice, even if it meant sacrificing her heart?

She only had questions and no answers.

40

GIRIDHAR

Giri stood before the girl he loved, draped in a ridiculous sari that felt like it might unravel at any moment. He had laid himself bare, revealing the truth of who he was, only to be met with doubtful stares. He had naively believed that simply telling her he was a prince would be enough—that the title alone would make her accept him. But now, as her uncertainty lingered in the silence between them, he realized his mistake. Titles meant nothing without trust, and he had lost hers.

Instead of the lightness he had imagined, Giri felt like he was plummeting, falling fast and unsure of what to do next. Desperation gnawed at him as he walked over to her window, where a tree limb stretched out like an offering. He scanned the darkness, searching for a sign—anything to guide him. The night sky was a deep blue, and the stars sparkled like pearls woven into a girl's hair. For a brief moment, he caught himself admiring the view, but then a thought echoed in his head, cutting through the stillness.

Giri turned toward Suri and gestured to the window. "Look," he said softly. "With you, I can share my innermost thoughts—

like how the night sky reminds me of a woman's hair, with stars twinkling like gems woven into it. I won't be ridiculed or mocked for such things. You will understand me."

Suri glanced at him, and he saw the beginnings of understanding in her eyes.

"And it's not just my thoughts I can share with you," he continued, his voice steady but full of emotion. "You understand the duties of being a prince—the need to place the kingdom above ourselves. With you, I can be myself, without having to hide any part of who I am." He could have explained it a thousand times, but with Suri, he didn't need to. That was why he was falling deeper in love with her. She made him want to be better—to become worthy of her.

A smile spread across her face like the moon emerging from behind a cloud, soft and radiant. He ached to kiss her, to feel her heartbeat against his, to trace the curve of her back with his fingers. Instead, he cupped her face and gently touched his forehead to hers, savoring the warm breath that filled the space between them. As her arms wrapped around him, everything felt right.

"It is time for you to leave," Kanika's voice cut through the moment, bringing them back to reality.

Reluctantly, Giri stepped back, his heart still tethered to Suri. "When do we meet again?" he asked softly.

Suri gestured with her hand, a slight wave.

"Tomorrow night?" he guessed.

She nodded.

"Where?"

Here, she indicated with a subtle motion.

"I'll come in disguise—with Kanika?" he asked, already planning. His voice softened. "But please, keep my identity secret until I'm ready to reveal it."

They nodded, sealing their agreement.

Giri barely slept that night, his body alive with anticipation.

Time seemed too valuable to waste on sleep when he could be spending it with Suryavati, discussing a story about a snake who transformed into a prince at night. Not just that one tale—countless stories swirled in his mind, waiting for her poems to breathe life into them.

At the rehearsal for the play, all Giri could think about was the night ahead, when he would see Suryavati again. He tried to push thoughts of her aside, but they only took deeper root. When the actors flawlessly performed a scene, he wished she were there to witness it too. He missed her, even though they had just been together the night before.

For so long, he had lived a lie, pretending to be someone he wasn't. But with her, he no longer had to hide. He could be both a prince and a storyteller.

After the castle quieted for the night, Giri transformed himself again, donning the sari and tucking a fragrant jasmine flower into his hair. He waited for Princess Kanika, growing more restless by the minute as the sari began to itch against his hip. Just when he was ready to give up, she finally appeared.

"We were at the temple with the queen," Kanika explained, rolling her eyes. "She wouldn't leave until she'd prayed to every known god—and a few new ones—for blessings on the upcoming wedding between Suryavati and Rangapani." She glanced at him with a teasing smirk. "I hope you've been saying your prayers too. Otherwise, you're in big trouble."

Giri smiled wryly, but inwardly, he knew the truth. If the gods truly favored him, he wouldn't be a prince with this maddening desire to write. No, this was a dream he would have to achieve on his own, without divine intervention.

As they walked, Kanika rambled on about some hairstyle she wanted to try. Giri assumed it was part of their pretense, keeping up the appearance that he was merely a maid, and he tuned her out. His thoughts drifted to Suryavati, and just imagining seeing her again sent his heart racing.

However, instead of heading straight to Suryavati's chambers, Kanika led him to her room. When she opened the door, they stepped inside, and there, rising from a bench, was Suryavati. The soft glow of the lamp illuminated her, and for a brief moment, Giri felt like the world narrowed down to just the two of them.

"I have letters to write," Kanika said, settling at a nearby table, giving the couple their privacy.

Giri moved toward Suryavati, his heart pounding with anticipation, the thought of kissing her vivid in his mind. She lowered herself onto the bench, and he slid as close as he dared. A soft blush crept across her cheeks, making his pulse quicken.

"Beautiful," he whispered warmly, removing the flower from his own hair and gently tucking it into hers.

She laughed, a light, melodic sound that seemed to erase everything else in the world, leaving only the two of them in that fleeting, perfect moment.

"What do you think of this story?" Giri asked, his voice gentle. "A girl finds a snake and brings it to her hut. At night, the snake transforms into a prince."

Suryavati's eyes lit up with interest. She reached for the plate of rice she kept nearby and quickly wrote,

Where can I find this snake?

Giri chuckled softly. "You don't need that beast. You have a real prince dedicated to you," he said, his heart lighter than it had been all day.

4 1

SURYAVATI

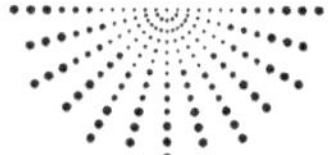

The story of the snake prince took on a life of its own,
growing limbs and leaves, with flowers blossoming
from its branches as they nurtured it together, their minds
entwined as one. Suryavati had never felt more alive, realizing
she'd found something rare—a man who could share both her
body and her mind.

"That's a wicked curse, Suryavati. You have a devious mind,"
Giri said with a grin, lounging with his legs spread wide, oblivi-
ous to the sari slipping from his shoulder. She couldn't help but
wonder what it would feel like to be nestled in his arms, her
head resting beneath his chin.

"A curse that requires a sacrifice to break," he mused,
watching her intently, as if searching her face for more than just
the story's answer—perhaps a glimpse into what she might be
willing to give up for him.

She nodded, reaching to secure the slipping folds of his sari
back onto his shoulder. This disguise was endearing to her now;
he'd worn it just to be near her, and in that, he was making
sacrifices of his own. Would she be able to make one just as
great? Could she leave her beloved home to follow him to

177

Nidhapur? And what if she failed to produce an heir? It was not unusual for royal princes to take many wives. What would happen to her if he married a woman who could speak and claimed his heart?

As if sensing her unspoken thoughts, he asked a peculiar question. "Suryavati, while revising the play about your parents, a thought struck me. King Vibudha had a previous wife before he married your mother. What happened to your stepmother?"

Her stepmother? Suri's memories of her were faint—she had passed when Suri was very young, leaving no one to keep her memory alive.

She died.

Her hand lingered on the words. A new curiosity flickered within her, wondering what her stepmother's life had been like when her father brought her mother as his new bride.

Later that night, she crawled beneath her silk sheets, her mind drifting to her stepmother and mother, vying for her father's attention. She doubted he had truly loved either of his wives; his sole concern had been for heirs to secure the throne. Slowly, she slipped into a dream. Giri hovered close, like a bee circling a blossom.

"I taste nectar," he murmured, his lips brushing hers and sending a shiver through her stomach.

Suddenly, dark clouds gathered, and lightning tore across the sky. "You're cursed!" Giri shouted, his voice twisted with terror. "The demon stole your tongue. I must vanquish you before you bring my downfall."

She jolted awake, drenched in sweat, her heart pounding in terror.

As if mocking her fears, sunlight filtered into her room, casting everything in a golden glow. She tossed her sheets aside and rose, a new determination to uncover more about her step-mother filling her.

She found her uncle in his chambers, where two matching wooden flutes were mounted on the wall behind him. She wondered about their story—whether her uncle played them or if they had another significance. Her silence kept her from asking too many questions, and this one would remain unanswered for now. Perhaps this was why she was drawn to writing poems; it allowed her to use her imagination to fill the gaps. But she could not rely on her imagination to understand what had happened to her stepmother.

Her uncle looked up as she entered and smiled warmly. With a slight hesitation, she unrolled the scroll she had brought with her and held it out.

Can you tell me about the former queen?

"Your stepmother?" His expression shifted briefly, a strange flicker of emotion crossing his face. "I haven't thought about her in years. She was a troubled woman, more absorbed in her silks and jewels than the affairs of the kingdom. In the early days of your mother's marriage, she made life difficult for her. But when your mother bore your brother—a feat the old queen never managed—she seemed to lose all resolve. She fell ill shortly after and never recovered."

Suri felt a pang of despair as the tale settled in her mind. A once-powerful queen, reduced to sickness and sorrow simply because she was childless. What if her own childhood illness, which had robbed her of speech, had also taken her ability to bear children? What would become of her then?

She trusted Giri, but he was a prince with duties and expectations. If she couldn't give him an heir, he'd marry again to fulfill his role. The woman who bore his son would become queen when Giri ascended the throne, while she would be set aside—perhaps reduced to no more than a servant in her own household.

* * *

SHE SAT on an ornate bench in her mother's chambers, the carved legs fashioned to resemble those of an elephant. Their midday meal had just been cleared by the servants, and her mother hummed softly as she sifted through her jewelry.

Rising from the bench, Suri picked up her plate of rice and approached her mother. She traced her finger through the grains to spell out her question:

How did you manage Father's first wife?

Though her heart held more questions, her silence limited her to only what she could fit within a plate of rice.

Her mother's expression shifted, flickering with sorrow, fear, and finally, a steely resolve. "The old queen was filled with bitterness, and over time, it consumed her," she murmured, gently stroking Suri's back. "You need not fear for your own safety, Suri. I will not allow Rangapani to take another wife, nor will your brother. That is why I've chosen him as your husband —to keep you safe, here, in your own home."

Was that reason enough to marry a man she could barely tolerate? Unlike a royal prince, she would only marry once. The thought of spending her lifetime with Rangapani felt like a fate worse than losing her tongue.

She spotted the man himself as she strolled through the palace gardens. Cursing herself for not ducking behind a bush in time, she kept her expression neutral and prepared to greet Rangapani.

180

"Suryavati," he called, striding toward her like a bull. His easy familiarity with her given name irked her in a way that Giri's never did.

She dipped her head, hoping the small gesture would help her regain her composure. If she married him, she reminded herself, he would be entitled to call her by her name, whether she liked it or not.

"Did you receive the earrings I gave you?" he asked.

She nodded, silently grateful for her inability to speak. At least he wouldn't expect her to give elaborate answers. Nor would she have to pretend to find something positive to say about the jewels.

"I may not have your wealth, my lady, but I bought those coral earrings with my own hard-earned gold," he added earnestly.

A pang of guilt stirred in her chest for her unkind thoughts. Rangapani wasn't a bad man—just an ill fit for the creative spirit she longed to nurture.

"Would you wear them on our journey to the Goddess Parvati temple by the lake?"

Suri's eyebrows lifted in surprise. Her mother hadn't mentioned anything about this trip when they'd shared their midday meal.

"Our men captured the bandits who roamed near the lake," Rangapani explained. "The king asked me to meet with the villagers to convey that there are no more thieves threatening their roads. I sought his permission to bring you along." He hesitated, then added, "Of course, the prince and your cousin will accompany us as well."

42

GIRIDHAR

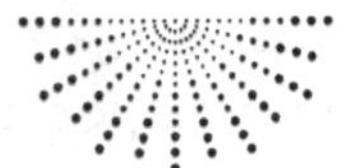

After a quick morning meal, Giri settled into his small room, ready to rewrite a few scenes. His concentration broke at a knock on the door.

"Prince Abhayan requests that you join him this morning. He's waiting at the stables." For a moment, Giri wondered if Suryavati or Kanika had shared his identity with the prince. He would find out soon enough.

"Could you deliver this to the lead actor?" he asked, rolling up the scroll with his edits and handing it to the servant, who nodded and left.

Giri dressed quickly and headed outside.

The stables were bustling with activity. Stable hands moved briskly, leading horses from their stalls and preparing them with saddles and harnesses. Several grooms worked in unison, polishing a grand carriage with elaborate gold trim, ensuring every detail gleamed in the morning light. Hooves stamped the ground as the horses tossed their heads, adding to the hum of anticipation. Nearby, a few men loaded supplies into an ox-driven cart, securing provisions for what seemed to be a lengthy journey. The air was thick with the scent of hay and dung.

"My lord," Giri said, dipping his head respectfully as he approached Prince Abhayan.

"Playwright, a few of us are headed to the Goddess Parvati temple by the lake. Join us," said the prince, extending a hand to feed his horse a cube of jaggery. The horse nuzzled the prince's palm, nickering in appreciation.

Giri opened his mouth, ready to decline, prepared to explain that he needed the day to work on his play. But then he caught sight of Rangapani striding toward them, flanked by the two princesses. In the fresh morning air, with sunlight dancing in her hair, Suryavati looked so enchantingly beautiful that he nearly forgot to breathe. His resolve shifted in an instant, and he found himself nodding.

"I would be honored to join you, my lord," he replied, his eyes lingering on Suryavati as he spoke.

Suryavati glanced at him, a mixture of emotions flitting across her face—joy, yes, and then worry. Did she think he had lied to her about being a prince? He wouldn't blame her if she did; he hadn't been entirely truthful with her from the beginning. So focused was he on the princess that he nearly forgot his rival standing nearby.

Unfortunately, Rangapani spotted him and noticed his lingering gaze on Suryavati. His face darkened, taking on the stormy hue of a rain cloud. "What are you doing here?" he demanded, his tone thick with irritation.

"Joining the outing to the lake," Giri replied, meeting Rangapani's stare without a hint of hesitation. What he truly wanted to do was punch the man hard enough to crack his teeth, but he knew that would be unwise.

Rangapani's voice rose. "I did not ask you to join us," he bellowed, his fists clenching at his sides.

"I did," Prince Abhayan interjected calmly, casting a steady glance at Rangapani. "I would enjoy his company."

Rangapani shot a dark scowl in Giri's direction. "He cannot

be trusted, especially around young women," he said, his voice taut with barely concealed frustration as he tried to keep his tone respectful in front of the prince.

Prince Abhayan raised an eyebrow, a hint of amusement flickering in his eyes. "Nonsense. Are you implying that you're not capable of keeping him in line should he misstep?" Abhayan had quickly learned how to keep Rangapani's temper in check.

"No, my lord," Rangapani stammered, his gaze lingering on Giri's nose as if picturing his fist colliding with it. At least they were alike in their dislike for each other.

Their party set out soon after, with Giri riding beside the prince on a brown mare. Despite the conversation around him, his heart was keenly aware of Suryavati sitting in the carriage. Just being in her presence filled him with a warmth that made him want to grin like an idiot. Even Rangapani's scowl, which darkened to the color of a crow, amused him.

As they arrived outside the temple, Giri swiftly dismounted, his eyes fixed on the approaching carriage. The chariot slowed to a stop, and Rangapani was at its side in an instant, grasping Suryavati's arm with more force than finesse. Giri tensed, worried Rangapani might pull her arm out of its socket. Instinctively, he stepped forward, angry at Rangapani's heavy-handedness.

"Gently, my lord. Our princess is no match for a warrior like you," murmured Princess Kanika with a calm but pointed smile. Rangapani flushed, adjusting his grip more delicately. Suryavati, serene as ever, simply dipped her head, allowing him to assist her without resistance, though her eyes briefly met Giri's with an unreadable expression.

As they entered the temple courtyard, Giri trailed behind the group, keeping his distance. The priest hurried forward to greet the royal family, bowing deeply before guiding them to the sanctum. Inside, the statue of Goddess Parvati radiated under the glow of oil lamps, adorned in a silk sari and garlands of fresh flowers.

The priest recited a prayer, his voice echoing softly off the temple walls. Giri's gaze wandered over the intricate murals, each one depicting scenes from the goddess's life, ending with her marriage to God Shiva.

He recalled verses from Poet Kalidasa's epic poem *Kumarasambhava*, about the birth of the war god. The lines described Goddess Parvati's beauty before she wed God Shiva:

As when the flowers are budding on a vine,
Or white swans rest upon a river's shore,
Or when at night the stars in heaven shine,
Her lovely beauty grew with gems she wore.

Giri longed to ask Suryavati if she had read this poem and which verses she cherished most. He himself was especially fond of the lament of Rati, the devoted wife of the God of Love, Kama. Her sorrowful verses over her husband's loss had always struck him deeply, each line steeped in longing and devotion. Would Suryavati, too, find her heart stirred by such words?

Her opening eyes were fixed with anxious thought
On every spot where he might be, in vain,
Were gladdened nowhere by the sight she sought,
The lover she should never see again.

But here in the temple, surrounded by watchful eyes, Giri knew he had to restrain his curiosity—and his longing.

Soon, the priest approached with a silver plate, an oil wick lamp flickering atop it. The warm glow danced across the polished metal, casting soft light over each face.

After presenting the *aarthi* to the crown prince, the priest turned to the princess, his gaze settling on Rangapani beside her. "You have come with your future husband," he observed, nodding approvingly. Rangapani straightened at this, a self-satisfied smile spreading across his face.

Giri's eyes flickered toward Suryavati, who glanced back at him briefly before facing the priest, her cheeks flushed.

"You will be blessed with many offspring, my lady," the priest continued, extending the *aarthi* plate toward her. Suryavati lifted her hand, cupping it over the flame to receive the blessing. The soft blush deepened, reaching down her neck, and her gaze stayed low, as if the weight of the priest's words lingered in the air around her.

Giri hadn't managed to speak to Suryavati or even draw near her during their time in the temple. Instead, he circled the courtyard restlessly, anticipating the moment his servant would return with his mother's blessing. Then he could finally abandon this disguise and ask for her hand openly. When the group gathered outside, preparing to ride to the village center, Giri mounted his horse, resolving to find a chance to be alone with her.

Just then, some commotion startled his horse, causing it to rear suddenly. Too late, Giri realized Suryavati stood directly beneath the horse's hooves, her hands raised in frantic gestures.

43

SURYAVATI

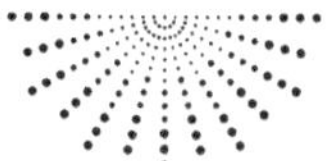

Seeing Giri at the temple stirred her emotions, with fear at the forefront. Suri dreaded leaving her home to travel to Nidhapur with Prince Giridhar. If he was the Crown Prince, why would his mother think Suri—a mute—could be queen? Her own mother thought her weak and defenseless, and didn't Suri's worries prove her mother right? Her other choice was to remain in Jaisalpur as Rangapani's wife, a man who would consider writing poetry an unsuitable occupation for his wife. Yes, her brother would offer her protection, but she couldn't run to him for every family quarrel.

When they entered the inner sanctum, Rangapani chose to attach himself to her side. As the priest chanted his prayers, Suri was acutely aware of Giri standing across from her, just off to the side. To distract herself, she glanced at the walls, studying the scenes from Goddess Parvati's life. Her gaze lingered on the depiction of God Shiva opening his third eye to burn the God of Love, Kama.

She recalled reading Kalidasa's verses on the anguish of Kama's wife, Rati, and wondered what Giri might say about the lament.

She rose and cried aloud:
Dost thou yet live,
Lord of my life?
And at the last she found
Him whom the wrathful god could not forgive,
Her Love, a trace of ashes on the ground.

Just then, the priest held out the *aarthi*, blessing her with many offspring. Keenly aware of Giri's gaze on her, warmth crept up her cheeks. It struck her as odd—Rangapani, the man beside her, whom the priest had assumed was her future husband, stirred no such intensity within her. In his presence, she felt only a quiet despair.

Deciding she needed some time alone, away from Rangapani, she lagged behind under the pretext of adjusting her sari, then hid behind a large pillar. Making sure no one saw her, she slid down to the floor, savoring the shadows that concealed her from view. She shut her eyes to ponder her future, but the quiet did not last long. She heard two men whispering.

"Slip this into the saddle, and when he climbs on, the horse will get agitated and throw him off."

Who were they talking about? Was her brother in danger? Suri peeked around the pillar and saw the men walking away. Was one of them Rangapani's man? She quickly stood up and began to follow.

"Suri! I was just looking for you," Kanika said, slipping her arm through Suri's elbow.

Suri gestured urgently, indicating she needed to move forward.

"What's the hurry? Abhayan is still talking to some devotees about how safe this place is now that the thieves have been captured."

Suri tugged Kanika along. Sensing her urgency, Kanika quickened her pace. "What is it, Suri?"

Suri searched the crowd but couldn't spot the two men. Instead, she noticed a lone figure heading toward the horses. She scanned the area, confirming that her brother's horse was closely guarded by one of his attendants. No one could approach it without being seen. Just then, she caught sight of the lone man adjusting the saddle on a brown mare. Who rode that horse? Suri couldn't recall.

Her brother soon arrived at her side. "One of the merchants thanked me for taking care of the bandits. Your suitor, Rangapani, did most of the fighting to round up those men." Suri only half-listened, her attention drawn elsewhere.

Just then, she saw Giri marching toward the tampered horse, climbing into the saddle. Panic surged within her as she feared for his safety. Without stopping to think, she sprinted toward him, cursing her inability to speak. As she approached, the horse reared its head, and she realized the danger she was in— one misstep and its hooves could land on her. In that instant, Giri saw her and yanked the reins to turn the horse around, saving her from harm. But in doing so, he was thrown from the saddle, landing with a bone-jarring thud on the ground, the fallen leaves providing little cushioning for his fall.

"Playwright!"

Suri felt movement beside her, and her brother and Kanika appeared at her side.

"Prince Abhayan?" Giri groaned, rolling onto his side.

"Tell me where it hurts," her brother urged.

"I'm all right," Giri gasped, though it was clear to Suri that he was anything but fine.

"Don't move," Kanika ordered firmly.

Giri ignored her and began to move his limbs. "Just a few bad bruises," he said through clenched teeth.

"You must be in pain," Kanika insisted, her concern evident, while Suri wished she could check him for injuries herself.

"Some," Giri admitted, grimacing.

"What were you doing? I thought you were a good rider," her brother asked as he helped Giri to his feet. Giri winced as he stood, his body protesting the movement.

"You shouldn't get back on the horse. Come join us in the chariot. There's plenty of space for you," Kanika said gently.

Her brother nodded in agreement, but Rangapani shouted, "No!"

Her brother's brows knitted in irritation. "Rangapani, would you explain why you disagree with me?"

"Is it wise to allow him to travel alone with two unmarried ladies, my lord?" Rangapani protested, his tone filled with concern.

"What exactly are you worried about? Don't you trust my sister?" her brother snapped, his protective instincts flaring. Suri felt a wave of affection for him; she would have embraced him right then if not for her consideration of Rangapani's feelings. A small smile tugged at her lips as her brother helped the playwright into the carriage. Kanika and Suri took their seats across from him.

Suri's gaze lingered on the large bruise on Giri's arm, and she subtly gestured toward her own arm to ask if he was all right.

"It looks worse than it feels," Giri assured her, glancing down at the mark. Suri clenched her fist, resisting the urge to cross over to his side to comfort him.

"Too bad you're stuck with us instead of riding with the wind," Kanika teased, leaning back against the chariot seat with a playful smile.

Giri settled deeper into his seat. "It would only be a problem if I weren't enjoying myself." His gaze drifted to Suri as he added, "The company's not that bad."

Suri focused on a carved bird on the wooden paneling, fighting to keep an absurd smile from creeping onto her face.

"Did you know Poet Kalidasa composed an epic poem about

the life of Goddess Parvati and her warrior son, Kumara?" Giri said softly.

Kanika shook her head. "No, I've never heard of this poet."

Suri's lips twitched as she glanced at Giri. She, too, had thought of Poet Kalidasa while studying the murals on the wall. Was this a sign that they were truly meant for each other? Just then, a breeze ruffled his hair, igniting an inexplicable urge to weave her fingers through it.

Giri began reciting a few lines from the poem, describing Goddess Parvati blossoming into womanhood. His gaze stayed fixed on her face, and warmth spread across her skin, each word sending a soft shiver along her spine.

As pictures waken to the painter's brush,
Or lilies open to the morning sun,
Her perfect beauty answered to the flush
Of womanhood when childish days were done.

"You already have my approval to marry my cousin," Kanika teased, a playful glint in her eyes. "No need to charm me with poetry."

"But I doubt everyone would support your union," she added, casting a quick glance at Rangapani, who still glared at the carriage as it moved along.

"If you mean the belligerent Rangapani," Giri replied, "I might find his agitation amusing—if he hadn't just tried to throw me from my horse." He met Suri's gaze, as though seeking confirmation that he had identified the culprit correctly.

"Rangapani was behind this?" Kanika asked, tilting her head to look at Suri.

Suri gave a quick, firm nod, recalling how she'd seen the man who had tampered with the horse exchange a look with Rangapani. A pang of guilt hit her, knowing Giri's life had been at risk. Yet, as a prince, he could end this charade and claim her hand at any time. Did she truly want that?

"You came to warn me," Giri said, his voice low, an intensity in his tone that made her shiver. Suri met his gaze and nodded again.

"Suri, we can't let Rangapani get away with this. We have to tell Abhayan; otherwise, someone could end up seriously hurt," Kanika urged.

However, Suri's eyes remained locked on the man across from them, wishing that choosing him could be easy for her. Nothing this important ever was.

GIRIDHAR

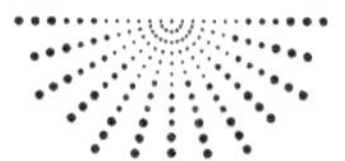

Giri said, "No," just as Suryavati shook her head. He glanced at her, sensing they shared the same thought: confronting Rangapani would only stir more trouble, especially with his jealousy simmering just beneath the surface. Better to stay vigilant for a few days than risk provoking him further. Giri felt a twinge of guilt over taking Rangapani's intended bride, though not enough to stop him; his love for Suryavati was too strong for that.

The chariot smelled faintly of flowers, a welcome change after hours spent on horseback. Suryavati absently rubbed her wrist, her expression soft and distant, like the moon peeking through drifting clouds. Her beauty shone in fleeting glimpses, though something still seemed to weigh on her. They sat in comfortable silence, but Giri's thoughts wandered, imagining the warmth of her fingers tracing softly along his bare skin. The thought sent a flutter of heat through him.

Soon, they arrived at the village center. Sparrows flitted among the tree branches, chirping excitedly at the approaching horses. A crowd had gathered to greet the royal siblings, with Prince Abhayan leading the way to meet the village elders. Giri hung back, watching the prince, a pang of guilt shooting through him. There were people in Nidhapur who depended on his leadership, awaiting his guidance and support. Yet here he was, caught up in this disguise and distant from his duties. But once he secured Suryavati's hand, he promised himself he would return to his kingdom, ready to fulfill his responsibilities with renewed dedication.

"My lord," an elderly man greeted, "you have restored order to our lives after the chaos inflicted by bandits, bringing peace after the strife."

Prince Abhayan accepted their gratitude with a gracious nod. "Rangapani here," he said, gesturing to the man as Rangapani strode confidently to the front, "led the fight to wipe out the thugs." The crowd's eyes shifted curiously toward Rangapani. "He will be my future brother-in-law and will help me bring harmony to this kingdom."

It was shrewd of the prince to praise the warrior, though Giri felt uneasy at the implications of Rangapani's marriage to Suryavati, even if only hinted at. He glanced at Suryavati, noting the way her face had become an unreadable mask.

The low beat of drums reached his ears. Giri turned and saw a funeral procession moving slowly down an alley a few yards away. Almost without realizing it, he found his legs carrying him toward the small crowd. They wound through a deserted alley—most of the village had gathered around the prince—and emerged at a quiet cemetery. Giri's eyes caught sight of a young boy wearing only a dhoti around his waist, standing solemnly by the pyre. The pallbearers lowered the body onto a pile of dried wood, and someone passed the boy a lighted stick. He stepped forward, igniting the pyre.

Giri took a deep breath, steadying himself as the boy reminded him of his own brother at ten years old, suddenly burdened with the weight of the kingdom. How selfish he had been, thinking only of his own needs. His brother had become king the day their father passed, bearing responsibilities no child should carry—and without complaint. Any dreams his brother might have held had dissipated like smoke from a pyre, sacrificed to ensure the continuity of their line. He had married two wives in the hope of an heir, and when that hope had faded, he had named Giri crown prince.

Giri glanced down at his disguise, the rough, plain fabric meant to help him blend in as a commoner so his brother's men wouldn't recognize him. He was a prince, not a street urchin, and he had responsibilities to uphold. Guilt twisted inside him for even briefly abandoning his duty. Resolving to set things right, he decided to visit his brother and mother in person.

Tonight, he would speak to Suryavati in private, letting her know of his plans. In the morning, he would leave, trusting the actors to continue rehearsing and, perhaps, even perform for the king and queen in his absence. Whatever punishment his brother deemed fit, he would accept. He deserved it, after all. As long as he was allowed to marry Suryavati, he could bear any consequence.

He returned to the village center to join in the feast offered by the merchants and farmers in gratitude for ridding them of the bandits. The aromas of fried plantains, gourd stew, tamarind rice, coconut rice pudding, and ripe mangoes filled the air, tempting his senses. He ate heartily, feeling resolved in his decision.

On the way back, he rode his horse despite Princess Kanika's protests. Before they departed, he managed a quick word with Suryavati as she mingled with the villagers. Leaning close, he whispered, "Meet me tonight at our usual spot," using the crowd to shield their conversation from prying eyes.

Later that night, he stepped outside. Soft murmurs drifted through the hallways as servants retired for the night. A few wall sconces lit the garden path, but he soon slipped deeper into the trees, guided only by the moonlight. He moved silently, savoring the cool breeze after the stale air in his cramped room.

As he neared the cluster of trees, he immediately spotted Suryavati standing beside a broad trunk, her fingers absently tracing the rough bark.

"I wish I could see the stars tonight," he said softly.

Suryavati turned to look at him, her expression thoughtful.

"The clouds aren't cooperating," he continued, stopping beside her and leaning against the tree.

For a long moment, they simply gazed at each other, the silence thick with unspoken words. Giri saw the shadows in her eyes, and he longed to banish them, to erase every trace of sorrow. If only she would let him.

Without realizing it, he swayed closer, his gaze locked on hers as if pulled by an unseen force.

"Suryavati," he whispered, his voice barely audible.

She tilted her head, her lips parting slightly. He closed his hand over hers, and when she didn't pull away, he drew her closer, his pulse quickening with each step.

His fingers brushed her cheek, and he found himself whispering her name again, as if savoring the sound of it. He couldn't tell exactly when he'd decided to kiss her—it felt as natural as breathing, as inevitable as the pull of the earth.

His hand trailed slowly up her arm, tracing the warmth of her bare skin, skimming past the edge of her sari until it settled at the small of her back, drawing her closer. She softened against him, her body molding perfectly to his, her chest pressed against his ribs. He wanted to stretch this moment, to make this closeness last forever. Beneath his fingers, the fabric of her sari felt as soft as a whisper, but it was her presence— warm, real, alive—that made his heart race.

Somehow, he found the strength to step back, allowing the cool night air to slip between them. But the separation was short-lived. Suryavati's eyes widened, a silent plea shining in their depths, and she shook her head, pulling him back, her hands firm around his neck.

Did she realize the hold she had on him? How she haunted him, her presence searing him even from across a crowded room, her image setting him ablaze in his dreams?

Giri's hands moved to cradle her face, his thumbs brushing gently over her cheeks. It was too dark to see the precise shade of her lips, but he knew they would be soft, welcoming, like a promise he had yearned to fulfill.

When his lips met hers again, all restraint vanished. His kiss was fierce, desperate—the kiss of a man who had been starved for far too long. He poured everything into it—every unspoken word, every unsatisfied longing, every promise he dared not speak aloud. His hands tightened around her, pulling her even closer, as if he could press her heart into his own.

"You traitor!"

Suryavati, recognizing the voice before he did, shrieked and jerked away.

"Rangapani?" Giri gasped, his heart racing as he pulled away from Suryavati, instinctively shielding her.

SURYAVATI

Rangapani was only a few feet away, closing the distance with terrifying speed. His brows were furrowed, his face twisted into a mask of fury, and with a guttural, primal cry, he lunged at Giri.

Suri barely had time to react before Rangapani's body slammed into Giri with such force that the shockwave sent her sprawling to the ground, caught by the violent flailing of someone's arm. She gasped, trying to regain her bearings as the sounds of grunting and the heavy thud of bodies filled the air.

"I will kill you—" Rangapani's words were cut short as Giri swiftly flipped him over, the impact knocking the breath out of him. But Rangapani was relentless. Like a man possessed, he fought back fiercely, his rage evident in every blow he landed on Giri.

Giri, perched on top of Rangapani, defended himself, blocking the punches, but he wasn't striking back. His expression was unreadable, though his body was tense with the effort to maintain control.

Suri stood frozen, her heart pounding as the violence unfolded before her. She couldn't just watch. Realizing she had to intervene, she took a shaky step forward, her mind racing for a way to stop the madness before it escalated further.

She reached toward the man she loved, her heart swelling with a moment of clarity. Yes, she loved Giri, and the thought of seeing him hurt was unbearable. But before she could act on that, the two men rolled over in their struggle, and a floundering limb sent her sprawling against a tree trunk.

She howled in pain, the sharp cry freezing the scene.

"Suryavati!" Giri exclaimed, again on top of Rangapani. He rushed to her side, his face etched with concern. "Are you all right?"

Suri whimpered, agony radiating from her body in waves, stabbing at every inch of her.

But before Giri could do anything more, Rangapani lunged at him, his fist raised. With swift reflexes, Giri blocked the strike. "Stop! The princess is hurt. We need to get her help."

Rangapani, still filled with fury, snarled, "Don't you worry about her," continuing to ignore Suri as if she were nothing more than a mere obstacle in his path.

Giri punched Rangapani in the chest, sending him stumbling backward. Without hesitation, he followed up with a swift kick that sent the man crashing to the ground. His curses rang out, harsh and unprincely—more akin to the rough speech of a stagehand than a royal.

Giri hurried back to her side. "Hold still while I check you," he murmured, his fingers gently probing her limbs. "Nothing seems broken. I'm going to help you stand up."

Suri nodded, and his hands carefully circled her waist. His gaze was fixed on her face as he supported her, allowing her to lean on him as she stood.

Just then, the sound of footsteps broke the quiet. Two palace guards appeared, and Rangapani, still on the ground, yelled, "Throw him in the dungeon!"

Making sure Suri could stand on her own, Giri stepped

away. The two guards stood still, watching her, but made no move to restrain him or place him in chains.

With a loud grunt, Rangapani pushed himself up, his bruised chin twisting in a snarl. He didn't check on Suri; his focus was solely on Giri. Without warning, he drew his fist back and slammed it into Giri's face.

Suri gasped, horrified, and instinctively moved to intervene. But Giri gently pushed her aside. "Stay out of it, my lady," he murmured, his eyes never leaving Rangapani as he squared off with him.

"You betrayed our trust!" Rangapani screamed, his voice filled with rage. "You defiled my bride!" He charged at Giri, throwing a punch, but Giri effortlessly sidestepped, the blow missing him entirely.

Suri's mind raced, and she knew what she had to do to protect him. With a swift gesture, she signaled to the guards, instructing them to bind Giri's arms. They nodded in understanding and moved to carry out her command. Giri remained still, not resisting as they tied his arms behind him, his gaze flickering to Rangapani.

Then Rangapani did something even more cowardly. With Giri defenseless—his arms bound and unable to fight back—Rangapani balled his fist and, with a cruel sneer, struck Giri directly in the eye.

Suri's breath caught in her throat as she watched Giri stagger from the impact. His eye instantly began to swell, the bruise already darkening. The sound of Rangapani's fist connecting with Giri's face echoed in her ears, filling her with a deep sense of helplessness.

"Take him away!" Rangapani barked, his voice dripping with venom. His fury was palpable as he glared at Giri, clearly relishing the moment.

Rangapani's eyes shifted toward Suri, and with a grim

expression, he approached her. "You, come with me," he commanded, his tone authoritative and possessive.

Before he could touch her, Suri swatted his hand away, her fingers trembling with the effort to remain composed. For now, she outranked Rangapani—at least until she married him. With a defiant glint in her eyes, she turned away from him, casting one last fleeting glance at Giri.

His bruised and swollen face filled her vision, and the look he gave her was one of heartbreak, as if his heart were being torn in two. In that moment, she made a silent promise to herself that she would make things right. But for now, she had no choice but to heed Rangapani. With a heavy heart, she walked away, Rangapani trailing behind her, smug satisfaction on his face.

46

GIRIDHAR

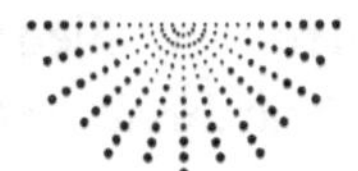

Suryavati's lips trembled as she gazed at him, and the sight pierced him like a knife. He felt her sorrow before a mask slipped into place, hiding her pain. Giri stood battered and bloodied, his eyes tracing her silhouette as she disappeared into the night.

A sharp tug on his bound arms jolted him, the guard's force nearly knocking the breath from him. He didn't resist, knowing he deserved every painful reminder of the situation he'd caused. He had compromised the princess's honor by kissing her—a deeply dishonorable act. Yet even now, the memory of her in his arms brought a guilty rush of happiness he couldn't deny.

A cool breeze swept around him as he marched between the two guards. He felt no fear about being held as a prisoner—he was a prince, after all, and Jaisalpur would hardly risk a war with Nidhapur. No, he knew he could free himself once he spoke with Prince Abhayan. His plans would simply need to shift. He'd abandon the secrecy, reveal his true identity to the prince, and seek his support. Together, they could approach Suryavati's father, allowing him to ask for her hand with honor and transparency.

No, he was not worried for himself. His thoughts were all for Suryavati. She was typically level-headed—except when it came to poetry. That was when she'd take risks, like disguising herself as a man to meet a stranger. But there would be no flights of fancy with Rangapani. The man would never read her poetry. He was wounded and humiliated, which could drive him to harm Suryavati in ways beyond words. If he dared to hurt her, Giri would hunt him down and make him regret ever setting eyes on her. But none of that would help Suryavati if he couldn't protect her now. Not that she was helpless. She had surprised him time and again, finding ways to sidestep conventions and become a poet despite every obstacle in her way.

Yet she couldn't escape this marriage. Perhaps she didn't want to. Did she truly believe her marriage to Rangapani would benefit her? Giri couldn't imagine her entering into it without carefully weighing all the consequences. Likely, she had made her decision before learning his true identity, when she thought he was merely a playwright and not her equal in rank. He had hoped to share his plan—to visit his home, return with his mother's blessing, and then formally ask for her hand. But he never got the chance—he had acted like a man under a spell. He remembered the feel of her lips, mirroring his own longing. He wanted to spend an eternity with her. Did she feel the same? Not knowing her desires gnawed at him.

A sharp bark cut through the night, jolting Giri from his thoughts. His eyes swept the area until he spotted Mooka emerging from behind a cluster of bushes, body taut, a low growl rumbling from deep within his chest.

Mooka!

But Sangu, his loyal guard, had taken Mooka back to Nidhapur. Giri hadn't expected his guard to return for days. Could he have come back so soon from Nidhapur? Or had he never reached home? Giri peered into the darkness, searching for any sign of his guard. The men dragging him to the dungeon tugged him forward, but he craned his neck, straining to see. Then he heard a soft, familiar whistle echo from somewhere nearby. In an instant, Mooka melted back into the shadows, disappearing into the night.

Giri worked to steady his breathing, forcing calm as he processed the situation. *Sangu is back*, he reminded himself, and the guard would have surely noticed his bound arms by now. Sangu was sworn to protect him at all costs. But what might he do?

Giri cursed inwardly. How could he have let this happen? He had no regrets about kissing Suryavati—that moment was worth everything. No, his only regret was letting that oaf, Rangapani, catch them.

Now a new worry crept in: would Sangu attempt something reckless and foolhardy to save him, believing his life was in danger? Giri's pulse quickened again, not from fear for himself but from fear that Sangu would make a needless sacrifice.

Giri's heart sank as he was shoved down the stone steps, each one echoing in the cold, damp dungeon. The walls closed in, pressing a suffocating weight on his chest as he was led into a small, windowless cell barely large enough to turn around in. The guard yanked the rope binding him, sending sharp jolts of pain through his arms before finally removing it. Giri rubbed the sore skin, easing the ache. His legs gave way, and he sank to the floor, hugging his knees to his chest in the utter darkness.

He pressed his forehead against his knees, and his thoughts spiraled, tugging him deeper into despair. He could almost see Sangu bursting into the dungeon, sword swinging—only to face guards with raised axes and spears. *Stop*, he willed himself, but his mind betrayed him, painting vivid scenes of Sangu's valiant, doomed rescue attempt. Giri clenched his eyes shut, hating his own helplessness.

He remained that way for what felt like a long time, though it was difficult to tell in the darkness of the room.

Footsteps echoed down the stone steps, growing louder until a small slot in the door swung open, spilling blinding light into the cell. Giri shielded his eyes with his hands, then squinted through his fingers.

"Playwright," Rangapani hissed, venom dripping from the word. "Ungrateful fool. That girl is mine—" his voice broke slightly. "I'd strangle you with my bare hands if I could. The only reason you're still breathing is because you're working on a royal play." He pressed his face against the iron bars, his eyes gleaming with malice. "Tomorrow, I'll demand the king's justice in honor of my future wife," he sneered. "And then, I'll have your head."

Giri closed his eyes, forcing down a flood of curses. He couldn't let this man harm Suryavati. Not her. As Rangapani's footsteps retreated, silence closed in, the walls seeming to press tighter, as if the very stones conspired to keep him trapped. His heart pounded with anger and dread, not for himself but for Suryavati, who was now caught in this ruthless game. The thought of Rangapani's hands on her, his possessive threats, filled Giri with a protective fury he hadn't known he was capable of.

He took a shuddering breath, forcing his racing mind to still. He had to bide his time, steady his thoughts, and, if nothing else, summon the strength to make it through the night—or was it already day? All for her.

Usually, Giri would retreat into his imagination, crafting stories to calm the anxiety that gnawed at him. But tonight, the events around him felt too real, too tangled, to turn into a tale. Instead, he closed his eyes and let his mind drift to her. His beautiful poet.

The sound of a key turning and the scrape of a bolt sliding echoed in his dreams. He stirred, the faint rustle by the door pulling him from his slumber. Opening his eyes, disoriented, he felt the cold of the stone floor against his cheek, shocking him awake. Rising onto his elbows, he blinked, squinting through the darkness just in time to see two pairs of eyes peering in.

"Open the door," Kanika's voice cut through the silence, softer than usual. "The princess wants a word with the prisoner."

The events of the past flooded back with crushing clarity. As the two girls stepped inside, he had eyes for only one. Surya-vati's tear-swollen, red eyes tore his heart in two.

47

SURYAVATI

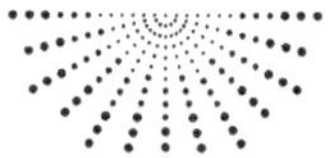

Suryavati didn't wait for Rangapani. She walked swiftly into her room, shut the door, and slid down to the floor, resting her head on her knees. Outside, she could hear Rangapani berating Nanmaran for letting her slip away on her own.

A deep worry weighed on her heart. When the guards had bound Giri's hands, he hadn't resisted. What would happen to him now? And what would become of them both?

Suri closed her eyes. She couldn't let him be hurt—not because of her. If it came down to it, she would marry Rangapani to ensure Giri's freedom. Tears pooled in her eyes as she swallowed her disappointment. She couldn't give up so easily. She clung to a sliver of hope that it wouldn't come to that. With effort, she forced herself to push aside the fear gnawing at her heart. Tomorrow, she would visit her uncle and tell him the truth about Giri—about him being a prince who had stolen her heart. Perhaps she would leave out that last part.

Exhausted, she slumped in the center of her bed, yet sleep evaded her. Her mind filled with images of Giri—his kiss, so intense, like he'd been thinking about it all day—interwoven with the thought of him lying on the cold floor of a cell. A faint light crept through the window, and she realized dawn had arrived. Her eyes felt raw and itchy.

Suryavati rose and dressed quickly, brass lamps catching the sunlight that filtered into her room. Her mother had never understood her desire to craft poems that allowed her to escape reality—words that could transport her from her stifling life. Her mother had never accepted her; her father cared little, and her brother was too young to understand. Suri pushed away her familiar resentment toward her parents. Her uncle, though, had encouraged her in subtle ways, never openly enough to defy her mother's wishes. She hoped now that she could persuade him to free her prince.

Suryavati went straight to her uncle's chambers, but a servant cleaning the room looked up as she entered. "Prince Vikaran is in the council room, my lady."

She strode through the palace hallways, acknowledging the maids with a brief nod, as smiling was beyond her that morning. When she reached the council room, a guard swung open the doors. Inside, her uncle sat behind an ornate wooden desk.

"Suri!" her uncle exclaimed when he saw her enter the room. He wasn't alone; the minister was there, and her uncle waved her toward a chair.

"I will speak to the merchants, my lord," the minister said, resuming their discussion. As her uncle and the minister continued talking about matters of state, Suri sat silently, rubbing her thumbnail with her finger. Because she was mute, people sometimes forgot she could hear. But today, she was barely aware of their conversation. Her mind remained inside that cold prison cell, and the weight of worry kept her thoughts fixed on Giri's fate.

She wondered what she would tell her uncle, and, more importantly, how. In her rush to get here, she had forgotten to write down her message. She scanned the room, searching for a plate of rice, scrolls, or anything she could use.

A sharp knock sounded on the door.

"My lord?" the guard called from the other side.

"Yes," her uncle responded.

The door opened, and a messenger entered.

"Our scouts have spotted King Bhadri of Nidhapur approaching the city."

"King Bhadri?" her uncle repeated, as if he had misheard the messenger.

"Yes, my lord. With a small army."

Her uncle stood immediately. "Gather the council," he ordered, and the minister vanished without a word. Her uncle nearly strode out the door when he turned back toward Suri. "Suri, whatever it is you want to tell me has to wait. I must find the king." With that, he hurried away, leaving Suri alone in the room.

Confusion swamped her mind. King Bhadri of Nidhapur. That must be Giri's brother. Why was he here with an army? Was Giri spying on them, allowing his brother to invade their kingdom? No, Suri could not believe him capable of such deception.

But why was King Bhadri here? Giri had mentioned he was hiding from him. Perhaps his spies had finally found him, and now his brother had come to take him back. But that didn't seem right. Why would the king himself come all the way to Jaisalpur to fetch his brother? Her frown deepened.

There was only one way to find out the truth. She rose and headed straight to her cousin's chamber. Kanika sat before a mirror, her maid weaving flowers through her hair.

Suri gestured sharply for the maid to leave. Kanika turned to look at her and gasped. "Suri, what is the matter?"

Prison, she wrote on a plate of rice.

"Who's in prison? Giri?" Kanika stared at her in disbelief.

Suri nodded and motioned for her cousin to follow. Without hesitation, Kanika rose and walked beside her, asking no questions. Suri was grateful for her silence. King Bhadri was here in Jaisalpur. Something was very wrong, and she was determined to find out what it was.

4 8

GIRIDHAR

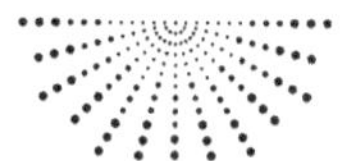

"*P*laywright, why are you in prison?" Kanika asked.

Instead of answering her, Giri turned toward Suryavati. Her troubled expression unsettled him. He almost reached out to touch her elbow but pulled back at the last moment, uncertain.

Before he could say anything, Suryavati gently touched his upper arm, her face full of feelings, causing his heart to skip a beat. Then, using her finger, she began writing on his palm. Giri's eyes shifted between her face and the motion of her hand.

"Bhadri?" His brow furrowed in confusion.

Suryavati nodded, her expression tense, as if she was holding something important inside.

"King Bhadri of Nidhapur is here?"

She lowered her head in a confirming gesture.

"Why is your brother here?" Kanika interrupted.

Giri's thoughts raced, remembering seeing his guard last night. Had his brother come to Jaisalpur with Sangu? If Sangu had seen him bound and reported it, what would his brother do? Giri gasped, clutching his head in distress.

211

"I need to go see him and set everything right before he decides to attack the city for imprisoning me."

Suryavati's lips thinned into a frown.

"My guard, Sangu, saw me last night as the men brought me into prison. My brother might think Jaisalpur has captured the crown prince of Nidhapur."

"We have to go see the king to have you released. We need Abhayan's help at the very least," Kanika said.

"There's no time for that," Giri burst out, frustration rising in his chest.

Suryavati glanced at him, then pointed at herself, tugging at her sari before pointing at him.

Kanika looked at her cousin in confusion, but Giri's eyes widened as understanding dawned. A thrill shot through him amidst the confusion. "You want me to wear your sari and leave, while you stay here in my clothes," he said.

Suryavati smiled at him, her eyes sparkling with the plan.

Giri turned toward the wall, removing his upper garment and holding it out to her. "Hurry," he whispered.

He assumed Kanika took the garment from him and, without a word, handed him a sari. He quickly wrapped it around his waist, stepped out of his dhoti, and handed it to her. He draped the sari over his waist, letting it cascade over one shoulder. The sensation of wearing Suryavati's sari stirred emotions he didn't have time to process.

"You can turn around," Kanika said.

Giri spun to see Suryavati adjusting the dhoti around her waist—his dhoti, which likely still held the faint scent of him. A strange warmth stirred in his chest as he watched her, the loose folds of fabric draping over her slight frame. It took all his will to pull his gaze up.

"My lady," he said urgently, taking a step toward her. "I'll return after I get my brother's blessing for our marriage."

She nodded, but the weight of everything unspoken lingered

between them. Instead of saying more, he cupped her cheek, his heart pounding in his chest. "You are everything I've been searching for—and more. I will come back. Wait for me." He wrapped his arms around her and kissed the top of her head.

"Don't we have to hurry?" Kanika's voice broke through the moment.

With one last, lingering look at Suryavati, Giri turned to leave.

"We're done here," Kanika called to the guard who stood a few feet away. "You can lock the prisoner up."

Hoping no one would notice the sudden change in his height, Giri held his breath as they walked through the dungeon, his nerves taut.

"Quick!" Kanika ushered him into a room. "Stay here, and I'll bring you some clothes."

She was gone for only a few moments, but in that time, Giri couldn't help but inhale the scent of Suryavati's sari, imagining her in his arms. He quickly changed into the clothes Kanika had brought and reluctantly handed the sari back to her.

This was the perfect opportunity to slip away from the castle, with the hustle and bustle of daily life providing the ideal cover.

"Do you need a horse?" Kanika asked, her voice urgent.

"No, I'll be safer on foot," Giri said, glancing at Kanika, his expression grave. "Will you return to free her?"

There was a note of pleading in his voice that surprised even him.

"Don't worry about her," Kanika assured him. "No harm will befall her in her own kingdom."

All he could manage was a quiet, "Please go back to her."

As Giri approached the fort entrance, he was taken aback by the sight of the large doors shut tight. If his brother's forces were truly nearby, it explained the heightened security. A smaller door within the main gates remained open, allowing people to leave, though the guards were preventing anyone from entering. Taking advantage of the moment, Giri slipped through and stepped into the daylight.

Leaving the castle behind, he avoided the forest that stretched along one side and made his way across the open grounds. He skirted the small village where he'd lived as a play-wright and continued toward a creek winding beside a hill. He knew this hill would offer his brother's forces an ideal vantage point over the area. The sun was directly overhead by the time he reached the creek, its waters murmuring at his feet.

"Sangu!" Giri called out, eyes sweeping over the trees scattered along the hillside.

A voice he hadn't heard in months echoed back, "Giri."

King Bhadri, along with a few men, stepped out from the shadows. Dressed in simple attire and without his crown, Bhadri blended seamlessly with his men.

Giri crossed the narrow stream, hitching his dhoti up to his knees but still managing to soak the fabric. As he reached the shore, his brother nearly ran to him and pulled him into an embrace. They stood eye to eye, and Bhadri's gaze darkened, his jaw clenched as he released Giri.

"Fool," Bhadri muttered, his voice tinged with restrained anger. "You've caused me no small amount of grief."

Giri's heart tightened with a mix of relief and guilt. "Forgive me, Brother," he muttered. Then, he bent to touch his brother's feet in respect.

"May the goddess grant you wisdom," Bhadri intoned, a trace of frustration woven through his blessing. "If not for Sangu, I might never have found you. I met him on his way back while I was searching for you. You've taken years off my life."

That explained how Sangu had returned so quickly.

"Brother—" Giri began, nervous as always in his brother's presence. Though his lips moved, and his heart longed to share the tale of the girl who had captured it, no further sound emerged.

"Sangu told me they had imprisoned you. How did you escape? I didn't bring enough of an army to attack them."

"I was not imprisoned, Brother. It's a long story—"

"You can tell it to me on our way to Nidhapur. I came with Sangu to ensure you travel back with us. Our mother is ill," Bhadri interrupted, his tone urgent. "She's been asking for you. We have no time to delay if you want to see her alive."

Giri froze, staring at his brother in shock. His mother? He banished all thoughts of Suryavati to a corner of his mind as he swallowed hard, dread settling in his chest. He could never forgive himself if his mother passed before he had the chance to see her.

"Come, we leave at once."

Giri took one last look at the path leading back to Jaisalpur, where he had left his heart behind. But his duty—and his love for his mother—pulled him toward home.

4 9

SURYAVATI

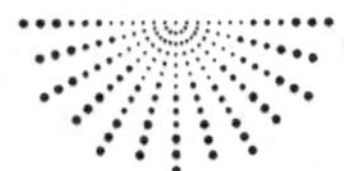

Suri looked up from her spot on the floor, still wrapped in Giri's clothes, which carried his scent. She inhaled deeply, wishing she could feel his arms around her instead of just his lingering presence in his clothes. But her heart leapt as the door opened, revealing not Kanika, but Rangapani and her younger brother.

She scrambled to her feet, eyes wide with shock.

Her brother's expression matched her own surprise. "Ranga-pani, did you throw my sister in this cell?" For a boy of fourteen, his voice held an unexpected menace.

"No, my lord," Rangapani stammered. "I threw that no-good playwright in prison for—" He hesitated, rubbing his chin, as if searching for a suitable reason. Suri blushed, recalling how Rangapani had found her, kissing Giri as though her very life depended on it.

Abhayan glanced at her and noticed her flushed cheeks. With a resigned sigh, he said, "Let's get you out of here."

As they made their way up to the living quarters, they encountered Kanika in the hallway, holding Suri's sari.

Abhayan muttered under his breath about conniving

216

women, casting a sidelong glance at both Suri and Kanika. Outside her chamber, he dismissed Kanika and Rangapani. "I'd like to speak with my sister alone."

Once they were by themselves, Abhayan began pacing, his agitation clear. Suryavati sat calmly in her chair, arms folded, watching him with a steady gaze, waiting for him to speak.

When she cleared her throat, he halted, turning to face her. "Judging by your embarrassment, I'm guessing I don't want to know what Rangapani caught you doing—" He broke off as she shot him a sharp glare, thinking of the time she had caught him sneaking a kiss with a girl, though he was only fourteen and far from marriageable age.

His face turned somber. "But, Suri, how could you let your guard down like that and drag us into this mess?"

Before she could respond, a knock sounded at the door. Her uncle entered, his gaze landing on her with raised eyebrows. Suri suddenly remembered she was still dressed in Giri's clothes and silently cursed herself for not changing back into her sari.

But her uncle's attention shifted to Abhayan. "King Bhadri of Nidhapur is preparing to attack us."

"What?" Abhayan shouted, his face a mixture of disbelief and alarm.

Suri stood quickly and tugged on her uncle's hand to get his attention.

"Not now, Suri," he said, pulling his hand back gently. "I'm sure I'll regret not asking why you're wearing a man's clothes, but whatever it is will have to wait."

Suri let out an exasperated growl that sounded surprisingly fierce. She hurried to her plate of rice and quickly wrote,

Giri is a prince.

Her brother followed her, reading the words as they appeared.

"Giri is a prince?" Abhayan repeated, his brow lifting as realization dawned. "Prince Giridhar of Nidhapur?"

Suri nodded.

Their uncle's gaze shifted between them, clearly puzzled. He didn't yet know the full story of Giri's imprisonment.

"Was Giri spying on us for his brother? So Nidhapur can conquer Jaisalpur?" Abhayan's anger blazed.

Their uncle's eyes widened. "That playwright? We had a spy among us?"

Suri shook her head firmly and wrote on the rice plate,

Giri sent a message about marrying me through his guard.

Abhayan's expression softened as he pieced it together. "His guard must have returned to Nidhapur and brought his brother back with him."

"Marriage? Suri?" her uncle repeated, still baffled.

"I'll explain everything, Uncle," Abhayan said quickly. He glanced back at Suri, sensing there was more. "What else?"

She wrote hastily.

Guard saw Giri bound.

Abhayan cursed under his breath. "King Bhadri thinks we've imprisoned his brother."

"Wait—why was the playwright fettered?" her uncle demanded, glancing between them.

Abhayan didn't answer, focusing on Suri. "Is that why you freed him? So he can explain this to his brother?"

Suri nodded, hoping Giri had reached King Bhadri by now.

"Abhayan, can you tell me what is going on before I throttle your neck?" her uncle exclaimed.

Abhayan quickly summarized the situation: Suri's interest in Giri, his true identity as a prince, Giri sending a messenger to his brother, Rangapani seeing them together and throwing Giri into prison, Giri's guard finding him restrained, and Suri freeing him so he could explain matters to his brother.

"Imagine that—our Suri winning the heart of a prince," her uncle said with a broad smile. "I'll summon your parents to the council room. Change quickly and join us."

When she arrived in the council room, everyone had gathered around the ornate table. She traced her fingers along the carving of a male elephant etched into the table's surface, feeling the weight of all their gazes. She knew they knew the truth about her heart. She wished she could tell them her bond with Giri surpassed reason. What had happened to her before—her illness that stole her voice, her elder brother's death, her father's indifference—did not matter anymore. They were in the past, and she decided to concern herself with the future.

"Suri could have been deceived. We should not let our guard down," her mother said, stepping toward her and clasping her arm. Suri avoided her gaze, knowing her mother likely resented her for keeping all of this a secret.

"Our general and his son Rangapani are preparing to defend our fort against any attack," her uncle added. Suri noticed that Rangapani was not among them, and she felt a sense of relief. After the way she had abused his trust, she lacked the courage to face him just yet.

"King Bhadri has no male heirs. His brother, Prince Giridhar, is the crown prince. That means Suri's son will sit on the throne," her father said, stroking his beard.

"Giridhar is an ideal match for Suri," said her uncle, gazing at her fondly. "We should hold their wedding soon."

"I will invite the wedding guests. Vikaran, get the priest and prepare the feast for the wedding. Urmila, you get Suri ready."

A swirl of emotions tightened in Suri's stomach—the joy of marrying Giri mingled with the fear of leaving Jaisalpur. Kanika stepped toward her, wrapping an arm around her waist. "I can just picture it," she whispered softly in Suri's ear. "Scrolls spread all over your room as you and he trade stories back and forth, refining each one together."

A warmth crept into Suri's chest as she imagined shaping their lives around a shared love for storytelling, crafting tales that would become their own.

A knock echoed through the room.

"Enter," called the king.

A soldier stepped inside. "The Nidhapur retinue has left, Your Majesty."

"Left?" Abhayan asked, confusion lining his voice.

"Yes, my lord. We saw their horses head west."

"All of them?" Kanika's voice mirrored Suri's growing dread.

The soldier nodded.

"Did you see the playwright with them?" Abhayan asked, his eyes locking with Suri's.

"He was among the riders in the front," the soldier replied.

All color drained from Suri's face.

5 0
GIRIDHAR

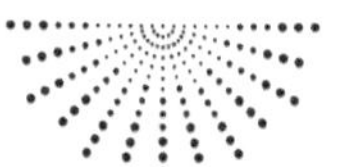

A faint scent tickled his nose, so subtle that Giri wasn't sure he wasn't imagining it. It was like a whisper of lotus over river water. Almost unconsciously, he lifted his arm and caught the lingering fragrance of Suri's sari. The image of the princess rose in his mind—her gentle smile, the way it set his heart racing every time.

He still hadn't told his brother about Suryavati, and with his mother seriously ill, now didn't seem like the right time to bring it up.

His thoughts shifted to his mother—the woman who had raised him and his brother and ruled the kingdom until his brother came of age. He recalled her telling him the story of a warrior who fought on despite knowing certain defeat because he refused to abandon his companions. Armed with bravery and pride as his armor and spear, the warrior fought fiercely, only to lose and rise to fight again. She had taught him that every day in the life of a king was a battle.

Yet he had run from that life and from her teachings, yielding to defeat.

One night, when he was seven, just after his father's death, he'd woken in the middle of the night to find his mother sitting on the floor beside his bed, her shoulders shaking, her face turned away. Wordlessly, Giri had crawled from his bed, placing a small hand on her back, staying there until he fell asleep beside her. His mother had remained strong for her sons, always concealing her tears from them.

Now, two months had slipped by, and he'd barely thought of the woman who had sacrificed everything for him. A surge of guilt washed over him, threatening to consume him.

Then, the part of him that longed to soar above the confines of duty argued back. He was no mere soldier, unlettered and bound to the sword. His mind brimmed with more than strategies of war—it held stories, half-formed and waiting to be told. Why should that side of him remain hidden? If his body and limbs embodied his warrior spirit, while his mind housed his creative soul, it made no sense to torment one while pampering the other. They needed to exist in harmony, each strengthening the other, to truly define the man he was meant to be.

He understood now that his mother's teachings came from her hard-won experience as a queen without a king, guiding two young boys through the treacherous currents of court politics. She had shielded them from the grasping ambitions of nobles who sought to shape the young king—or marry their daughters to him. And indeed, his brother had made that sacrifice, taking a Nidhapur noble bride, freeing Giri to pursue the desires of his own heart.

His thoughts circled back to Suryavati as his horse leaped effortlessly over a ditch. He had promised her he would return immediately. What would she think if he didn't? King Vibudha's spies would undoubtedly report that he had left with his brother. The thought of her heartbreak—believing he had betrayed her—cut deeper than any blade. Resolving to send her a message as soon as they made camp that evening, he tried to ease his mind. Yet guilt surged anew, crashing over him for even thinking of her when his mother lay on her deathbed.

He had given his mare free rein, letting her gallop across the open plain, but now he reined her in and waited for his brother to catch up. Bhadri rode up alongside him, casting a sidelong glance. "Two months! Hiding from me. What were you thinking?"

"Brother, I didn't really—what I mean is—after the fiasco with Princess Lalitha, when she rejected me for King Dushyant, I needed time to think." Giri's voice trembled, and a pang of old embarrassment surfaced. Lalitha had good reason to reject him; he had never truly won her heart. After meeting Suryavati, he understood why—Lalitha had never captured his either.

Bhadri snorted. "And you couldn't do your thinking at the palace? You're always brooding anyway."

Giri ignored the jab and asked, "What happened to our mother? She was in good health when I left." His voice faltered, and he swallowed hard. The fear that his absence had worsened her condition twisted in his chest.

Bhadri's expression softened as he noted Giri's anxious face. "It came on suddenly. The royal physician hasn't been able to find a cause. That's why I was leading the search for you. My spies had tracked you to Jaisalpur. Thankfully, Sangu spotted us —saved us a lot of marching."

They rode on, even as the dim rays of the setting sun faded, for Bhadri was determined to put as much distance as possible between them and the palace of Jaisalpur. Only when the darkness thickened to the point where they could barely see a few feet ahead did he finally call for a halt. They made a modest camp, with no grand royal tents to betray their presence.

Giri guided his horse alongside Sangu's. "I need to send a message to Princess Suryavati. Let her know I will return soon."

Sangu nodded. "My lord, please write it on a scroll. I will

find a trusted courier to deliver it to the temple priest outside the Jaisalpur fort. He can ensure it reaches the princess."

He studied Giri closely for a moment, as though searching for words, but said nothing more. Sangu had forged many connections during his time in Jaisalpur to aid him in his duty of protecting him, and Giri assumed the priest was among them.

Giri settled by the cookfire, the flickering flames casting shadows on his face as he prepared to write his message. The men of Nidhapur, accustomed to seeing their prince lost in his thoughts as he penned his tales, respectfully left him undisturbed.

Wait but a while, my fragrant lotus bloom,
Till this bee returns to drink your sweet perfume.

Giri was confident that Suryavati would grasp the meaning hidden in the missive. He sealed the letter with the imprint of his fish-emblem ring and handed it to Sangu, silently willing her to find a way to delay her impending wedding to Rangapani.

For the next few days, they rode tirelessly from dawn to dusk, pausing only once to change horses. By midday, they finally arrived in Nidhapur. The palace, set in the middle of a vast lake, shimmered in the sunlight, its reflection sparkling on the water's surface. Home.

They left their horses at the shore and boarded the waiting boats. Giri stood at the prow, facing the majestic palace as the wind tousled his hair. His heart raced with prayers that he had not arrived too late. Meanwhile, his brother turned his attention to the court officials who had gathered at the dock, eager to discuss urgent matters of state with their king.

Soon, they set off—King Bhadri and his royal retinue in one boat, with Giri in another. As they reached the shore, Giri didn't wait for the anchor to drop. Without hesitation, he leapt into the water, using the ropes hanging from the boat to swing down and land lightly on his feet. He hurried up the landing steps and entered the palace through the royal entrance, scarcely acknowledging the men who recognized him and bowed in respect.

Reaching his mother's chambers, Giri pushed open the doors without waiting for the guard. "Mother," he whispered, bursting in, his heart heavy with dread at what he might find.

His mother rose from her chair, a look of surprise crossing her face at the sight of him. "Giri," she said, rushing forward to embrace him.

Relieved to see her up and moving, Giri hugged her tightly, then bent to touch her feet, seeking her blessing.

"May you find a bride of your heart," she said softly, her hand resting gently on his head. Her words felt as though they reached into the depths of his soul, touching a wish he had barely dared to voice to his family—a gift his mother had always possessed.

"I'm glad to see you've recovered from your illness," he said as he straightened.

"That illness was just a ploy to get you here," she said, her words shocking him.

SURYAVATI

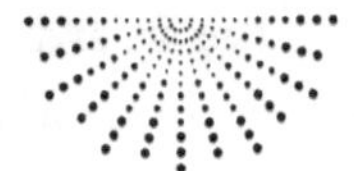

Suri only half-listened to the conversation swirling around her. Giri would not have left with his brother without a reason—that much her heart was certain of.

But her parents were in no mood to entertain her thoughts. Just moments ago, they had been celebrating the prospect of her wedding to Giri. Now, they were back to planning her union with Rangapani.

"No need for any of this Prince Giridhar talk to pass beyond these walls," her mother said firmly. "We should proceed with Suri's marriage to Rangapani as planned."

Her brother and cousin exchanged glances, their eyes flicking to Suri's downturned face, but neither spoke up.

To Suri's surprise, her father broke the silence. "Wouldn't it be wiser to send word to Nidhapur and propose Suri's hand in marriage to Prince Giridhar? A union with their kingdom would strengthen our alliance."

Her mother's eyes narrowed. "Have you forgotten our daughter is mute? I will not risk her safety for politics!"

Her father quickly lost interest in the matter, leaving the decision in her mother's hands. When the family dispersed, instead of retreating to her chamber, Suri wandered aimlessly through the palace halls.

As she passed an open doorway, the moonlight glinting through a window caught her eye. Drawn by the silvery glow, she stepped into the room. Her gaze fell on the faintly visible curtains near the window, and recognition sparked. This was the room where she had hidden that day when her mother and uncle met in secret.

Drawn to the memory, she walked to the window and gazed at the waning moon. Her life, too, felt as though it were fading, shrinking into something beyond her control.

A faint sound broke her thoughts. By instinct, she slipped behind the heavy curtain, her heartbeat quickening.

Footsteps approached, pausing just outside the room. A second set followed, heavier than the first, and then the door creaked shut.

"Urmi, you are making a mistake," her uncle said firmly, his voice low.

Suri remained hidden behind the curtain, her breath shallow, her mind racing to piece together the meaning of their hushed conversation.

"Vikaran," her mother whispered, her tone heavy with frustration, "the world is not filled with men like you. It is filled with men like your brother."

"You are underestimating Suri. She carried on this courtship with Giri right under our noses, and none of us were the wiser," her uncle said, his voice tinged with admiration.

"She did that with Kanika and Abhayan's help," her mother replied sharply. Suri heard the rustle of her sari as she moved. "She will have no one to help her in Nidhapur."

"You're forgetting the prince who stole her heart," her uncle countered.

"That is her story," her mother retorted, her tone clipped. "And you know how wild her imagination can be. What if the prince doesn't reciprocate her feelings and had truly come to spy on us?"

"Abhayan and Kanika didn't doubt her words. And why would King Bhadri risk the life of his heir by sending him to spy on us?"

"Maybe the prince wasn't spying on us, but that doesn't mean he wanted to marry Suri. A mute girl is hardly suited to be a queen. Besides, Abhayan, Kanika, and Suri are just children. What do they know about love and the sacrifices it demands—"

Her mother's words broke off suddenly, as though she had been silenced mid-sentence. But Suri's thoughts raced. Had her mother just declared her unfit to be a queen? The realization hit her like the weight of an elephant pressing down on her chest. She fought the urge to leap out from behind the curtain, shake her mother, and prove her worth. It would only make her mother furious.

Suri heard more rustling fabric, followed by a soft sigh.

"You know how to quiet me," her mother said softly, her tone transformed.

Her uncle laughed—a low, intimate sound that made Suri's heart skip. Curious and uneasy, she risked peeking around the curtain.

What she saw sent shock waves through her. Her mother stood close to her uncle, her head resting gently on his shoulder, while his chin tilted down to touch her hair. They looked... entwined.

Memories of Rangapani catching her in a stolen kiss with Giri flashed through Suri's mind. But this wasn't her. This was her mother.

Had they just kissed?

Her chest tightened as the realization sank in. Adultery committed by a queen was punishable by beheading, and her uncle would face a similar fate. Why would they risk such a perilous act?

"Urmi, I've never demanded a say in such matters before, but I insist now. Don't rush into marrying Suri to Rangapani. You'll crush her spirit. Let us send a message—"

What did her uncle mean by demands? And what matters? Suri's mind swirled with questions, trying to piece together fragments of conversations and glances she had overlooked in the past.

"Vikaran, do you not trust me to act in my daughter's best interest?"

"I do," he replied.

"Then allow her marriage to Rangapani to proceed as planned. He is beneath her in status and will respect her wishes far more than a prince in a distant land."

Her uncle sighed, his voice heavy with resignation. "As you wish," he stated. Moments later, Suri heard the door creak open and the fading sound of their footsteps retreating down the hall.

The silence that followed was deafening. Suri remained hidden behind the curtain, her heart pounding. She was alone now—alone with her unanswered questions.

Later that night, as she leaned out her window with the breeze murmuring in her ears, she worried about her mother getting caught. Her mother and uncle had not been particularly cautious when meeting in that dark room—any servant could have stumbled upon them. She wondered why they had never been caught before. Then, a strange thought wormed its way into her mind: What if her father already knew and chose to turn a blind eye? But why? No answers came to her.

Reluctantly, she climbed into bed and nestled under the silk sheets. Was it because her mother had given her father what he wanted—heirs—that he left her alone? Her thoughts turned to her older brother, who had died at twelve. He had been a sickly child for most of his short life.

As she thought of him, sleep claimed her, and her dreams, in that strange and unpredictable way, shifted. The image of her brother faded, replaced by her uncle and mother, their shadows merging in the dim light of the secret room.

"It is him. Any child of his will be sick. That is why his first wife never gave him an heir."

"My love, there is nothing we can do about it." He stood at a safe distance from her, though longing to close the gap.

She moved toward him, her voice low but insistent. "You are wrong. There is something you can do about it." She placed a hand gently on his shoulder. "Allow me to carry your child," she whispered.

Suri jolted awake from the dream, her heart pounding in her chest.

5 2

GIRIDHAR

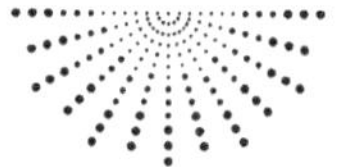

"Giri," his brother called as he walked in.

"The general constantly complains to me about bandits, exaggerating the details to demand more money and men. The minister is forever discovering new ways to help me rule, drafting policies no one bothers to read. My spy chief drones on about plots and rebellions all day. Even the head poet keeps pushing me to spend more money on the arts. I could handle them all—except for the poets and sculptors. They've been drowning me in petitions, accusing me of neglecting art. While you've been hiding from me, I've had a very difficult time keeping everyone content. You were like an elusive fish in the sea, disappearing for months!"

Giri's guilt deepened as his brother prattled on, reminding him of how he had left his elder brother—just three years older than himself—to shoulder the burden of the kingdom while he indulged in his desires. Then he remembered his brother and mother had lied to him.

"I've been worried sick about Mother's health, and now I find out there was no reason for my concern," Giri said, carefully avoiding calling them liars.

"What option did you leave us but to entice you back with falsehoods?" their mother interrupted, her voice sharp with bitterness.

"I agree with Mother," his brother admitted, turning to Giri. "I know you love your freedom, and if I were in your place, I wouldn't want to return to court either. But I need you, Giri. I'd rather you help me carry the burden of administration than leave me to manage it all alone."

Giri thought of his broken promise to Suryavati, shame weighing heavily on him. "Brother, permit me to speak freely. Yes, I've behaved like a wild boar, charging aimlessly, rather than a buffalo steady at the plow," he admitted, his voice low.

"I have indulged your desire to remain untangled from politics for far too long," his mother added, her tone tinged with disappointment. "I want you brothers to get along with each other. Support each other. Not find ways to avoid each other," she said firmly.

"I am so sorry, Mother," Giri replied, regret in his voice. "I apologize for my errant ways. I promise to aid my brother in ruling this kingdom. But do not mistake me. To love both of you does not mean I want to give up my will." He paused, his eyes fixed on the ground before lifting them to meet his mother's. "I met Princess Suryavati in Jaisalpur." He took a deep breath. "Unexpectedly, love blossomed between us. Please, give me your blessing to take her as my wife."

"What?" his brother asked, incredulity straining his voice.

Giri's face went through a complicated series of contortions as he struggled to answer. For a man so fond of writing, words seemed to elude him when it came to speaking to his brother.

"Princess Suryavati helped me escape from Jaisalpur's prison," Giri said.

"Prison?" exclaimed his mother.

"You never told me the story behind this imprisonment," added his brother.

Heat rose in Giri's face as he remembered Rangapani finding Suryavati in his arms. "It was a misunderstanding, Brother. One that Princess Suryavati helped clear up."

His mother frowned. "If I recall correctly, Princess Suryavati had some disfigurement that made her less than an ideal match. I gathered information about all the eligible girls in the neighboring kingdoms."

"She is not disfigured, Mother," Giri blurted out. "She is mute."

And to him, she was perfect. He had no doubt she would make a magnificent queen—purposeful, graceful, and compassionate. She was the flame that lit his heart, and he would not let anyone dim her light.

"Mute? She is cursed. That hardly makes her an ideal queen. I must ask you to ignore your feelings and forget about this girl," his mother said firmly.

To Giri, Suryavati was anything but cursed—she was a girl blessed with poetry, her silence a canvas for profound expression. Yet his mother's words darkened his mood, her dismissal striking a chord of frustration.

Giri watched her, his happiness fading like morning mist before the rising sun. He had allowed his aunt to manipulate him into kidnapping Princess Lalitha, a decision he now deeply regretted, and he wouldn't let himself be coerced into actions that contradicted his beliefs. Taking a deep breath to steady himself, he replied, "I am not a sculpture carved out of wood. I cannot simply ignore my feelings."

"Mother," his brother interjected, "let him marry her. He isn't restricted to taking only one wife. She can remain by his side, even if not on the throne."

Giri winced but did not look away. He understood that if Suryavati could not bear him heirs, he might be compelled to marry again. Yet, he had no intention of taking multiple wives simply because it was permissible. It was not right to indulge one's desires unchecked. Even his passion for weaving stories required restraint. He understood that now.

Giri turned to his mother. "Without realizing it, my heart has grown to make room for Suryavati, and I know I have a place in her heart. Many married couples yearn for this bond but never achieve it."

His mother scrutinized his face and sighed, satisfied that he was telling the truth. "King Vibudha of Jaisalpur struggled to produce an heir. His elder son succumbed to illness. Princess Suryavati comes from such weak stock. Still, I will not prevent you from marrying her. But first, you must marry one of the noble daughters of Nidhapur and produce an heir to the throne. I have already arranged for eligible girls to visit us in the next few days. We can hold a wedding within a fortnight."

Giri felt a surge of anger and disappointment. Four years of marriage, and his brother had yet to produce an heir. Who knew how long he would have to wait? "Mother, by then, Suryavati will already be married off. Please, allow me to return to Jaisalpur—"

"No," his brother declared firmly.

Giri flinched. When they were boys, huddled under a table with mischief dancing in their eyes, Giri would have argued endlessly. But now, he respected the authority of the crown glimmering on his brother's head and swallowed the retort that rose to his lips.

"I went to great trouble to bring you here," his brother continued, "and I'm not letting you out of my sight. It is customary for weddings to be planned by the elders of the two families, not the couples themselves. Leave this in my hands."

Giri's heart sank at those words, a small storm swirling within his chest as the image of Suryavati in Rangapani's arms tormented him. "Please, Brother," he begged, bowing deeply.

"Send a royal messenger to Jaisalpur," his mother relented,

"to seek the princess's hand for Giri. We can arrange for a long betrothal."

Giri had no illusions that Queen Urmila would agree to this. His eyes bulged as he struggled against the conditions imposed by his mother. He had failed spectacularly to convince them. Closing his eyes, he sank into despair.

A voice inside him urged him to be valiant. Princess Suryavati would have been more resolute in finding a solution. He opened his eyes, his voice trembling with fury. "I will seek monkhood and celibacy if you force me to marry anyone other than Suryavati."

SURYAVATI

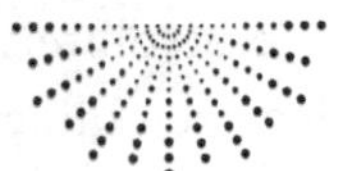

Suri sat on her bed, still shaken by her vivid dreams. She had always admired her mother, but imagining her engaging in a clandestine affair with her uncle shattered the illusions she had built in her mind about a woman's role and morality.

The maid entered the room to clean, and Suri watched her with a pang of envy. The maid was free to live by her own merits, while Suri's worth was dictated by her birth, confined to a palace and groomed for a future marriage to a man she could not esteem. But the feeling faded quickly as she recognized the futility of her envy. Few people enjoyed the privileges she did. Though she had occasionally disguised herself as a commoner, her life bore no resemblance to the maid's. She lacked neither material wealth nor education nor comfort.

Her thoughts turned to her mother's actions. Married off at a young age, her mother had arrived in a city already ruled by another queen. Yet, she had found a way to endure, securing both her survival and the affections of Suri's uncle. With limited agency, she had used her wits to stabilize her position. While others might see her as cold and calculating, Suri viewed her actions in a kinder light.

Suri had feared leaving Jaisalpur, uncertain of her survival in a strange land. Now, she found courage in her mother's resilience. Though Suri had no intention of violating the marriage vows she had yet to take, she believed she could carve out her own path, especially with Prince Giridhar's love as her anchor. In that way, she was more fortunate than her mother, who had been wed to a stranger who never grew to love her. Her father had merely tolerated her mother, but Suri had the rare blessing of a prince who truly loved her. All the uncertainty she carried—the constant fear that she would fall short of the ideals of a queen—melted away. She would not allow her fears to stand in the way of her heart.

Her cousin, Kanika, burst into the room, flushed and breathless. "Suri, I am so sorry about Giridhar. That miserable prince betrayed our trust! What worthless scum he is," she ranted, sitting on Suri's bed and clutching her hands. "I swear, I have half a mind to have my brother hunt him down and eviscerate him for hurting you."

Suri shook her head, but Kanika didn't pause for breath. "He should be thrown into a cage with a starving tiger and shredded to pieces!"

Leaning forward, Suri pressed a hand over Kanika's mouth and shook her head emphatically, her eyes pleading for silence.

Kanika's expression softened, her eyes filled with pity. Suri wanted to scream, to tell her cousin she didn't need anyone's sympathy. Instead, she rose from her bed and walked to her writing table. Kanika followed, her curiosity evident.

Using her finger, Suri wrote a single word on the plate of rice.

Swayamvara

Kanika read it aloud. "Swayamvara." She paused, meeting Suri's gaze. "Are you asking about what I told your mother? About my brother agreeing to host a Swayamvara for me?"

Suri nodded, her eyes urging Kanika to elaborate.

Kanika turned to face her. "A Swayamvara is a ceremony where a princess gets to choose her future husband from among the eligible men invited to attend. My brother has agreed to host one for me. He'll invite nobles, warriors, and princes from across the kingdom and beyond."

Kanika's eyes sparkled with a hint of mischief as she added, "Since I won't know most of these men, I'm thinking of organizing some kind of contest. A way to test their skills, perhaps their character, too, and find the right man for me."

Suri's heart quickened at the thought. She didn't need to search for the right man—she already knew whom she wanted to marry. Prince Giridhar. The problem was getting him to attend the Swayamvara. Her cousin's idea of a contest, however, sparked something within her. It was a chance to grab Giri's attention. She would not be a passive player in her own future.

But first, she needed to convince her mother. Suri hesitated for a moment, considering going to her uncle for help, but quickly dismissed the idea. She knew that if she wanted her mother's support, she would have to win her over herself. She had one weapon at her disposal, and she intended to use it.

Her thoughts solidified. The Swayamvara was her chance. And with it, she would make her mother see that Giri was the man she chose, not just by heart, but by right.

Soon, Suri dressed and left to find her mother. She was in her chambers, speaking with a priest who performed the rituals at a temple outside the palace fort. The priest handed a scroll to her mother as Suri walked in. Her mother's nose wrinkled as she read the message, and her eyes narrowed when they landed on her daughter.

"Don't say anything about this message to anyone," Queen Urmila ordered the priest. The man bowed and departed.

Her mother tucked the scroll into the folds of her sari and sat on a bench, patting the space next to her to invite Suri to sit. There was something about the way her mother had tucked the scroll away so quickly, as if guarding a secret, that piqued her curiosity. Suri sat down, propping her elbow on the back of the bench so she could see her mother.

Queen Urmila sighed and placed her hand gently on Suri's. "You made a mistake," her mother said. "A grave one with terrible consequences. You trusted a stranger with your heart. Luckily, before any lasting damage was done, the man revealed his true, dark nature, sparing you from lifelong agony." Suri swallowed back a lump in her throat at how her mother characterized her love.

"It's okay to feel guilt and regret," her mother continued, mistaking her emotions.

Suri could stand it no longer. She rose and went to find the plate of rice her mother kept in her chambers. Bringing it back to the bench, she wrote with an anger-propelled finger.

Uncle or father?

Her mother read the words and recoiled as though she had been whipped. Though Suri had come prepared to use her newfound knowledge to her advantage, her mother's reaction plunged a knife into her heart. She felt ashamed of causing such pain.

Queen Urmila's eyes narrowed as she studied her daughter. "What do you mean by that?" she asked, her voice sharp as a blade.

Suri took a deep breath, her heart pounding. She swept her hands across the rice to wipe her letters and wrote.

I saw you and uncle last night.

There was a long, pregnant pause as her mother's expression faltered for a moment.

"Suri," she whispered. "You are not old enough to understand my actions. You may even respect me less when you learn the truth." Her voice cracked. "Some of my decisions were not made by weighing the merits but by taking a leap of faith for a better future for me and my offspring."

Suri shook her head, but her mother paid no heed and continued.

"I don't claim to be perfect. I have made many mistakes. I loathe myself on many days, despising myself for my actions." Her mother paused, and Suri saw her hands tremble slightly as grief and rage washed through her face before they became steady again. "But I cannot undo the past, nor can I permit you to damage your brother." Her mother's voice grew stronger. "I will not let my sacrifices go to waste." Even as her mother spoke, Suri saw a grim determination to survive on her face.

Morbid curiosity stirred in Suri's chest as she wondered if her father was Prince Vikaran. She assumed King Vibudha had fathered her elder brother, the sickly child who died young. Her mother had likely taken no chances with her younger brother, and Suri suspected he was Prince Vikaran's son—hale and healthy. But what about her? Yet, as she looked at her mother's guilt-ridden face, her curiosity faded. What would she gain by learning the truth other than twisting a knife in her mother's gut? She knew her uncle loved and cared for her, overlooking her many flaws. They were bonded by blood, no matter their true relationship.

Suri decided not to threaten her mother with revealing what she knew to bend her to her will, because she could never carry out such a deed. It would be wrong to take the way of a coward, especially if she harmed an innocent like her brother. Suri did the only thing she could: she leaned into her mother's shoulder, silently telling her that she did not come to accuse her and that she forgave her for her mistakes. Suri knew there was no changing the past; the only choice was to move forward.

Her mother was silent for a moment, and Suri could sense her struggle. Then, slowly, she wrapped her arm around Suri and kissed the side of her head.

Suri lifted her head and gazed at her mother with teary eyes. Then she wrote on the plate.

I want a Swayamvara. I want to choose my future husband. And I want Prince Giridhar to be there.

GIRIDHAR

Giri stood atop the raised dais, his eyes scanning the powerful noblemen, generals, ministers, priests, and poets assembled in the Grand Throne Room. His brother, King Bhadri, sat on the golden throne, resplendent in his full regalia, while Giri stood a step behind him, a silent observer of the proceedings.

Below the dais, the assembly had arranged itself in a deliberate pattern, reflecting the hierarchy of influence within the kingdom. Those closest to the king's throne were the ones with the greatest sway over his decisions, their positions a silent testament to their power.

The minister, bent at the waist in a deep bow, addressed the king. "Wise ruler of Nidhapur, on this auspicious day, permit this humble servant to present the revised education protocol."

When Bhadri first ascended the throne, he could barely lift the ceremonial sword, let alone understand the workings of the court, so he relied blindly on the advice of others. But as he grew older, he began to see the flaws in the policies he had enacted. The wealthy prospered while the poor remained trapped in their struggles. Over a year ago, he had discussed the matter with Giri, who shared his observations. Giri explained that unlettered farmers were often exploited by merchants who paid them meager sums for the fruits of their labor. Determined to bring change, Bhadri had resolved to compel noblemen to educate more of their people.

A month ago, the minister had presented a protocol draft so voluminous that it dwarfed the entire written history of their kingdom. Bhadri had scowled as he skimmed the document, thinking, *No one will read this, let alone follow it.*

Frustrated with the process, Bhadri handed the task over to Giri upon his return, ordering him to work with the minister and simplify the cumbersome document.

Treating the task as though it were a script for a play, Giri approached it with creativity and focus. Over several days, he collaborated with the minister to condense the sprawling document into a scroll roughly his own height. They debated each subject fiercely, with Giri discarding unnecessary classical references and enduring the minister's relentless protests.

Immersing himself in this work served as a refuge from his worries about Suryavati. It allowed him to momentarily set aside the fear coursing through his veins and the anger that simmered at the thought of Rangapani. Though he trusted Suryavati's strength and ability to take care of herself, the anxiety swirling in his stomach never fully eased. This task kept his mind occupied and his hands busy, offering some solace in the midst of his turmoil.

Today, the minister began with guidelines for appearance and etiquette, which Giri mentally likened to costumes in his plays. Next came lettering, which he equated to his scripts, and then numbers. Each section felt more like stage directions than a syllabus to Giri, making the process oddly satisfying.

As the minister droned on about the latest revisions, Bhadri stifled a yawn. Giri caught it and resisted the urge to smile. His brother had always preferred the straightforward speech of ordinary people, and the simplified protocol would no doubt appeal to him more than the original tome.

"Are you falling asleep?" Giri whispered with a sly grin.

"Asleep? The man could bore us to death," mumbled Bhadri, keeping his voice low.

"His style is... flowery," Giri offered diplomatically.

"Tedious is a better word," Bhadri countered.

"He does take ten sentences to say what could be said in one."

"Does he know I'm not paying him by the word?" his brother quipped, his tone edged with dry humor.

Giri stifled a chuckle as the minister finally neared the end of his interminable speech.

"You'll have to summarize it for me," Bhadri admitted, leaning slightly toward his brother. "I confess my mind wandered to pleasanter things."

Giri leaned closer, whispering back, "I ensured that basic education would be accessible even to a farmer who might only spare a few moments a day for it, unlike the son of a scholar who could dedicate his entire life to learning. A farmer who can count is less likely to be cheated out of his earnings."

Bhadri raised a brow, his expression softening. "Formal education should benefit all people, not just nobles and schol-ars. I'm glad we're partners in this. The kingdom is stronger when we work together."

A look of joy slowly brightened Giri's face as he silently agreed with his brother. The minister had argued endlessly about requiring the masses to read tomes of classical literature written in an obscure language no one used anymore to learn proper behavior. Giri had kept those only for advanced students who were truly interested in deepening their knowledge. For the masses, he believed stories were far more effective than archaic verses in inspiring the right thoughts and behavior.

Back in his chamber, Giri paced restlessly, his steps quick

and forceful as he shoved one foot in front of the other. He moved from one wall to the opposite, his thoughts oscillating between the princess and his plans for educating the masses.

He knew he should focus. Taking the heartfelt stories of compassion, loyalty, and kindness from their traditions and staging them across the kingdom could inspire people. These tales could serve as both entertainment and moral guidance, weaving lessons into the fabric of daily life.

Yet Suryavati lingered in his mind, her presence as vivid as the stories he longed to share. How could he champion a kingdom's soul while his own heart smoldered like a dying ember, yearning for a spark only she could ignite?

As he held steadfast to his threat, his mother had relented, allowing Giri to marry Suryavati. But she insisted that he also marry a girl of her choice at the same time. "It is my duty to protect you from bad choices, whether you like it or not," she had claimed. Giri had reluctantly agreed to her condition, allowing his brother to send a messenger to Jaisalpur. The absence of news stabbed him in the chest like a thorn. Concern knotted in his stomach.

He was slow to wake in the morning, his head caught between dreams and nightmares, his limbs heavy with lingering drowsiness. Blinking up at the ceiling, a ray of sunlight streaming through the large windows greeted him—the only sign of time moving forward.

Loud footsteps echoed outside the door, jolting him to full awareness. His guard, Sangu, barged in with an intensity that left no room for pleasantries. "Jaisalpur is holding a Swayamvara for Princess Suryavati."

For a moment, the room spun, the world tilting as his gut plummeted. Then, slowly, clarity returned. He had to attend the Swayamvara—to allow her the chance to choose him. A coil of fear wrapped tightly around his belly. *She might not choose me*, a whisper of doubt crept in. But another thought burned brighter.

If she intended to marry Rangapani, she wouldn't have pushed for a Swayamvara—a ceremony designed to grant her the power to choose her groom.

"I heard she is holding a poetry contest," Sangu continued.

A poetry contest meant Suryavati wanted him to compete and win. The flicker of hope ignited action. He rose swiftly, washing his face with cold water to chase away the last vestiges of sleep. Changing hurriedly, he slipped into the cool hallway, his footsteps echoing as he made his way toward his brother's chambers.

The guard stationed outside bowed but hesitated before speaking. "He is with the queen."

Heat of embarrassment crept up his neck as Giri realized he could not disturb them now. Frustration simmered beneath the surface, his resolve tested by the urgency he felt. Every fiber of his being protested against waiting, screaming for immediate action, yet he knew better. Timing was everything. He had to be patient, even if it felt like a battle against his own restless spirit.

5 5

SURYAVATI

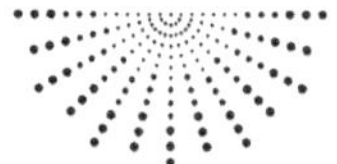

"Are you ready?" asked her cousin, King Dushyant, his tone gentle as he studied her.

Suri shook her head, unable to muster a smile. Convincing her mother to hold a Swayamvara—a groom-choosing ceremony—had seemed like the hardest challenge. With the help of her brother, uncle, and Kanika, she had accomplished it. But the man she intended to choose as her husband, Prince Giridhar, had yet to arrive. The ceremony was tomorrow, and the thought of his absence sent waves of unease through her.

Guests had been arriving steadily over the past few days. Her cousin, King Dushyant, and his new bride, Queen Lalitha, had arrived yesterday from Vidarpur. Suri had heard countless tales about Dushyant and Lalitha from Kanika, but seeing them together was another matter entirely. Watching the couple exchange loving glances across the crowded hall filled Suri with equal parts joy and despair.

At the far end of the hall, Lalitha stood engaged in conversation with Suri's mother, Queen Urmila. From the moment she arrived, Lalitha had been diligently observing the queen, as though intent on gleaning every lesson she could about queenship during her brief stay. Yet even amidst her attentiveness, her gaze frequently drifted toward her husband.

Dushyant, standing beside Suri, was clearly no less smitten; his eyes sparkled whenever he mentioned Lalitha, and a subtle, involuntary smile graced his lips each time his gaze fell upon her. Their connection was undeniable, a palpable thread of love weaving through the crowded hall.

"If Giridhar isn't here tomorrow," Dushyant said in a fiendish whisper, "I will ride to Nidhapur without stopping, tie him to my reins, and drag him here myself."

Suri blinked, startled by Dushyant's vehemence, though she appreciated his fierce desire to help. Having grown up alongside her after her aunt's passing, Dushyant and his sisters had always treated her as family, with Dushyant being particularly protective of her, much like an older brother.

She also knew that Giri shared a history with Dushyant—he had kidnapped Lalitha once, an act Giri deeply regretted. She had promised herself to unravel the full story if he showed up.

If.

That word loomed heavily in her mind, an unwelcome guest in her thoughts. Had she imagined his regard for her entirely? Suri could only hope she would have her answers tomorrow.

When a shadow crossed the entryway, Suri's heart leaped into her throat. Was it him? Every beat of her heart cried out for it to be him—rushing in, his face etched with longing, begging her to forgive him.

But no. It was only a guard stepping forward, leaning in to whisper something into her father's ear. The flicker of hope she had allowed herself to feel was snuffed out, leaving her chest hollow and aching.

Queen Lalitha wandered over, her presence as calm as the soft swish of her silks. "Has Giridhar arrived yet? I want to make sure he knows I harbor no hard feelings."

"Speak for yourself," Dushyant growled, his expression darkening. "If he hurts Suri, I'll cut him to pieces and feed him to the eagles." His tone carried a sharp edge, and Suri noted the deliberate mention of eagles, the emblem of Vidarpur.

Lalitha rolled her eyes, unfazed by her husband's dramatics. "Ignore him," she said lightly, addressing Suri. "The Giridhar I knew was kind, compassionate, and sensitive. His love for poetry always put me at odds with him, but from what Kanika has told me, those very traits would make him an ideal match for you."

"Yet he is not here," Dushyant snarled. Suri felt her hopes wavering, the weight of her uncertainty pressing heavily on her chest.

Her cousins, Kanika and Ambika, joined her just then. Ambika had traveled with her brother, while Kanika had plans to return home with them. Suri already dreaded parting with Kanika's boisterous and comforting presence.

"Suri, dusk is the perfect time to pluck jasmine flowers for your garland," Kanika said with a teasing grin. Her words, instead of lifting Suri's spirits, seemed to churn her fears, like rain-swollen waters surging against a riverbank.

Reluctantly, she allowed herself to be led to the garden. Around them, birds cooed as they settled into their nests. Maids moved about lighting oil wick lamps, their glow casting soft, flickering light over the lush greenery. Yet none of the tranquil beauty around her could soothe the storm in her heart.

She had dared to dream of a future with Giri, but now, it felt as though those dreams might shatter before they had a chance to bloom.

Kanika, sharp-eyed as ever, studied Suri's sullen face. "Suri, the prince will come," she said, her voice steady and full of conviction. "There is no excising him from your life."

"Are you really going to recite two verses from a poem and ask the gathered suitors to complete your verses?" Ambika asked in awe, her eyes wide with the curiosity of her youthful innocence.

"Don't be silly," Kanika interjected before Suri could respond. "Suri isn't going to recite anything. She'll be standing on a raised dais, looking extraordinarily beautiful while her uncle reads the verses she prepared."

The easy banter between the sisters made Suri's heart ache with a pang of jealousy she couldn't entirely suppress. Kanika and Ambika, two years apart, shared a bond that seemed effortless.

Suri pulled her thoughts back to the Swayamvara. The verses weren't just hers; they were hers and Giridhar's—words they had shaped together. Only he could complete them as she intended.

The others will make fools of themselves. None of them were poets. They'd probably commission some court bard to cobble together uninspired lines about love or marriage and recite them with no regard for her words.

The thought filled Suri with equal parts dread and determination. If Giridhar didn't arrive, she wouldn't just endure the humiliation of hearing her carefully crafted verses mangled— she would also confront the harsh reality of a future without him, a future she wasn't sure she could face with the same courage she wore like a veil before the world.

After plucking the jasmine flowers, the girls settled by the edge of the garden pond, their feet dipping into the cool, rippling water. The surface of the pond was a mosaic of lotus leaves, and above them, giant pink blooms swayed like rubies glinting on a crown. The gentle breeze carried the scent of flowers as they wove the blooms into a garland.

Kanika and Ambika flanked Suri, their arms draped over her shoulders in a gesture of sisterly comfort.

"I'm going to miss our adventures," Kanika whispered.

"Sneaking out dressed as boys, leaving behind the palace, the guards, the maids, and the endless duties of being princesses."

"We should do it in Vidarpur," Ambika suggested mischievously.

Kanika laughed. "Our brother would tear his hair out and marry me off just to stop me."

It would still be worth it, Suri thought, recalling how one of their escapades had led her to meet Giridhar.

"Queen Lalitha would never let him forget his vow to let you choose your groom in a Swayamvara," Ambika said with conviction.

Suri smiled, though her heart ached. She would miss Kanika's unwavering loyalty, their shared sense of adventure, and having a friend who truly understood her heart.

"I don't care much for love," Ambika declared in a haughty tone, her innocent candor on full display. "I want to travel to faraway lands and sail eternal seas."

Suri wished she could dream as freely as Ambika. Instead, her thoughts circled back to the looming uncertainty of her future, heavy and unyielding.

Kanika seemed to sense her despair. She reached for Suri's hand, her grip warm and reassuring. "Suri, your happiness isn't tied to any boy, no matter who he is. If you don't like the way your story is unfolding, then write new chapters."

Suri closed her eyes, allowing herself to imagine her heart as a vessel, emptying of bitterness and filling with the possibility of both joy and sorrow. The world was vast, and perhaps there was still space for her dreams to flourish. The thought calmed her momentarily, though the weight of the Swayamvara still pressed on her.

Her mother had insisted she sleep early to be fresh for the morrow, but Suri had tossed and turned, haunted by memories of Giri and the uncertainty of his arrival. Silver moonlight now seeped through the windows, outlining the shadows of her room. She sat up, rubbing her eyes as her blanket slipped from her shoulder, startled by the soft creak of the door opening.

Abhayan entered quietly, already dressed for the day. His alert eyes scanned the room as he walked toward her bed.

Why are you here so early? Suri asked silently with her gaze, her brows knitting in confusion.

Her brother sat on the edge of her bed, his face serious. "I wanted to see you before Mother."

She reached out and traced *Giri* on the back of his hand with her finger.

"He's not here," Abhayan said softly, frustration and confusion in his voice. "It makes no sense."

The dread that had been lurking in her chest all night swirled to the surface.

"What do you plan to do if he doesn't come?" he asked, his brows drawing together in worry.

Suri swallowed hard. The same question had echoed relentlessly in her mind throughout the sleepless night. Despite all her efforts to push it aside, she had no answer to offer—not to Abhayan, not even to herself.

5 6

GIRIDHAR

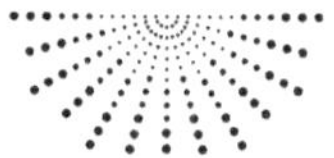

Giridhar leaned against the balcony railing, gazing down at the palace gardens. The flowers—red, white, and yellow—unfurled in a vibrant, endless carpet of color beneath him, swaying slightly in the morning breeze. Their beauty, however, did little to soothe the restlessness within him.

Footsteps echoed down the corridor outside his chambers, each step reverberating in the air.

Giri straightened, turning toward the sound just as his brother entered. He bowed respectfully.

"I heard you were looking for me, Giri," Bhadri said.

Giri stepped back into the room, his heart racing. "Brother, Jaisalpur is hosting a Swayamvara for Princess Suryavati."

Bhadri's expression softened, a knowing glint in his eye. "The girl who stole your heart." A statement, not a question.

Heat climbed Giri's face, and he dipped his head. Was it so wrong to long for the one person who truly understood the stories that danced in his mind? Suryavati was that person, and he considered himself blessed to have found her. Slowly, reverently, he raised his eyes to meet his brother's. "Please grant me permission to take part in the Swayamvara."

Bhadri studied him, his brow furrowing. "Why would a girl who cares for you hold a Swayamvara?"

Giri hesitated, then said, "Her mother arranged for her to marry the son of their general. This is likely her way of escaping that arrangement."

Bhadri stared at Giri, jaw clenched and eyes narrowed. "Out of attachment to this unknown girl, you would risk our kingdom?"

Giri blinked, startled, worry flickering in his chest like a restless flame. Was he no longer in control of this journey? "I do care for our kingdom, but I am not willing to throw away my heart," he said, struggling to stay calm. Disappointment washed over him like a sudden downpour.

Bhadri scoffed. "What does the heart have to do with royal marriages?" he asked. "Forget this princess and marry the one chosen by our mother."

Giri frowned, irritation tugging at his features. "I don't need another bride," he mumbled, his voice low.

If he were seven and Bhadri ten, playing hide-and-seek in the palace gardens, he might have argued endlessly, their laughter ringing through the corridors. But that fatal day, when the crown had been placed on his brother's head, had changed everything. Their bond, once marked by playful rivalry, had shifted into something more restrained, weighed down by responsibility and the unspoken reverence that came with it.

"That's not up for debate," Bhadri countered, folding his arms. "You've been known to let your heart lead you into some unique situations. Mother and I have sacrificed much for this kingdom, so I'm not asking anything more from you than what I have already willingly given up."

Heat crept into Giri's face, but he bit back a retort. Instead, he nodded reluctantly. "As you wish, Brother."

Bhadri clapped him on the shoulder. "You will see the wisdom of what I'm saying soon enough."

Giri harbored other ideas in his mind. He went to find Sangu and hatched a plan with him.

That night, Sangu, adorned in Giri's finest clothes and jewels, set out on a boat beneath the stars. On the opposite shore of the lake, Giri watched as his brother's guards spotted Sangu and gave chase in their own boats. Earlier, Giri had swum partway across the lake before climbing into a small boat Sangu had left in the middle, far from the guards' prying eyes. From there, he silently rowed across the water.

Hoping Sangu could elude the guards long enough for his escape, Giri walked for a mile before finding the horse Sangu had hidden for him. Each passing moment of delay tightened his chest, draining him with anxiety.

What if he arrived too late? What if Suryavati, forced to choose among the gathered suitors, had already made her decision by the time he reached her? The thought tightened his chest.

Giri despised having to deceive his brother. His mind drifted back to when he was eight years old, standing in the training yard. He had watched his older brother parrying with a sword, his admiration plain. Giri had been training with another partner, but in a moment of childish vanity, he struck Bhadri on the shoulder with a blunt blade and laughed, eager to show he could fight too.

Perhaps it was the force of the blow, or perhaps the guards failed to recognize him as a prince—or cared only about their oath to the new king.

The next moment, Bhadri's personal guards had thrown Giri to the ground, swords pointed at his neck.

It had taken Bhadri a moment to understand what had happened. He had looked as confused as Giri before his eyes widened in horror at the sight of blades threatening his younger brother. "Don't hurt him!" he had screamed. Bhadri could have easily reversed the order and thrown him into the dungeon. Their respective positions and powers etched themselves into young Giri's mind.

The memory lingered, its taste bitter. Giri swallowed hard. If Suryavati's garland ended up around another's neck, he would never forgive himself.

He could not live in his brother's shadow forever. It was not unreasonable for him to demand that his brother treat him as a grown man.

"Bless me, Mother and Brother," Giri prayed as he mounted his horse in one fluid motion.

The cool night air enveloped him as he rode under the canopy of stars, his heart beating in sync with each hoofbeat as he prayed he would arrive in time.

5 7
SURYAVATI

Suri sat in front of the mirror, her reflection betraying none of the turmoil raging inside her. Her maid deftly added the final touches to her intricately woven bun, but Suri wanted to shout, to curse, to tear at the elegant red sari draped around her. Instead, she sat still, composed, like a woman in mourning.

Kanika and Ambika hovered behind her, their voices offering small comforts.

"You look regal in the red sari," Kanika said, her tone gentle. The silver-embroidered elephants lining the border caught the light, a symbol of majesty that mocked Suri's internal chaos.

"Dazzling," Ambika agreed, admiring the pearls woven into Suri's dark hair. But Suri felt anything but dazzling; waves of grief crashed over her, each one carrying the bitter sting of Giridhar's absence.

How did her face remain serene while her mind spiraled with despair? She had sent her guards to search for him several times that morning, but the answer was always the same: Prince Giridhar was not in Jaisalpur.

What would she do when she stood in the great hall, staring

at the eager faces of strangers? The thought made her stomach churn. Suri took a deep breath, forcing herself to hold steady. If Giri had truly abandoned her, she would face this alone, as she always had. Yet the knowledge brought no solace, no softening of the sharp ache in her heart. It felt as though a part of her had been hollowed out, leaving only the echo of her longing and the bitter sting of his absence.

Her mother arrived in her room to give her view of what she expected Suri to do.

"Kanika and Ambika, head to the Swayamvara hall and wait for us. I will escort Suryavati myself."

The sisters obeyed, leaving her alone with her mother. The older woman waited patiently as the maid wrapped a flower garland around Suri's hair, then dismissed the servant with a curt nod.

"Child, you look like the divine goddess herself," her mother said, coming to stand behind her.

Suri swallowed hard, the words catching in her throat. She didn't feel remotely divine. She felt like a storm caught in human form, ready to unleash chaos at any moment.

"I listened to you and organized this Swayamvara, though your father opposed it," her mother said, rubbing her wrist as she spoke.

Suri knew the gesture well; it was her mother's tell, a sign of inner turmoil. She could imagine her father's displeasure at the idea of a Swayamvara. He had likely been reminded of his own rejection at her aunt's ceremony all those years ago.

Her mother didn't particularly like the idea either, Suri knew. She had acquiesced only because Suri had uncovered a dark secret—one that still weighed heavily on her heart. A secret that whispered unsettling questions about her true parentage.

Suri had never mustered the courage to confront her mother directly. The closest she had come was hinting at her suspicions, but even then, her mother's sharp deflections and the sadness in her eyes had stopped her from pressing further.

Now, as her mother's words hung in the air, Suri couldn't help but feel the unspoken tension between them—a chasm filled with truths they were both too afraid to name.

"Your prince is not here," her mother whispered, her voice low but each word a thunderclap in Suri's ears. "I don't think he is coming, Suri. He has had many days to send word if he truly cared about you."

Her mother's eyes searched hers, softening. "It is hard to see clearly when you're at the center of a storm, but we tell ourselves the most convincing lies. I know you are hurting, my child, but this may be a blessing in disguise. It's better to learn his true nature now than after it's too late."

Suri's throat tightened, the weight of her mother's words sinking into her heart.

"Grieve for him if you must," her mother continued, her hand warm but unyielding on Suri's shoulder. "But when we step into that hall, I need you to lift your chin and turn your face toward the future. Rangapani may not be a poet, but he is steadfast. He will care for you, Suri. He will keep you safe. Choose him."

Her mother gave her shoulder a reassuring squeeze, but Suri felt no comfort. The churning storm inside her only grew, threatening to drown her mother's words in a flood of despair.

Suri blinked back her tears, willing them not to fall here and now. Her face shifted through a cascade of emotions—a storm brewing, cresting, and crashing—before settling into a calm, expressionless mask. If her mother was correct, it was not worth shedding tears for a man of fickle nature. Yet her heart rebelled, clinging stubbornly to the belief that Giridhar's regard for her was genuine.

Did his mother forbid him to marry her? Was he trapped in

some obligation he couldn't escape? Why wouldn't he send her a message, even if only to explain?

Her mother's voice cut through her thoughts, low and tinged with a vulnerability Suri rarely heard. "It is the duty of a mother to sacrifice so her children can live in peace. Don't waste my sacrifice, child."

Suri swallowed hard, sensing her mother's unspoken words. She guessed what that sacrifice was and what it had cost her mother over the years.

A knock broke the silence, and Nanmaran peeked in. "They are waiting, my lady."

Suri stood, dust motes dancing in the light streaming through the windows. Her legs felt leaden, refusing to obey her will. Her mother stepped forward, stopping to glance back. Suri drew a shaky breath, forcing herself to move and follow.

The sounds of the Nadhaswaram drifted in, mournful and melodic, an echo of her own turmoil. They paused at the side door to the hall, her mother turning to her one last time. "Do you remember the plays I took you to as a child?"

Suri nodded, the memories vivid. Those plays had sparked her love for poetry, for words that sang and wept.

"The first act always ended in tragedy," her mother murmured, her hand resting lightly on Suri's arm. "But there is always a second act. Do not forget that."

The doors opened, and the light hit Suri's eyes, momentarily blinding her. She stepped forward, the murmurs of the gathered crowd washing over her.

As Suri stepped into the grand hall, her thoughts drifted to the play Giri had once crafted, inspired by her own poem. It was a story that had bound them together, their shared love for words forming the thread. In that play, the first act had ended in happiness—a triumph of love and destiny, just as Giri and her tale had once seemed to promise.

But the second act had followed, darker and unrelenting, and it had ended in tragedy.

Now, Suri couldn't help but wonder if their story was destined to mirror the one they had woven together. Had their first act—their laughter, shared verses, and fleeting glances—been all the happiness they were allowed? Was this moment, standing before the gathered crowd with her heart splintered, the beginning of her second act?

5 8

GIRIDHAR

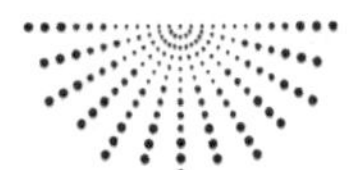

At the sound of hooves, Giri turned in his saddle and saw Sangu's brother riding swiftly to catch up with him. He, too, wore Giri's clothes.

"King Bhadri will soon realize I have left the Nidhapur Palace. Let the king see you, then lead them on a chase away from me," Giri said. He wanted to slow his brother down and had stationed Sangu's brother at a hideout for this very reason.

Traveling with the king would take time, so Giri hoped he could reach Jaisalpur before his brother closed the gap.

"I will ensure no harm comes to you or your brother," Giri said with a curt nod. The weight of his mission pressed heavily on him. He turned his attention back to the road ahead, urging his horse forward, the pounding of hooves matching the frantic rhythm of his thoughts.

The stars vanished for a moment before reappearing, their light flickering through a shifting canopy of clouds.

Rain clouds, Giri thought, squinting against the darkening sky.

"Let us hope I reach the Jaisalpur palace before the sky sheds

262

its tears," he murmured to himself, his voice tinged with both urgency and weariness.

Prince Giridhar, accustomed to riding for days on end, would have endured the journey without complaint. But playwright Giri, more familiar with ink-stained hands than reins, was feeling the toll. His thighs chafed against the saddle, his back ached, and his hands had lost all sensation from gripping the leather too tightly.

He blamed his condition on the days of inactivity spent immersed in crafting stories and composing verses. Yet, despite the pain, he refused to slow his pace. The thought of Suryavati waiting—or worse, choosing another—spurred him onward, forcing his body to obey the demands of his will.

Soon, Giri felt the weariness of his horse. He feared the animal might overheat from the strain of the long journey.

For the sake of the horse, Giri knew he had to switch mounts. He slid off awkwardly, his legs unsteady as he landed, and immediately began stroking the horse's head.

Alone on the quiet roadside, Giri leaned against a nearby tree, his eyes half-closed, the weight of exhaustion pressing down on him. The soft rustle of leaves and the distant hum of nocturnal insects were his only companions.

Pushing himself upright, Giri guided the horse on foot, searching for a stable. It wasn't long before he found one. Carefully, he eased the door open, keeping a firm hand on his horse to prevent any noise. Inside, he spotted a mare, likely used for pulling carts.

"Who's there?" a man's voice called out, startling Giri. He noticed a club resting on the man's shoulder.

Half-turning so the moonlight illuminated his face, Giri intoned imperiously, "I am a royal messenger." He held out the messenger ring he had taken from the palace. In Nidhapur, messengers were entitled to swap horses, and citizens were expected to provide shelter and food for them.

"Messenger," the man acknowledged with a nod but remained still. Panic flared in Giri's chest; a confrontation would only delay him. He needed to act quickly.

"I'm swapping my horse for yours," Giri declared, gesturing to his magnificent steed, far superior to the man's mare. "Do I have your permission?"

The man's eyes lingered greedily on Giri's horse before he nodded. Giri swiftly exchanged the animals, pressing a silver coin into the man's palm.

Before the man could reconsider or follow, Giri disappeared into the darkness, the new horse carrying him away.

Deeply grateful for the fresh mount, he muttered a silent thanks to the gods. As he settled into the saddle, he winced at the renewed strain on his body. He couldn't shake the feeling that he was just as exhausted as the horse he had left behind.

Giri managed a faint smile, allowing determination to course through his weary limbs. "I'll rest when this journey is done—and not a moment sooner."

With that, he urged his new mount forward, the horse galloping beneath the darkening sky as Giri pressed on.

The sky god seemed to pity Giri's weary body and shed tears in a relentless downpour. The rain soaked him to the bone, his clothes clinging uncomfortably to his skin. The wet fabric chafed against his already raw body, each movement a fresh sting. He gritted his teeth, swallowing his discomfort, unwilling to voice his misery.

When the storm finally relented and the night surrendered to dawn, the world seemed transformed. The first rays of sunlight broke through the horizon, gentle and tentative, like a child rubbing its eyes after a long sleep. The fresh scent of rain lingered in the air, and droplets hung from the leaves like tiny jewels.

But the beauty of the moment was lost on Giri. His lungs burned, and his arms and legs felt heavy and weak. He scanned his surroundings and realized, with a pang of dread, that he still had many miles to cover. Panic surged in his chest, sharp and unrelenting. He wasn't going to make it. What if Suryavati stood in the Swayamvara hall, surrounded by eager suitors, and thought he had abandoned her?

Giri gripped the reins tightly, his knuckles white. "We ride harder," he said, his voice hoarse but resolute.

The horse, though weary from the night's ordeal, was urged into a faster pace. Giri leaned forward in his saddle, ignoring the pain in his body and the doubts in his mind. He could not afford to fail—not now, not when Suryavati's happiness and his own future hung in the balance.

5 9

SURYAVATI

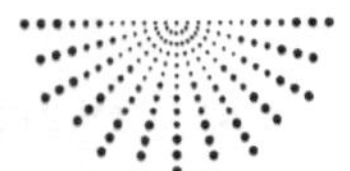

The auspicious time for the Swayamvara had been carefully chosen by their minister, an esteemed astrologer. Yet, as Suri stood near the entrance to the grand hall, her legs trembling with fear, she felt anything but favored by fate.

Her mother, sensing her hesitation, leaned closer and whispered, "My sister chose the wrong man because of love. And what came of it? She and her husband perished—she first, and he in a drunken stupor mourning her. Don't make her mistake, Suri. Choose wisely and marry Rangapani."

Suri's chest tightened at her mother's words. *Love does make fools of us all,* she thought, unwillingly agreeing. But without love, what were they? No better than cattle, she decided.

Her thoughts drifted to her aunt, the mother of her three cousins—Dushyant, Kanika, and Ambika. She had defied expectations and lived a fulfilling life. *Perhaps love is worth the risk,* Suri mused, *if the man reciprocated.* Giri's absence at the moment led her to wonder if he ever had.

Suri walked to the raised dais alone, the jasmine garland trembling slightly in her hand. From the corner of her eye, she stole glances at the gathered noblemen and warriors, her heart sinking with each step. Despite her longing, her mind failed to conjure Giri's face among the crowd.

You are on your own, the walls seemed to whisper, their silent taunt echoing in her ears. Suri felt like a solitary plank adrift on an endless ocean, aimless and uncertain of where the currents might carry her.

As she climbed the two steps to join her father, his voice cut through her thoughts, low and sharp. "Your aunt made a fool of me once," he whispered, his tone laced with bitterness. "I will not tolerate a repeat of that. Your prince is not here. If you do not place the garland around Rangapani's neck, I will not hurt you. But your mother is a different story."

The words struck her like a blow, and Suri swallowed hard, her throat tightening. She didn't dare look at him, fearing the cold determination she would see in his eyes. Instead, she focused on steadying her breath, her fingers tightening around the garland as she fought to suppress the storm rising within her. She could not let him hurt her mother—not if it was within her power to prevent it.

Her uncle, standing a few feet away, smiled at her reassuringly, unaware of her father's threat, and then turned to address the gathered assembly. "Honored guests, esteemed ministers, and valiant generals, we gather today to seek a suitable groom for our beloved princess. I thank you all for your presence on this auspicious occasion."

His voice carried an air of authority tempered with warmth, and the crowd listened attentively. "The princess has entrusted me with a few verses from her poem. She wishes for those among you who seek her hand in matrimony to continue the poem by reciting the next two lines. How the princess will evaluate these lines is a mystery known only to her."

Here, her uncle chuckled lightly, his tone inviting a ripple of laughter from the crowd, though Suri's father remained stone-faced, his frown deepening. Suri quickly cast her eyes down, her heart pounding.

Her uncle's voice softened as he began to recite the verses she and Giri had written together:

I am determined to find her place
Crawling around the shrubs blind
I can never see any face
Maybe it is all in my mind.

The words hung in the air, a delicate thread binding her to memories of Giri. Her chest tightened as she glanced at the crowd, knowing the one voice that resonated with her soul was absent.

"Have your verses ready. She might recognize a regal soul in your verses."

One by one, the gathered young men were introduced and presented their poems. As Suri had suspected, they had come prepared with verses that did not align with hers.

"This is Kripa, son of our minister, a student of history and literature," her uncle announced, his voice carrying over the hushed crowd. A young man with delicate features and a carefully composed demeanor stepped forward, his palms pressed together in greeting.

He began to recite his lines, his voice soft yet clear:

Gazing at your face, a breeze touched my heart,
Whispering of days where love plays its part.

Excited murmurs rippled through the hall. Some of the older ministers nodded in approval, while the younger warriors exchanged knowing glances. It was an elegant verse, artfully composed, and many seemed to think it worthy of admiration.

Her uncle turned to Suri, his expression a mixture of

encouragement and expectation. But Suri kept her gaze fixed firmly on the floor, her face obscured so no one could see the despair etched into her features, nor the heavy weight pressing on her heart.

Since she showed no inclination to place the garland on Kripa's neck, her uncle offered him a kind smile and a slight bow. "Thank you, young Kripa. A beautiful offering indeed."

The young man stepped back, his expression faltering slightly, though he recovered quickly, bowing gracefully before retreating to his place among the crowd.

Her uncle gestured to the next man. "Step forward," he said. The Swayamvara continued, each hopeful suitor presenting their verses, but none managing to tie their words to the poem Suri and Giri had crafted.

Rangapani stepped forward, his voice steady but devoid of the earlier arrogance that had marked his demeanor. "I am no poet, Princess Suryavati," he began. "What I seek is not a verse, but an alliance—a bond as unyielding as that between a warrior and his sword. Allow me to be your sword, to stand as your shield, protecting you all your life."

Suri's gaze flickered to him, her expression unreadable. His words were straightforward, unadorned, yet they carried a weight of sincerity she had not expected.

"If this is to be a contest of words, then here are mine."

Daughter of Jaisalpur, hear my plea,
It is my destiny to seek thee.
Let you bloom in my nurturing soil,
Shielded from strife, untouched by toil.

What she shared with Giri was unique, a bond that could never be replicated. No matter how deeply she longed for him, the reality was clear—he was beyond her reach. Perhaps, in time, a friendship could grow between her and Rangapani, a companionship that might eventually blossom into something more. Maybe cradling a mewling child in her arms would be enough to fill the void.

She took a hesitant step forward, then another, the jasmine garland trembling in her hands. Descending the dais, she approached Rangapani, her heart heavy with the weight of tying her future to this man. As she raised her hand, a gut-wrenching sob threatened to erupt from within. She gulped air to mask her turmoil and raised the garland to slip over his neck.

A sudden commotion erupted near the entrance. The guards parted reluctantly as a figure, drenched and caked in mud, stumbled into the hall.

Her breath caught in her throat, her heart pounding wildly as her eyes locked onto his face.

"Wait!" Giri's voice rang out, raw and urgent, from the doorway.

6 0

GIRIDHAR

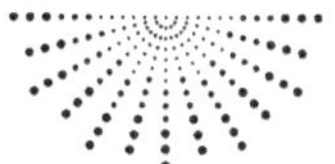

The world had shrunk to just one face etched in his memory, and Giri thought only about taking one step. Then another. He had lost count of how many steps he had taken from the moment he jumped off the horse outside the palace steps. The possibility of arriving after the Swayamvara seemed a worse tragedy than death and kept him moving forward.

Prince Abhayan had left word with the palace guards to bring him to the Swayamvara hall upon his arrival, so he had a couple of escorts accompanying him, matching his tottering steps.

When the doors to the grand hall came into view, he used his remaining energy to hasten his way. What he saw as the room came into view stalled his heart. Princess Suryavati stood ready to place her garland around Rangapani's neck.

"Wait!" he screamed, and the guards at the entrance turned to observe him. But he had eyes only for the princess, who froze as she shifted to view him. Coated in mud, he barely resembled a human, let alone a prince.

Before the men guarding could throw him out, King

Dushyant rushed to his side. Clutching his elbow tightly, he asked, "Are your feelings for Suri sincere?"

Giri nodded as if his life depended on it.

"Do you intend to take her as your wife and treat her with love and respect?"

Giri gazed at the princess, who watched him, a mix of emotions racing across her face. A temporary dizziness seized him as he imagined a life without her, and he swayed unsteadily on his feet. *I love her.* Like a mirror, he saw her face reflect his sentiment, as if their hearts sang the same tune.

"I will cherish her till my last breath and gladly give up my life before I allow anyone to hurt her."

She lowered the hands that held the garland.

Startled, Rangapani dashed toward him, his hand gripping the hilt of his sword.

Dushyant waved off the guards and the approaching Rangapani.

"Idiot," Dushyant muttered, whether about Giri, Rangapani, or both. "For whatever reason, Suri loves you. She would not want you to sacrifice yourself for her. She would want you to fight for her."

Somehow, the mocking tone of Dushyant infused life into his legs. Giri walked forward.

"I am here for the Swayamvara," he said in a clear voice.

Rangapani glowered at him, but Giridhar ignored the warrior.

Prince Vikaran gazed at him and then at his niece.

"Tell us your name, young man," Prince Vikaran asked.

"Prince Giridhar of Nidhapur, brother to King Bhadri. I have also masqueraded in Jaisalpur as Playwright Giri."

Could he still claim to be a prince of Nidhapur after defying his brother's wishes?

Silence reigned in the hall after he introduced himself. He sensed Rangapani startle upon learning his identity.

Her uncle's face settled into a mask as he gave him the instructions. "Princess Suryavati wants the suitors to recite the next two lines in her poem. If she finds your words to her liking, she will choose you as her husband."

Prince Vikaran then went on to recite the lines that Giri knew very well, having written the first two himself.

I am determined to find her place
Crawling around the shrubs blind
I can never see any face
Maybe it is all in my mind.

Giri realized he had never set the next few lines to ink, though the words swirled in his head as he observed the princess.

In a clear voice that echoed around the room, Giri completed their poem, which had started as a mere play of words and had turned into a vessel for their authentic emotions.

When all my hopes flee
I saw her in shimmering light
Waiting to be set free
Our love bringing back my sight.

Suryavati ran to his side, forgetting all decorum. Giri staggered a few feet forward to meet her in the middle of the hall. He looked down to meet her eyes. The sound of his pounding heart filled his ears, and his vision narrowed into a tunnel. She looked more beautiful than what his tired mind had conjured on the way here, like the sun shining through a spiderweb touched with drops of dew.

With all the eyes of the audience on them, Suryavati raised her garland, but Giri placed a hand on her elbow to halt her.

"I come without the blessings of my mother or my brother. I

may not have a kingdom to return to after this. Will you accept a humble playwright as your husband?" Although he wanted her to choose him, he did not want to deceive her about his prospects.

Determination shone in her eyes as she pushed his hand away and lifted her garland once more. Giri bowed his head, accepting the flowers with quiet reverence.

Tears welled up in Suryavati's eyes after she placed the garland around his neck and straightened. Like a flooded river breaking through restraining walls, a sob broke out of her as she began striking his chest in anguish. He bore it silently, like a rock absorbing the rage of a pounding wave, understanding the source of her pain, knowing she had been contemplating marriage to Rangapani just moments ago. When she stopped, he reached out, squeezed her hand, and watched as her rage soon dissipated into tenderness.

"To be with you means everything to me," Giri said, his expression intense.

She let her hand rest in his grip, feeling his joy merge with hers, their eyes reflecting their hope for the future.

King Dushyant led a chant that was soon echoed around the hall. "Long live, Princess Suryavati. Long live, Prince Giridhar."

Princess Kanika and a girl who looked remarkably like her rushed to their side with huge smiles on their faces. "Playwright Giri, I'm glad this story did not end in a tragedy like one of your plays," said Kanika.

Prince Abhayan strode over, looking very annoyed. "You kept my sister waiting on a thorn bed."

The corners of his lips twitched at the young prince's outrage on behalf of his sister, but Giri kept a stern face. He had grown fond of the prince during his time in Jaisalpur, but it was never too early to assert the respect due to him as Abhayan's soon-to-be brother-in-law. "I could not refuse my brother's order to return to Nidhapur, Abhayan," Giri said, his tone edged with authority, his courtly accent deliberate—a reminder that he was no longer merely a playwright. Yet something else nagged at him. "I sent a message through a temple priest. Did you not receive it?"

At his words, Suryavati frowned. That was all the confirmation he needed—someone had ensured his message never reached her. Someone powerful.

Before Abhayan could reply, the queen approached. Giri's instincts whispered that she was the one who had hidden his letter. Her gaze swept over him, pausing at the mud-streaked clothes he had yet to change out of. He had shed most of his royal insignia during his journey, a precaution against detection by his brother.

"How do we know you are Prince Giridhar?" she asked sharply.

Giri bowed his head. "My guard has my other jewels, but here is my ring bearing the Nidhapur fish emblem." He held out his right hand, where he wore the ring.

Queen Urmila squinted her eyes to peer at his hand, while Abhayan reached out to lift his hand higher. "You are an expert in disguises, so I am not sure I will trust a mere ring. We will hold the wedding when we can ascertain your identity beyond a doubt."

Dushyant stepped in to defend him. "Aunt Urmila, I met Prince Giridhar in Garthapuri and can vouch for his identity." Giri hoped this meant Dushyant was starting to forgive him. Queen Lalitha added, "I can attest to this as well." Giri nodded at them in silent gratitude.

Reluctantly, Queen Urmila said, "We will hold the marriage ceremony tomorrow."

Fearing his brother might arrive to disrupt the event, Giri urged, "Please, let us hold the ceremony today."

Queen Urmila glanced across the room at King Vibudha and gave a nod.

After his tiring journey, he took a hot bath to cleanse himself of the road's grime and restore his mental tranquility. The room assigned to him was much larger than the one he had occupied as a playwright and was located in the royal visitors' wing. Prince Abhayan soon arrived to guide him to the wedding hall.

"Brother, I hope you can forgive any disrespect in my words or actions," Abhayan began earnestly.

Giri let out a quiet chuckle. "Abhayan, if anyone should be seeking forgiveness, it is I—for my deception. And you treated this playwright far better than most princes would have." His grin turned teasing. "But don't worry, I promise to be a far better elder brother than my own has been to me."

"As long as you don't smack me like my sister does," Abhayan mumbled, causing Giri to smile.

As Giri and Abhayan walked side by side through the palace halls, their footsteps echoing against the stone floors, Giri's smile faltered into a frown. "How's Rangapani taking all this?" A shadow of concern crossed his face, knowing Abhayan needed the man's sword to defend his kingdom, and Giri's own actions hadn't made it easy for Abhayan to retain Rangapani's loyalty.

Abhayan paced beside him, drumming his fingers thoughtfully on the hilt of his sword. "My mother and uncle have already worked their matchmaking magic," he replied with a sly grin. "They've arranged a marriage for him with one of my cousins—nothing like a little family entanglement to keep him tied to the royal fold." He chuckled, clearly entertained by the turn of events. "When he found out you're a prince, the fight just... evaporated. Apparently, royalty has that effect on people."

"At least there are some benefits to this burden of the crown we wear," Giri said darkly.

Abhayan shrugged, glancing at Giri. "If nothing else, Rangapani still gets a beautiful wife out of it."

Giri's thoughts drifted to Suryavati. No one would ever

compare to her. If Rangapani was willing to settle for less, then he never truly cared for her at all.

The noble families of Jaisalpur had gathered to witness the union of Giri and Suryavati. Giri sat on a mat laid before the sacred fire, eagerly awaiting Suryavati. Draped in a red sari and looking like a goddess in human form, Suryavati arrived, her beauty surpassing even that of a sunset.

His mind filled with the scent of Suryavati as she sat down beside him. Giri's concentration lapsed for a few moments, causing him to miss a guard speaking in an urgent tone to Prince Vikaran, who quickly left the hall. Giri failed to notice the air crackling with tension.

"Halt this wedding!" shouted a voice.

Giri felt as though the ground had shifted beneath his feet as he turned to see his brother, King Bhadri, marching into the room.

6 1

SURYAVATI

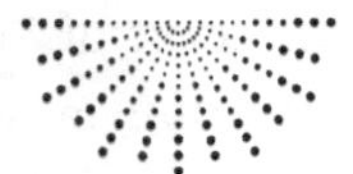

Suri glanced at the man standing at the door, then at Giri's shocked expression. Even without the striking resemblance between them, Giri's reaction alone was enough for her to deduce that the man at the door was King Bhadri.

"I intend to wed Princess Suryavati, with or without your blessing," Giri declared, his voice steady as he regained his composure.

"Will you defy your king for a mere girl?" King Bhadri retorted, his tone sharp and challenging.

Her cousin, King Dushyant, and her uncle hurried to King Bhadri's side. Though their voices reached her as indistinct murmurs, like waves crashing against sea cliffs, their animated hand gestures made it clear they were locked in a heated argument.

Giri made an attempt to rise, but she placed a firm hand on his thigh and shook her head. He regarded her curiously as she stood instead and walked toward King Bhadri. This was Giri's brother, his family, and she wanted to make a good impression.

The men fell silent, their attention shifting to her. Ignoring her cousin and uncle, she knelt before King Bhadri, pressing her

278

forehead to the ground in a gesture of respect. A dull throb pulsed in her head as blood rushed to her face.

A heavy silence filled the room as she remained motionless, her stomach twisting into a knot of panic. Then, she heard the soft rustle of movement, and King Bhadri's hand rested gently on her head. "Rise, Sister," he said.

As she stood, King Bhadri regarded her thoughtfully, and she was struck by how familiar his face seemed. Yet, as she looked closer, the differences became clear. Bhadri bore the look of a man carrying the weight of the world on his shoulders—a burden that came, no doubt, from being king.

"My brother spoke of your intelligence, compassion, and courage, but he failed to mention your beauty," King Bhadri said, a smile curling on his lips. "I can see why he is so bewitched." He glanced at Giri, still seated on the dais, and sighed. "Go ahead and marry that fool. Perhaps you can teach him some sense."

Suri released the breath she hadn't realized she was holding.

Before King Bhadri could change his mind, Suri quickly returned to the dais. As she approached, Giri's eyes shone with admiration for her, warming her insides. Together, they exchanged garlands and walked around the sacred fire seven times, hands clasped, binding themselves for seven lifetimes. She lifted her eyes to his, and an effervescent warmth spread through her, filling her heart with a gentle glow. A boyish grin spread across his lips, and she let the moment wash over her, shimmering with contentment. She was a mute girl, yet he loved her—not out of pity, but with deep and genuine affection. He loved her enough to defy the world, even to stand against his own brother, just to be with her. She tightened her grip, and he squeezed her hand in return. The gathered crowd showered them with flower petals and turmeric-tinted rice as they completed the ritual, sealing their union.

As a couple, Suri and Giri sought the blessings of her

parents, his brother, and then her uncle. Her mother hugged her tightly. "He was ready to defy his king for you, my child," her mother whispered, tears welling in her eyes. "Fortune favors you." Suri smiled at her mother's approval of her marriage, a weight lifting off her chest.

Her father clasped Giri's elbow. "Son, I hope this brings our two kingdoms closer together."

Giri glanced at his brother and replied, "You can count on Nidhapur's alliance."

His brother laughed as he approached them. "Look at your face—you look like a cat that caught its favorite mouse."

"Bad analogy, Brother," murmured Giri.

"How would the playwright describe his happiness?"

"Like a devotee blessed with the sight of his divine god," said Giri, gazing tenderly at Suri.

Bhadri laughed. "Welcome to our family, Sister. Giri, I am leaving for Nidhapur tomorrow. Make sure you return home with your bride."

Her uncle wrapped an arm around her shoulders and kissed her temple. "She is precious to us," he said to Giri, as if she were a rare gem. "Treat her well."

"Suri will no doubt tear me to pieces if I don't," Giri said with a small smile. "I will strive to be the husband she deserves."

Rangapani did not meet her eyes, his gaze shifting to her ears as he muttered a perfunctory greeting. Queen Lalitha, however, was more effusive in her joy as she approached them.

"Prince Giridhar, I heard you have found your match in Suryavati."

Suri gazed at Giri tenderly. He understood her need for stories, knowing they were not just composed of words but woven with the heart. The stories she cherished most offered glimpses of what she could become if she listened to her heart.

Giri smiled at her in a way that made her heart ache, light illuminating his face. In that moment, she felt as if she could hear the whisper of the gods in her ears, affirming that she had chosen the right path.

The feast afterward was a blur of flavors she barely tasted: mangoes, bananas, and jackfruit dipped in honey; a dozen different vegetables sautéed, stewed, or fried with pepper, ginger, and coconut sauces; millet and rice taking center stage alongside tender fish; and a sweet coconut pudding to conclude the meal. Giri, on the other hand, ate as if he hadn't seen a meal in days, savoring every bite. He probably hadn't eaten much during his hurried journey from Nidhapur to Jaisalpur. When he met her eyes, his facial muscles relaxed, as if he had finally come home. Suri admitted to herself that she loved it.

They sat side by side on a silk carpet to watch the play—one that Giri had created. Giri noticed the Head Poet standing near the stage. "Your Head Poet never liked me. Did he take over?" he asked.

Suri nodded. According to Abhayan, the Head Poet had made some significant changes. She worried he might have butchered their beautiful creation.

As the play began, Suri leaned her head against Giri's shoulder in the dim light. He shifted slightly to offer her better support. Gazing down at her, his lips curved into a soft smile. He looked as though he wanted to kiss her. Instead, he wrapped his arm around her waist, his attention barely on the scene unfolding before them.

Suri gasped as she realized the Head Poet had centered the play on her father. Giri's eyes narrowed, his focus shifting sharply to the stage. "He wanted to please the king he serves," Giri murmured, his tone thoughtful.

The tension of the last few days began to ebb from Suri's body. Her breathing deepened, and her muscles relaxed. Feeling safe in Giri's arms, she let her eyelids flutter closed and allowed sleep to claim her.

GIRIDHAR

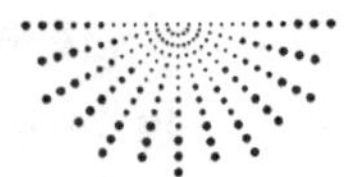

As the play—bearing little resemblance to the one he had originally crafted—came to an end, Giri noticed Suryavati had fallen asleep. He gently tried to wake her, but she didn't stir. With a smile, he lifted his wife into his arms, a warm sensation spreading through his limbs as the realization washed over him—she was his wife.

"Oh no, this is your wedding night. Wake her up!" Queen Urmila exclaimed from nearby.

"That is unnecessary," Giri muttered, heat rushing to his face at the mention of his wedding night. Ignoring further remarks, he carried Suryavati toward her chamber—their chamber for the night.

Once he placed her gently on the bed, a maid entered to remove her jewelry. Afterward, she glanced at him expectantly, noticing that Suryavati still wore her heavy silk sari. However, Giri didn't want to disturb her further and dismissed the maid with a nod.

Standing beside the bed, he hesitated, debating whether to sleep there or on the floor. His weary body quickly argued against the latter, and the large bed had ample space for both of them. Carefully, he climbed onto the bed, spread a blanket over them both, and surrendered to sleep almost instantly.

Giri woke to the sun's warmth on his face and the faint, intoxicating scent of Suryavati. Without opening his eyes, he burrowed deeper into the sheets with a contented sigh.

A sudden shove against his chest startled him, and he opened his eyes to find Suryavati's beautiful face inches from his, her hair cascading loose from its braid. Her gaze dropped to his arm, wrapped around her waist—her bare waist. She gasped and bolted upright. Giri realized he hadn't moved, as he was still lying on his side of the bed. She must have shifted toward him in her sleep, and in the dim haze of the night, his hand had naturally found its way around her.

A quiet sob escaped her, pulling at Giri's heartstrings. Fully awake now, he pushed up on his elbow. "Suryavati, what is it?"

She didn't answer. Instead, she turned away, her shoulders trembling. Concerned, he sat up and reached for her, but the moment his hand touched her shoulder, she flinched and shrugged him off. Her body was taut, wound as tight as a bowstring.

"My love," he said softly, his heart aching at the distance between them. "Tell me what's wrong."

She remained silent, and his mind raced for answers. She had woken up and seen him beside her—why would that upset her? Then, the realization struck him like a blow to the chest.

"Suri," he said, his voice gentle, "nothing happened between us last night."

She stilled. He had found the source of her distress.

Understanding dawned on him, and his stomach twisted. "Did you think I would ever—" He exhaled sharply, steadying his emotions. "Suri, I am your husband, not a monster." He longed to gather her in his arms, to reassure her with his warmth, but he held back, giving her space.

At last, she turned to face him, her dark eyes searching his.

"You fell asleep watching the play," he explained gently. "I carried you here, and your maid removed your jewels. I was exhausted from my journey, and the bed seemed spacious enough for both of us."

Slowly, the tension seeped from her body. She exhaled, her rigid posture softening. They sat mere inches apart now, so close he could feel the warmth of her breath. He remained still, letting her see the truth in his eyes.

She leaned forward, resting her forehead against his neck, inhaling deeply. He responded with a tender kiss against her temple. Gently, he brushed a few stray tendrils of hair from her face, his hand gliding to her wrist. Interlacing their fingers, he pressed their palms together and gave a reassuring squeeze.

A scar on his chest drew her attention, and she instinctively leaned closer to inspect it. Her hand lifted, hesitating mid-air before she glanced at him.

"You can touch me," he murmured, his voice low.

A blush crept up her neck as she bit her lip, then tentatively placed her hand on his chest. The moment her fingers met his skin, a jolt shot through him, straight to his heart. Her touch was hesitant at first, but as her confidence grew, her hand moved across his chest with a deliberate curiosity. He remained still, though every nerve in his body burned from the heat they shared.

Her gaze locked with his, and on a sudden impulse, she buried her fingers in his hair and kissed him. His legs went weak, and he wrapped his arms around her, pulling her closer still.

A sudden knock echoed through the door. "My lady." They sprang apart, startled, as if caught in a scandalous act.

"I can send her away," Giri whispered, yearning to hold her again.

Suri's lips curved into a soft smile, but she shook her head.

As she moved, the end of her sari slipped to her waist, revealing her bare shoulders. Giri quickly averted his gaze, forcing himself to focus elsewhere as he hurriedly climbed out of bed.

As the maid stepped in with her eyes respectfully downcast, Giri slipped past her, his pulse still unsteady, and strode toward his chambers on the far side of the palace. Marriage to Suryavati would test his restraint in ways he hadn't anticipated. How was he supposed to endure an entire day without touching her when every fiber of his being ached to do so?

The day passed in a blur after Giri bid his brother farewell, promising he would follow him to Nidhapur soon.

Later that afternoon, he found Suryavati standing with her shoulder against the wall, leaning toward the window, looking outside. The sky was blue with a tinge of yellow. She lifted her face to the wind and closed her eyes. Watching his wife, Giri felt something stir within him, a deep yearning to stay in that moment forever. She shifted and opened her eyes.

"It is beautiful," Giri said, his gaze shifting between her and the clouds drifting lazily in the wind. With her, he could speak his thoughts freely. With others, he was always cautious—they neither noticed the same details nor felt the need to express them.

She turned to face him, her eyes bright with unspoken words, and he instinctively stepped closer. She raised her hand, shaping it like a snake, then gestured toward the sky with a playful smile.

Following her gaze, he spotted the cloud she pointed to. "That one looks just like the snake in our story," he said. Her smile grew even bigger, lighting up her face in a way that made his heart feel full.

Glad to finally have a quiet moment alone with her, he spoke gently. "I understand the sacrifice you're making by leaving your family and traveling to Nidhapur with me. If you wish, I can stay here a few more days so you can savor these last moments in your home."

She gazed at him with warmth, her fingers brushing lightly against his hand before she made a simple sign for home.

His heart swelled as he interpreted her gesture. "I am your home," he murmured, the urge to fold her into his arms nearly overwhelming.

She nodded, her eyes shining with affection.

"Invite your cousins, Kanika and Ambika, to Nidhapur," he added. He knew she enjoyed their company, and they would help her settle into the unfamiliar world.

That night, when Giri stepped into Suryavati's chamber, she was awake—waiting for him. Eager, unhesitating, and bold in ways that caught him off guard. A thrill coursed through him at the realization. How was he ever supposed to leave her side to tend to the kingdom when she had become the very root anchoring him? Yes, this marriage would test him—but not in the way he had once imagined.

The next day, Queen Lalitha and King Dushyant prepared to depart. Giri managed to find a moment to speak with Lalitha before they left. She regarded him with an amused expression, a knowing smile playing on her lips.

"You've found yourself a poet, Prince Giridhar," she said warmly. "She truly cares for you. Make sure you treat her well."

Giri nodded, a small smile tugging at his lips. "And is Dushyant treating you well?" he asked, tilting his head toward the king, who stood a few yards away, deep in conversation with their uncle.

Lalitha's gaze softened as she looked at her husband, tenderness evident in her eyes. "If you are even half the husband he is," she said, her voice laced with affection, "then Suryavati is indeed a fortunate girl."

He intended to be the best husband he could possibly be.

When he returned to his chamber, he found Queen Urmila

waiting for him. Surprised, he hurried inside. "Queen Urmila, you should have sent for me. I would have come to you," he said.

"Prince Giridhar—"

"Please, call me Giri," he interrupted deferentially.

Queen Urmila rubbed her wrist, her expression conflicted. "Giri, my Suri is a special child. She is caring, loyal, and sensitive." Her voice wavered, and tears filled her eyes as her shoulders slumped.

The sight tugged at Giri's heart, and in that moment, he forgave her for all she had done against him. He stepped forward and took her hands in his. "I promise, I will never let anyone hurt Suryavati. But you should know—she is resilient and resourceful. She can take care of herself."

Queen Urmila took a ragged breath, her lips trembling. "A mother's heart still doesn't stop worrying," she admitted. Then, meeting his gaze, she squeezed his hand. "I entrust her well-being to you, Giri."

He nodded solemnly. "We will take care of each other, my lady."

The day of their departure arrived. Giri extended his hand, and Suryavati placed hers in his, allowing him to guide her into the carriage. He chose to forgo his horse, opting instead to travel by her side. As the familiar sights of her city faded from view, tears glistened in her eyes. Giri gently took her hand, interlacing their fingers. He remained silent, hoping his love would be enough to support her in this new chapter of their lives.

She wiped her tears and rested her head against his shoulder. He pressed a tender kiss to her hair. "You'll have to cross a lake to reach the palace," he said softly. "It's built on an island."

Her eyes brightened with curiosity as she looked up at him.

"When the sun sets, the water shimmers like molten gold. I can't wait to show you my home—our home."

A slow smile spread across her lips, and he couldn't resist

teasing. "I have always dreamed of bringing Poet Ravi back to Nidhapur."

She let out a silent laugh, her fingers tightening around his. His heart swelled with affection for the girl who had become his everything.

END OF PRINCE IN EXILE

COMPLETE POEM

Blinded by love, I go
To the place where nothing stirs
Charging through the brush, although
In fear my heart murmurs.

I hear a sharp howl of pain
Piercing the deep quietness
Cry of someone in chain
While I search around restless.

I hear her pitiful moan
But I cannot tell from where
While I go up the hill alone
All I hear are cries in the air.

I am determined to find her place
Crawling around the shrubs blind
I can never see any face
Maybe it is all in my mind.

When all my hopes flee
I saw her in shimmering light
Waiting to be set free
Our love bringing back my sight.

ACKNOWLEDGMENTS

The title *Avvaiyar* (also spelled *Ouvvayar*), meaning "the elderly lady," was bestowed upon multiple female poets in ancient Tamil lands. Unlike in many other historical societies, women in these regions were not denied education, as evidenced by the wealth of poetry that has survived to this day. Esteemed female poets flourished under the patronage of Chola and Pandiya kings, who respected and supported their work. These remarkable women from the Sangam period and beyond served as inspiration for Suryavati's character.

Avvaiyar's Words:

கற்றது கைமண் அளவு, கல்லாதது உலகளவு

(What you have learned is a mere handful; what you haven't learned is as vast as the world.)

Kalidasa, one of the most renowned Sanskrit poets and playwrights, likely lived in the fifth century under the patronage of King Vikramaditya of Ujjain. Reading his poetry, especially from *Shakuntala* and his other epics, has been a true delight. As a tribute to this literary legend, I have woven verses from *Kumarasambhava* (*The Birth of the War God*) into this book.

Here is another exquisite sample from his works:

The water-lily closes, but
With wonderful reluctancy;
As if it troubled her to shut
Her door of welcome to the bee.

Ratnavali is a play written by the Indian Emperor Harsha, who ruled in the fifth century. As a poet and playwright, Prince Giridhar would find himself in esteemed company among Indian kings—many of whom were not only patrons of art and literature but also accomplished writers of poetry and drama themselves.

Another towering figure in Indian literature, Rabindranath Tagore, whose plays left a lasting legacy in the 20th century, served as an inspiration for the theatrical scenes in this book.

James Stephens (1882–1950) and his poem *The Goat Paths* inspired the joint composition by Giridhar and Suryavati.

I am by no means an expert in any of their works, but I deeply enjoy reading and learning from them.

I am grateful to these extraordinary writers of the past, whose words continue to live on—guiding, inspiring, and illuminating our lives.

I also extend my gratitude to the incredible local authors in San Diego who keep the tradition of reading and writing alive. Meeting you at book fairs and festivals is always a joy, and your passion for storytelling inspires me every day.

To my parents, who nurtured my love of reading and indulged my curiosity by buying me used books as a child—thank you. To my brother, my extended family, and my cousins, I am grateful for your unwavering support of my passion.

To my dear friends, who show up at my book events, read my books, and cheer me on throughout my writing journey—my heart is full of gratitude. A special thanks to D, S, and L for coming to support me at the local library event—it meant the world to me.

To my husband and daughters, your unwavering love and support mean everything to me. I could not do this without you —your encouragement, patience, and belief in me fuel my passion for writing. Your love is my greatest inspiration, and I am endlessly grateful to have you by my side on this journey.

Lastly, to the readers who buy my books and take the time to read them—you are the heart of this journey. I hope my stories have touched your heart, sparked your imagination, or simply brought you joy. Your support means more to me than words can express, and I am deeply grateful for the opportunity to share my passion with you. Knowing that my words find a home in your hands is the greatest reward of all. Thank you for being a part of this journey with me.

ABOUT THE AUTHOR

The stories I read growing up inspired me to write. I am interested in historical fiction and within that society, examining the human heart in conflict. I like to place my female characters in difficult situations and see how they learn to survive with no actual power. And watch my male characters fall in love while fighting for king and land. I love exploring the struggle between love and duty.

I live in California with my family. Visit me at annabushi.com to learn about upcoming books.

Thank you for reading! If you enjoyed this book, I would love it if you let your friends know so they can experience the adventures of Suri and Giri. You can also leave a review so that other readers know what they're getting into when they pick up this book!

throne and an enemy horde.

Raised in ancient Indian tradition, Princess Meera neither wields a sword nor wears the crown. She is content to let her father and brother manage the affairs of the court. She performs her duties and knows her place.

When her brother disappears in enemy territory, her kingdom is left without an heir. As princes vie for her hand to capture the throne, her only use seems to lie in her ability to give birth to a son to wear the crown.

Afraid for her people's future and her brother's life, Meera can no longer accept her traditional role. As she fights to guard her heart and keep her kingdom safe, she struggles to navigate the royal game of chess without becoming a pawn.

Can she save what she holds most dear, or is her brother's disappearance a harbinger of worse to come?

This royal Indian saga weaves a tale of destiny and danger, forbidden love and courtly intrigue.

Heir to Malla is the first book in the epic Land of Magadha trilogy.

* * *

<u>War of the Three Kings</u> - Book 2

Jay promised not to kill him a decade ago. Now he stands between Jay and the throne.

Crown Prince Jay has grown into a legend with all his triumphs on the battlefield. While he is away helping a neighboring king, Jay is unaware of a new enemy who has emerged back home.

Jay fought with Nakul many years ago, but he believes the bitter past is behind them. Unknown to Jay, Nakul covets his crown. With chaos brewing in his realm and the lives of his people in peril, Jay stands exposed to danger as he cannot tell friend from foe.

Neither is Jay aware of the grave secret that binds him and Nakul together. Plunging into a conflict that might result in destruction, is he ready to pay the price for triumph? His failure would result in death—his and the kingdom he vowed to protect.

Malla siblings, Meera and Jay, return to face the consequences of their actions in War of the Three Kings, the second book in the epic trilogy, Land of Magadha.

Perfect for fans of historical fiction like Wolf Hall and Ponniyin Selvan or lovers of fantasy like Baahubali and The Lost Queen.

* * *

<u>Burden of the Crown</u> - Book 3

Blinded by despair, they fail to see the foe plotting their ruin.

His people revere him for the prosperity he has ushered. His enemies cower on hearing his name. Then, disaster strikes King Jay. He drowns in grief, forgetting his duty as a king.

When tragedy strikes, Meera thinks it is punishment for her past mistakes. One, in particular, rattles her. When she sets out to right her wrongs, she doesn't know if she can make up for the biggest mistake of all.

Anger festers in Jay's heart, threatening to ruin all he holds dear. The pain Meera inflicted on the one who captured her heart haunts her. A dangerous enemy seeking to seize the throne uses this opportunity to cause chaos in the kingdom.

Their foe has anticipated their moves to stay two steps ahead. Will the siblings heed the troubling signs? Or will they cause the downfall of their kingdom?

Burden of the Crown concludes the epic trilogy, Land of Magadha. Malla siblings face their gravest threat yet in their mission to protect their kingdom.